EATING ASPHALT

SACRED HEARTS PNW CHAPTER - BOOK V

A.J. DOWNEY

COPYRIGHT

∿

Editing & book design by Maggie Kern @ Ms.K Edits

Cover art by Dar Albert at Wicked Smart Designs

DEDICATION

To Carrie, I couldn't do any of this without you. Thank you for being my bestie – even from so many miles away. Love you lots.

*G*lass Jaw…

"Gah! Damnit!" Mace cried, and I frowned, looking up from my call with one of my suppliers.

"Alright now, thanks," I said and hung up the phone. I called out from the kitchen down the basement stairs, "What's the problem?"

Laughter filtered up, and I rolled my eyes.

"Quit fuckin' around down there and get it done!" I yelled. "The home buyer's coming today, and I don't need you all making us look like a bunch of fucking jackasses!"

We were working in the basement of a house built in the 1940s. It was a multi-tier repair, some foundational shit, new sump pump installation, mold removal – that sort of thing. The current homeowner? What a fucking bitch. I hoped the buyer, who was coming in from across the country, would be easier to deal with since the repairs were going to overlap and go past closing, which was supposed to be tomorrow.

I mean, honestly – who the fuck bought a house sight unseen from across the fuckin' country like that?

"Hey, boss!" Mace called. "Come and look at this and tell me what you want me to do."

"Fuck," I muttered and went down the stairs into the unfinished basement. That wasn't good. That was *never* good.

I went down to deal with whatever bullshit had come up and sighed.

"This cheap-ass white-trash fucking cunt ain't gonna pay for it," I said, looking up under the fireplace at the severely rotted wood. It wasn't too bad of a repair, not bad at all, but I wasn't about to do any more shit for this woman.

"What do you think?" Mace asked. "Point it out to the buyer after closing and go from there?"

"Yeah, maybe." I rubbed my chin and closed one eye, looking up at the flaking dry rot. The whole corner of the beam was starting to come apart.

"Man," Mace said, shaking his head. "I don't know what show this bitch watched to make her think flipping houses was a good idea, but she watched the wrong fucking one."

I barked a laugh and said, "Who you telling?" Finally, I sighed and said, "Let me look at this inspection report again. The buyer's inspector was really fuckin' thorough – I don't see how he could have missed this."

"Yeah." Mace nodded.

It was a really odd situation, this whole job. The *buyer's* agent had reached out to me for one – which that almost never happened and after meeting the current homeowner, I understood why.

She wasn't interested in anything except getting her money, period – gold digging hooker. She'd even had the nerve to get up in my face about shit and I was fuckin' trying to help her ass – giving her options. Not my fault she wanted top-tier everything at bargain-basement prices. That wasn't how this fucking shit worked.

"Jared?" a female voice called from upstairs, and I frowned and looked at my watch.

"Yeah, just a sec!" I called back.

"Holly?" Mace asked.

"Sounds like it. Also sounds like she's early."

"Fuckin' great."

I huffed a laugh and slapped him on the back.

"Time to be the bearer of bad news," I said, and turned toward the stairs. Holly was the buyer's agent – and thus, she was on our side.

"Hey, Holly," I said as I came up the stairs.

Holly was the quintessential bubbly blonde, buxom, too – which I could appreciate both. She blinked wide blue eyes at me and said, "Uh oh, you don't look happy. Homeowner or…?"

That was the other thing I appreciated about Holly – she was sharp as a tack. Today, that worked against me, some.

"I don't know yet. Give me half a second here," I said and went over to the kitchen counter. That was the one thing they'd done right in this place – or at least on the surface. Granite countertops, gleaming white cabinetry, and brick facing for the backsplash, the kitchen looked sharp, all except for the shitty, half-assed paint job in the same unrelieved gray throughout the whole fucking house.

I swear to God, the woman selling this place was painfully fuckin' *cheap*. She probably had her fuckin' kids paint the place.

Holly waited while I flipped through the fifty-four-page printout that the fuckin' inspector had handed her on the house. Yeah, it seemed like a lot, but a lot of it was penny-ante shit. Nothing to write home about when just about every fuckin' house in the history of ever had the same shit going on.

I tapped the third page and said, "Gah…"

"What is it?" Holly asked, looking over my shoulder.

"Your guy was maybe a little too thorough. This is a problem that really needs to be addressed but he's got so much penny-ante shit packed into this report it got overlooked."

"Oh no," Holly said, dismayed. "Show me."

I took her down into the basement and showed her. She covered her mouth with her hand and shook her head.

"Jared, this is really bad… the negotiations have been made, and the contract has been signed. How immediate of a repair is this?" she asked.

"It's bad," I agreed. "It really shouldn't wait."

"How much are we looking at, though?" she asked.

"There's the good news," I said with a sigh. "I mean, I could do it for…" I ran the calculations through my brain and shrugged. "Five-seventy-five, maybe."

Holly let out her breath in a whoosh. "Okay, that's not completely awful, but, Jared, I don't know if my client can do it," she said. She looked worried, and that was weird. Like, who was this woman that was buying that Holly was *this* invested?

"What's going on, Hols?" I asked her.

"She's a really nice lady," Holly said with a sigh. "And she's really been through it. Single mom, husband left her and tried to leave her cold. It's just her and her son. She got a job out here, but they weren't going to pay for her relocation fees. She's spent just about everything she's had on securing this house. Of course, we get so far into the process and the woman that owns this place—" I raised my hand to stop her.

"Say no more on that last one," I said.

Holly looked at her watch and said, "She's supposed to be here any minute."

"The seller?" I asked. "Or the buyer?"

"Oh, God no! The buyer! The seller was warned away from the walk-through. My client doesn't want to have anything to do with her. She's been jerked around so much. Between you and me." Holly made a cringy sort of face.

"Always, Hols. You know I take care of you," I said, and it was true; in a business sense, I did. Always had and always would. That was why she and her real estate group were one of my best repeat customers.

"Jared, she's really been through it, and I don't know that she can take much more bad news," Holly said. She genuinely sounded like her heart went out to this lady.

"Got pretty close with her, huh?" I asked.

Holly nodded. "She's an amazing person." She sighed, chewed her bottom lip, and drew herself up to her full height, which was only like five foot six, which to my six one, looked adorable.

"I'll pay for it," she said. "Out of my finder's fee."

"Shit, you're fuckin' serious," I said, wide-eyed and surprised as fuck. I'd never seen her do anything like this.

"As a heart attack," she said solemnly.

I sniffed. "You know, you've brought me a lot of business and shit over the years, but I can't do it for *free*. I'll go halves with you. Two seventy-five." I stuck out my hand, and she smiled and shook it.

"Thank you. I'm glad you're here," she said, and then her eyes went wide as her phone went off in her hand. "Oh!" She looked at the screen and smiled. "She's here!"

"Well, go on," I said. "I got some shit to handle down here. I'll be up in a bit."

"Okay."

She went up the stairs, and I put my hands on my hips and shook my head. Well, that was something.

"Hi!" I heard Holly's enthusiastic voice at the back door and a peal of feminine laughter.

"It's so good to finally meet you!" another woman's voice cried.

"Hi," a boy's voice said, cracking – so a teenager maybe.

Hm.

I went around looking at my crew's work, nodded and finally took myself upstairs. I had no idea where the women had got to, but there was a teen in the kitchen. Skinny, tall, hadn't equaled out yet, but maybe, sixteen? Seventeen?

"Hi," he said, and waved.

"Hey, how's it going?" I asked.

He tossed back his brown hair that was getting too long in the front, bangs sweeping into his brown eyes.

"Good to be stopped," he said with a reckless grin.

"Aw, yeah? Where you come from?" I asked.

"East coast," he said.

"Shit, that *is* a long way away," I agreed.

"Marc, who are you talking to?" a woman's voice called from the stair-well up to the second floor. Her flats hit the hardwood floor, and she stepped around the corner into the dining room where I could see her and holy shit… she left me eating asphalt.

She was fucking gorgeous.

Long, sleek-brown hair waved around her face, which was angular and supermodel perfect. Wide brown eyes swept over me uncertainly and softened when Holly came around from behind her and introduced us.

"Oh, Cadence, this is Jared. Jared, this is our buyer, Cadence."

"Hi." My brain finally caught up to what I was supposed to be doing versus what I *was* doing, which was staring gobsmacked at the woman.

"Jared Ronald Allen Smith," I said. She hesitantly put her soft hand in mine and barely gripped it, shaking it weakly.

"Oh, like the trucks outside," her boy said, and I startled slightly, forgetting he was even there.

"Yeah, I own the contracting company," I said.

"It's nice to meet you," Cadence murmured and without any more preamble, said, "How bad is my house?"

Direct. I liked that.

Shit, I was in trouble here.

2

*G*lass Jaw...

"Come on down to the basement if you'd like, I'll show you what we're doing." There was some flinching around her eyes.

"The basement?" she echoed.

"I'll go," her boy said, rolling his eyes. "Mom's afraid of basements and attics. That's why the attic room is gonna be mine." He grinned and his mother smiled behind his back. Damn, that small smile turned her from something beautiful into something out of this world. I was going to *keep* eating asphalt and start stumbling over my words – tripping over my own damn tongue if I didn't get away from her for a minute.

"Cool, come on downstairs, Marc."

Marc pushed off the granite countertop, and with a grin and a wink at his mom, turned toward the basement door which was standing open.

I nodded at Holly and Cadence and followed the boy down the stairs.

"Clean it up, fellas," I warned as we entered the basement. "Quit leaving your shit all over the place." I kicked a trowel lightly back, closer to the bucket of mortar where some of my guys were shoring up a janky set of blocks serving as part of the back of the foundation.

"What happened down here?" Marc asked, wrinkling his nose at the chemical smell.

"Previous owner let a busted sump pump go too long, and mold proliferated the basement and crawl spaces, but y'all got lucky," I said. "Up here we get something called black mold. Highly toxic, causes all sorts of breathing and neurological issues in a person if they live around it too long."

"This mold looks yellow," Marc said, peering at some of the timbers underneath the house up under the floor. I nodded.

"Same kind of mold they make penicillin out of," Mace said. "You get sick, you can just come down here and lick one of these beams here."

"Really?" Marc asked, looking skeptical. Mace laughed.

"No! I'm just fu— messin' with you, kid."

"Oh, it's alright. You can swear around me, I don't care," Marc said.

"I do. It's unprofessional," I said. I shook my head, grinning with Mace though. That'd been cute.

"What else are you guys doing down here?" Marc asked with mild interest, looking around.

I took him through all that we'd accomplished and had yet to accomplish down here.

"Well, we dug out this new trench, here. Put in this new sump pump," I tapped the top of the thing lightly with the sole of my work boot, "and the boys are back up in there, mortaring some bricks all the same size and shape in place for your foundation."

"What else needs to be done?" he asked. The kid was pretty shrewd. I liked that. Seemed his mamma didn't raise no fool. Also seemed his mamma had him pretty young. She didn't look much older than me – if she was even older than me – she could be a few years younger or even the same age. I was terrible at guessing a lady's age which had landed me in some hot water back when—

I stopped my mental meandering and focused on what the kid was asking me. "Gotta replace the wood up under here," I said, touching the rotting specimen, the wood flaking and shredding under my fingertips. "But no worries, there. That's already paid for. I just have to come in and do it."

"Okay, what isn't paid for that needs to be done."

"A few things. Those windows down here need replacing, but to be honest with you, I wouldn't replace 'em with *windows*. In my profes-sional opinion – which is what I'm here for, right –? I would put in some open grating to ventilate things down here. Keep the critters out but promote some airflow. I'd also look at a few other things, but not right now, maybe in the future when your mom's flush. You know?"

"Things like what?" he asked, and I smiled.

"Insulation up under these floorboards for one. Replacing all these galvanized pipes – but I'd wait a minute. The water heater was put in eight years or so ago, so when it needs to be replaced, that's when I would do the pipes."

"Okay." Kid looked like he was mentally taking all of this down. "Isn't there supposed to be plastic on these piles of dirt or something?"

"Don't worry!" Mace called. "It's on our list of shi—" I shot Mace a warning look over my shoulder. "Stuff to do." He changed what he was going to say in the nick of fucking time.

"He's right, it'll get done too. I didn't forget. I just forgot to mention it."

"Anything else we should know about?" the kid asked.

"Ask you something?" I raised an eyebrow.

"Sure."

"Where's your pops?"

He frowned. "Died." He said it flatly, and there wasn't a trace of hurt on the kid's face, but there sure was a whole lotta anger.

"I'm sorry to hear that," I said automatically. "My condolences."

He shook his head.

"Save 'em. He was a douche," he said, and I nodded.

"Okay."

"So, anything else we should know about?" he asked, changing the subject flatly.

"A few things," I said. "But those are all upstairs and I best take them up with your mom if she asks. Be happy to go through that report with her page by page if she'd like."

Marc frowned.

"You know about that?"

I chuckled. "Holly and I have been doing business for a good bit of years now. She knows I'm honest and it wouldn't look good on my business to cheat anyone. A lot of that stuff? Superficial. Some of it, though? It should be addressed, even if it's not immediately."

Marc studied my face for a second and finally nodded. I filed it away as interesting. He clearly had some trust issues, which, didn't we all? Still, interesting.

"Come on, let's head on back upstairs."

"Okay."

He turned and I followed him up, catching Mace's eye, who mouthed *what the fuck?* at me. I frowned and shook my head and waved him off.

He knew I didn't really like kids – which was true – I didn't like *kids*, as in little kids. Marc wasn't little and so far, he seemed alright.

When we got back upstairs, it was to an unwelcome surprise.

"Aren't you done yet?"

I frowned slightly, and Holly, who was standing on the other side of the counter in the dining room, looked helpless and at a loss for words.

Hillary McConnel, the current homeowner and seller, was standing in the kitchen. Cadence had evaporated. I frowned slightly.

"We aren't slated to be done for another few days yet," I told her. "I do believe that's laid out in the contract you signed."

Just like it was laid out that we didn't get paid until after the house was closed on, which was a big fuckin' favor where this bitch was concerned. I was already doing this shit at bargain-basement prices as a favor to Holly. This bitch, Hillary, could go fuck herself. She was constantly up our asses, getting these fucking ideas in her head and trying to foul up and change deals to suit her better mid-fuckin'-stream.

She was a royal pain in the fucking ass, thought she was better than she actually was, and could best be described as a white-trash princess. I meant what I said. From her ugly fucking little dog to her pink Juicy Couture velvet tracksuit that was probably the only one she owned or could afford. It was so old some of the fuzz was getting rubbed off in places.

Bleached-blond-Karen hair completed her look right along with a few trashy tattoos that look like she went for a chic-upscale look with a dollar-store artist.

Needless to say, I couldn't stand the bitch. I had no idea where Cadence was, but I was glad she wasn't here right this second.

"Who are you?" she demanded of Marc.

"Uh…"

"Marc is Ms. Mitchell's son," Holly said carefully. Marc just kind of looked nervous and waved.

"Oh, so she *is* here?"

Fucking bitch. She knew exactly what she was doing. She knew Cadence didn't want to see her, but fuck what anybody else wanted. It was all about Hillary, all the fuckin' time.

"Yes." Holly made eye contact with me and tilted her head back ever so slightly in the direction of the front door through the archway behind her. My phone did me a solid and chimed in my pocket at just that moment.

"Excuse me, ladies, for just a second," I said, and went for the front door. Marc stayed back with Holly, which was good. I checked the notification – an app I didn't care about – and I opened the front door and went out onto the front porch.

Cadence startled and turned to look at me, tears wetting her cheeks.

"Oh! Um…" She turned away and tried to wipe them away, but they just seemed to want to fall faster.

I have to say, my curiosity was piqued.

"You alright?" I asked, leaning on the railing overlooking the narrow patch of front yard.

She shook her head and sucked in a deep breath and held it, trying to get it together.

"It's just a lot," she said, finally letting it out in an explosion.

"Talk to me," I said gently, hoping that to her ears it sounded inviting.

I couldn't tell you how much I wanted to know more about her.

3

Cadence...

We'd been through so much – Marc and I – and I was trying to be strong for the both of us, but I just felt like falling apart. I was under so much stress, so much strain, and when Holly had rushed up to me and told me to go out front, that Hillary McConnel was coming in through the back, it was everything I could do to suppress the sudden wildfire inferno of rage tearing through my breasts.

I went out onto the narrow front porch, leaned against the railing, and just tried to breathe for a minute.

It was pleasant out here, at least. Cold, but clear. The sun shining, a nice breeze rolling through the trees along the idyllic little street. The neighborhood wasn't the best now that I saw it in person. It was certainly a far cry from the affluent neighborhood Marc and I had come from in Georgia. A definite step down, but then again, the house prices here in the Pacific Northwest were *insane* and I was lucky to get this home for what I did. God, but didn't it figure that buying this place would be more difficult than anything else thus far?

Tears sprang to my eyes, and I took several deep breaths and tried to get a handle on myself before I started crying and just couldn't stop.

I leaned harder onto the porch railing and sniffed, trying not to buckle under the weight and sadness, the *stress,* when the front door to my – well, my *soon-to-be* house, opened. I turned expecting my son or Holly, but it was the contractor, instead.

"Oh! Um…" I straightened, startled, and turned away, wiping the tears from under my eyes.

"You alright?" he asked, crossing his arms over a very nice chest and leaning his jeans-clad hip against the railing.

I shook my head to dispel the thoughts about just how attractive Jared Ronald Allen Smith was and let out my breath in a whoosh.

"It's just a lot," I said.

"Talk to me," he said gently, and I paused for a moment, the invitation a siren's call of sorts. I closed my eyes and looked away from those intense, hazel eyes – the mix of brown and green, earthy and vivid but the look in them... I don't know what to say about that. It held an edge of predator, but also an edge of something like protection. The intensity with which he looked at me left me wanting to spill all my secrets but stole the words from my lips.

I couldn't tell you how much I wanted to unburden my soul, but this was not the time, nor the place. Nor was this poor man the one I needed to dump on, either.

I finally pressed my lips together miserably and shook my head lightly.

"Thank you, um, that wouldn't be right or a good idea, I don't think," I stammered and was saved from my own awkwardness by the door opening once more and my son poking his head out.

"Mom, you okay?" he asked, and I did what I always did.

I put on a brave face, smiled brightly, and said, "Yeah, honey. What's up?"

He stepped out and closed the door.

"Holly's doing her best to fend off the cuntasaurus rex in there. She wanted me to give you these." He held out keys on a ring to me, and I frowned, temporarily forgetting to tell my son to watch his language.

"What are these?" I asked.

"The keys to the house. She says this one is the storage door out back and that one or both of these open the front or back door, she doesn't know which."

"Oh, God," I groaned. "I'm sorry, baby, you shouldn't have had to deal with any of that. I—"

"Mom, it's okay," Marc said, putting up his hands to ward off my babbling. "I'm a big kid, now," he said with a laugh. "She's awful, but she doesn't bother me the way she bothers you."

"You're iron clad, kid. She bothers *everyone*."

I shot a smile past my boy at Jared and said, "More like Teflon. Nothing sticks to my boy."

"Okay, so she came just for that?" I asked, and Marc rolled his eyes.

"No, she's got a bunch of her shit in the storage out back," he said, wincing and rubbing the inside corner of his eye. It was one of my son's tells. Unlike his father, he had a terrible poker face. Likely he got it from me. I was awful at lying, but that wasn't what this was. This was Marc, cringing at having to tell me something he knew I wouldn't like to hear.

I closed my eyes, let out a breath I hadn't realized I'd been holding, and felt my shoulders drop in defeat.

"How much stuff?" I asked.

"A lot. Most of it's garbage and stuff and I think she's planning on sticking us with it."

"Goddamnit," I uttered in frustration.

"Let her," Jared spoke up, and I jumped slightly. I had gotten so focused on Marc, and I was so tired, I had truthfully forgotten he was standing there.

"I'm sorry?"

"Let her," Jared repeated with a shrug. "I'll get it out of there for you. It's not worth the headache and it won't take much. Just let her haul out what she will, and I'll handle the rest when the job's done."

"You mean it?" I asked, holding out hope that just *one thing* in this whole process was about to be easy because nothing else about it had been.

"Yeah, but I need you to do something for me," he said.

"What's that?" I asked.

He pushed off the railing with his hip and put his arms down to his sides, stepping into a little circle with me and my son, pitching his voice low.

"Either tonight before you get back to wherever you're staying or tomorrow right after you close and before you head this way, I need you to stop at a hardware store and pick up new lock sets for the front door, back security door, back door, and the storage door. Do yourself a favor and get ones all keyed the same. Both knobs and dead bolts. I'll put them in for you."

"Why would you do that?" I asked, then realized it sounded rude. I stuttered, correcting myself and said, "I mean, why would I do that?"

"Because this bitch is crazy, and I don't trust her as far as I can throw her skank ass."

Marc sputtered a laugh, and I gave him a sharp look.

"Okay, she's a pain, I admit that, but there's no need to call names," I corrected my boy for laughing. Jared's lips quirked into a half-smile at me as his eyes roved my face.

"Point taken," he said. I blushed furiously and was grateful he didn't seem offended for what I had intended to be for my son, but apparently caught him, too.

"Oh, oh no! You're an adult, you can say whatever you'd like. My son, however, I would like to instill a little better than that in him."

"It's okay, Mom. No reflection on you. Let's call it Dad's genes."

I bit my lips together, closed my eyes, and drew in a long slow breath in through my nose and let it out through my mouth.

The door opened again, and I jumped. Holly poked her blond head out and looked apologetic.

"Coast is clear," she said.

"Did she leave a mess in my storage unit?" I asked.

Holly winced. "Afraid so."

I sighed.

"Perfect," I muttered. "Just perfect."

"It's nothing to worry about," Jared said, reaching out and pinching my jacket sleeve, giving it a gentle shake. "I'll take care of it," he said.

"I appreciate that, thank you," I said. "But you shouldn't have to."

It was the principle of the thing.

4

*G*lass Jaw...

"Heyyy – oh shit, what's wrong?" Marc held out a couple of bags from the hardware store, looking grim. I took them from him.

"Movers dicked us over," he said unhappily.

I looked past him up the driveway where Cadence was parked. She was on the phone, tears streaming down her face, her makeup running, her fingers under her nose, hand pressed to her lips as she tried to maintain her cool with her phone pressed to her ear.

"What do you mean?" I asked.

"Our stuff is still back in Savannah," he said unhappily. "It was supposed to be delivered today. We left over ten days ago – got here in six. They lied to my mom and now they're saying it won't be here until like the end of the month."

"Okay, hang on a minute here." I thrust the bag of lock sets into his hands and muttered, "Take these to Mace for me."

"Whose Mace?" he called at my back as I marched across the grass to Cadence's SUV with its little U-Haul trailer. I don't know what she'd brought, but at least she wouldn't be without nothing.

I opened the car door and could hear the guy on the other end of the phone screaming at her in a thick Boston accent.

"You callin' me a liar, you two-bit fuckin' cunt?"

I snatched the phone right out of her hand. "Who is this?" I demanded to a "fuck you" and the phone clattering on the other end. The call severed and the line went dead.

Cadence had both hands shoved over her mouth and was sobbing uncontrollably.

"Hey, come on now." I kneeled in her open car doorway and put a hand on the back of her shoulder, giving it a squeeze. "Don't waste any tears on that piece of shit."

She crumbled and lost her shit even harder, gripping the steering wheel of her car with both hands, breath sawing in and out of her chest too fast.

I switched tactics immediately.

"Breathe, honey. Just breathe," I said. Making eye contact with her, I mimed breathing in and breathing out slow and steady until she caught on and started doing it too.

"Right, that's right." I nodded. "That's good."

Holly's words from the day before came back to me – about this woman going through so much and how beautiful she was inside – I wanted to know. I'd seen her on the front porch yesterday afternoon. She sparked fire like an opal in the sun. She was tough. I could see it in her, so what the fuck had happened to bring her this low?

"I'm sorry," she said. "I'm so sorry!"

"Don't be," I chided. "Just breathe. Take your time."

"I don't know what to do," she half-wailed. "I don't have all the answers this time."

"Just take your time, honey. Just take your time, get it together, and we'll go from there. Okay?"

She stared at me, mascara running down her cheeks in muddy tracks, and nodded.

I think she was out of strength. It was the end of the line. I was half glad she'd landed in my lap – I had plenty of strength to spare. I would get this figured out.

Her phone rang in my hand, and I looked. *Movers* was emblazoned on her screen. I swallowed hard and had a bit of grim resolve settle in my chest before answering her phone with a warning look at her to stay in her car.

"Hello?"

"Who's this?" a guy with a decided middle-American accent asked. "I thought I was calling Cadence Mitchell."

"You are. This is her phone, but you got me."

"Who are you?" he asked.

About to be your worst fucking nightmare, if you don't answer my questions, I thought.

"This is Jared Smith. I'm working on Ms. Mitchell's new house. She's a little upset right now. Maybe you and I can sort things out, yeah?"

"Yeah, yeah, okay." He sounded a little relieved.

Fuckin' idiot.

~

"How you doing?" I asked and slid up onto the second stool at her kitchen bar on her dining room side.

She took a sip from the coffee I had one of my guys run out and get us. Her face was freshly scrubbed, her long, wavy, brown hair pulled up into a high ponytail. Her face was stark, her eyes red rimmed from crying.

"Better, thank you."

"Okay, good. That's good." I nodded.

She sniffed. "So did you get anywhere with them?" she asked.

I sighed heavily. "Not yet, but I think I got this shit figured out. You aren't the first person they've done this kind of shit to. I've seen it before," I said. Which was true, I had.

"What's going on?" she asked weakly.

"Well, one, the Southie piece of shit that had the gall to talk that way to you on the phone says he's sorry." She gave me a look, her facial expression dropping her green eyes, clearly stating without saying a word to drop the fucking bullshit with her. I smiled and laughed a little. "Fair enough," I said.

"So, what's going on?" she repeated, and I sighed.

"According to these assholes, the contract you signed states they have twenty-one business days to deliver your things to you from the date of when it was initially supposed to be delivered which is…?" I asked.

"That was supposed to be today," she said, sniffing, her voice cracking slightly.

"Okay." I nodded. "So, we look at a calendar, take out every Saturday and Sunday that means…" I clicked my tongue. "Friday, the second of next month."

She closed her eyes, her face dropping and her shoulders settling under the weight of defeat that landed on them like a ton of bricks.

"Next month?" she asked weakly.

"Not necessarily. They could bring it any time between now and the second without being in breach of contract. What it means, really, is that you can't do anything about it until after the second of next month. Meaning, you can't sue them, or anything like that."

She nodded morosely.

"What have you got in your car and trailer?" I asked.

"Um, boxes of important papers, clothes, uh… artwork and some odds and ends. They said they would have everything here today, so they have *everything* – our furniture, our *beds*, our kitchen stuff. I don't know what I'm going to do!"

"Deep breath," I told her and got up off the kitchen stool. There were two at the counter and they'd been left with the house, so it wasn't all bad. I mean, at least she had those to sit on at the counter to work or whatever for the time being.

I went to the basement door and called down, "Hey, boys, stop what you're doing real quick and let's give this lady a hand with her things."

"Oh, you don't have to do that!" Cadence cried, sitting up straighter.

"Ah!" I put up a hand and waved her back down into her seat. "Stay in the truck, we've got this. Many hands make light work." She looked taken aback, looking at the steering wheel of her SUV, like she was trying to figure out… truck? It was adorable.

My boys on today's work crew came up from the basement along with Marc, who seemed to be an inquisitive kid, wanting to learn anything that was in front of him. A good quality if you asked me.

"We unloading the car and trailer?" Marc asked curiously and looked to his mom. She held hesitation on her face, and finally nodded.

"Where do you want us to put it?" Jerome asked. He was a good dude, unrelated to the club. I tried hard not to mix club business with my business when it came down to it. If the club got picked up on bogus or even very real charges, I couldn't have the majority of my workforce going into lockup with me. Mace was the exception to the rule in that regard, but he'd really needed the work and I had been desperate for a reliable guy that I didn't have to train from the ground up, so that shit had just worked out.

"It's okay, Mom, I'll show them," Marc said helpfully. Cadence smiled at him and the tiredness radiated from her face.

"Thanks, honey," she said to him quietly and let us handle it.

"Where do you want this stuff? The office?" Jerome asked as some of the other boys got the back of the U-Haul travel trailer open.

"Uh, you mean the little room inside the back door off the laundry?" Mark asked.

"Yeah."

Marc shook his head. "That's not gonna be the office. That's supposed to be the guest room, Mom says."

"Well, whatever, gotta know where's it going."

"The guest room like Marc described, for now. His mom'll tell us if it goes somewhere else," I said, and Marc nodded.

Jerome hefted two eighteen-gallon plastic totes and headed for the back door of the house with an indifferent shrug. I stood by while the guys took things out of the back of the trailer until Marc made a face as I went to grab a flat thing up against the side of the trailer wrapped in a tough blue moving blanket.

"We gotta be super careful with this," Marc said, taking the other end.

"What is it and where is it going?" I asked.

"It's Mom's drafting table. She's had it since college or whatever and it means a lot to her. She was super worried it was going to break or whatever if the movers took it and is pretty much the entire reason we even have the trailer."

"Good to know," I said, walking the table backwards under the carport toward the back door. "Your mom an artist or something?"

"Architect. She draws building plans and stuff."

"Really?" I asked. I hadn't expected that.

"Yeah, she's really good at it. Won some awards and stuff for her designs."

"No shit?" I asked.

"For real. Step up!" he warned, and I looked back over my shoulder and took the two steeply pitched steps up into the back of the house.

"Mom!" Marc yelled. "What room do you want your drafting table in?"

"I'm coming!" Cadence called and appeared at my back through the kitchen.

"Front bedroom, please. The one with the most windows and the better light."

"Got it." I nodded, and we carefully guided the table through the doorway to the kitchen and around the corner into the hallway.

"Uh, left or right?" Marc asked.

"Right," his mother said decisively.

Past the bathrooms and into the front bedroom we went, Cadence letting out an audible sigh of relief when we set the table on its legs.

"My father bought me this table when I was nineteen," she said.

"Oh yeah?" I asked casually, eager to listen to any sort of personal tidbits or information she was willing to impart.

"Yeah," she said with a slightly sad but fond smile that made me wonder if her dad had passed.

"My dad died when I was twenty-three. Mom didn't remarry until five or six years later to my stepdad, who she met in a widow's and widower's support group."

"You don't mind me asking, how'd he die?"

"Brain cancer," she said, leaning way down to pick at the brown packing tape securing the blanket around the table.

"Here, let me," I said and whipped my folding Karambit knife out of its holster on my belt by its loop. I whipped it open and around on my finger with practiced ease and Marc let out a "Whoa." I kept my grin to myself as I slashed through the tape with the sharp tip and put it away.

"Thanks," Cadence murmured with a wry smile.

"What is that?" Marc asked, all but vibrating with curiosity.

"It's called a Karambit knife. Useful little tool if you learn to use it right."

"Marc, help me a minute," his mom said, and the kid was a good kid, stepping in and helping out without argument.

The table unfolded smoothly, and Cadence worked on twisting knobs underneath to tighten things up.

"Where do you want it?" Marc asked.

"Not sure yet, and I don't have the rest of the things that go in here so let's just leave it here for right now."

"I'm going to get started on those locksets. You have any trouble with my guys, you just let me know. I'll straighten 'em out," I said.

"Thank you," Cadence murmured, her large green eyes flicking over me, coolly appraising, as though she were trying to decide about me. I smiled a bit ruefully and gave a nod, ducking back out the door and down the hallway, heading for the kitchen and where the knob and locks were waiting on me.

My guys made short work of the trailer and the back of Cadence's SUV. By the time I was done with the front door, she and Marc were already sifting through their stuff, taking stock of what they had versus what they needed. She was meticulous, having found a notebook and pen somewhere in the midst of the chaos of her belongings, and was making a list quietly at the kitchen counter while Marc hauled what looked to be a tote of computer equipment upstairs followed by a television.

Kid had his priorities right, so it seemed.

"Mom, do you know when the internet is gonna be hooked up?" he asked.

"One thing at a time," Cadence said with a heavy sigh. "What time is it? I can maybe call now."

"Not even ten o'clock yet," I supplied. Marc retreated up the stairs back to his room.

"Really?" she asked stretching. "It feels so much *later* than that."

"I promise," I said, testing the latch on the knob I'd just installed. "One down, three to go," I said.

Cadence stared sightlessly in my general direction and chewed thoughtfully on her bottom lip.

"What's up?" I asked.

"Huh?" she asked and blinked as though coming awake.

"You look thoughtful. What's on your mind?" I asked.

"I just have *so much* to do. I need to go shopping to make this place even semi-habitable until our stuff arrives." She sighed heavily. "Air mattresses, shower curtains, towels... I have to return the trailer, too."

"Go do what you have to do," I told her. "We're gonna be here a while yet." I got up and went over to her and held out a set of the keys that'd come with the lockset. "If we're here when you get back, cool. If not, I'll lock up and you got keys so…"

She scraped her bottom lip between her teeth, and I felt my cock jump slightly in my damn jeans. She was just so naturally sexy… *fuck*.

"Thanks," she murmured judiciously and plucked the keys from my hand.

"No problem," I said with a nod.

"Marc!" she called, and he came bounding down the stairs from his room.

"Yeah?"

"Come on, let's go. We have things to do."

"Okay," he said and tossed his hair out of his eyes.

I watched them retreat out the back door, my eyes lingering appreciatively on the perfect curve of Ms. Mitchell's ass.

I needed to draw some boundaries for myself and quick.

5

*C*adence...

"Can I go to my room now?" Marc asked on our return to the house, all but vibrating with his need to set up his computer so he could go play with his friends. It was just about all he could talk about once he figured out that he could use his phone as a hotspot with our plan.

"Yes, go," I said with a tired smile. "Thanks for all your help today," I said.

My kid flashed me a grin and said, "No problem, Mom. Love you."

"Love you, too, baby." I murmured to the thunder of his sneakers against the tile of the kitchen and the hardwood of the dining room after that.

I sighed and closed the security door behind me, leaving the back door open for now with the pleasant spring afternoon outside.

The house needed fresh air, badly.

I set myself to the task of setting up both bathrooms for showers, etc. As far as I could tell, the house was empty until I heard a loud curse from behind the closed basement door. I went to it and opened it.

"Hello?" I called down the stairs.

"Yeah, I'm still here!" a grizzled male voice called back, clearly unhappy.

"Mr. Smith?" I asked.

"Yeah, it's me!" he called up, then absently followed it with a "God*damn* it."

I took a deep breath and went down the stairs into the musty unfinished basement.

"Everything alright?" I asked.

"Yeah, uh, just finishing up. I'll get started on this support tomorrow if that's okay with you."

"Yeah, um, staying awfully late, aren't you?" I asked, hugging myself. I was not a fan of basements. Never had been, never would be.

"Uh, yeah, well, you know… life of being the boss. First one in, last one out – always."

"Oh, um, well… it's not much, but I was just about to order Marc and I some dinner. Can you stay a little longer and have something to eat? Feels like the least I can do after you took the time out of your day to do all those locksets."

He gave me a tired half-grin and a nod. "Thank you," he said. "I'd like that. I'll uh, be up in a sec. Just have a phone call I need to make."

"Wife and kids at home?" I asked, steeling myself for the answer.

"No." He laughed and shook his head. "Just letting a buddy of mine know I'm gonna grab some dinner before I meet up with him at the club."

"Club?" I asked with a slow grin. "You don't strike me as the country-club type, Mr. Smith."

"Hey, none of that now. It's *Jared*, or Glass or Glass Jaw," he said.

"*Glass Jaw?*" I asked incredulously.

"Ah, yup. That's my club's name for me." He laughed a bit nervously and said, "I belong to a motorcycle club."

"Oh!" I cocked my head. I hadn't even considered such a thing. "What's *that* like?" I asked curiously.

"Busy," he said and looked down at what he was measuring on a big old, what looked to be cast or wrought iron table, the thick slab of wood on its top scarred with years upon years of use as a workbench.

"Good Lord," I said, going over to it and touching fingertips to its surface. "I wonder how they got this down here."

"If I had to guess; I'd say it's original. They built the damn house around it."

"That's *crazy*," I muttered.

"Useful though. Hope you don't mind we've been making use of it."

"Not at all," I said. "By all means."

He grinned slightly and checked off measurements against a notepad he had on the table.

"So, what's for dinner?" he asked.

I laughed slightly and said, "I have absolutely no idea. I was going to find something to order. Have any recommendations?"

We chatted briefly about dinner options, and I retreated upstairs to grab my phone. With a sigh, I pulled up local options from a food delivery service and I ordered for myself and called Marc down to put in his. By the time he was done pushing buttons and handing back my phone, Mr. Smi— I mean, Jared, was closing the basement door and looking it over critically.

"Here. I handed him my phone. He frowned, perusing the menu items and made his selections, handing back my phone. I put the order through, and he held out his hand.

"What?" I asked.

"Phone." He waggled his fingers, gesturing I should pass it over. I handed it over, and he swiped and tapped his way through and across screens. His phone rang in his pocket, and I jumped. He tapped my phone and the shrill noise stopped. He handed back my phone.

"In case you need anything. I get the impression you don't know anybody locally."

"My parents," I said softly.

"Oh, yeah? Where abouts are they located?"

I shifted slightly on my feet. "Gig Harbor," I said. He nodded.

"I'm closer, by a lot. Something breaks or something – call me first, okay?"

I swallowed hard. "Okay."

"You get yourself set?" he asked, looking behind himself at the floor of the laundry area just inside the back door. I sighed.

"Sort of."

"See a couple air mattresses," he said with slight disapproval.

"Best I can do," I said softly. "At least until the movers get here."

He nodded.

"What can I do to help while we wait for the food?"

"Oh, you don't have to do that," I said with a smile, and he looked over at me.

"What can I do to help?" he asked again, and his tone said he wouldn't hear of not doing anything at all.

"I got a folding table and a few folding chairs," I said.

"Dining room?" he asked.

"Yeah."

He nodded. "I've got it. Go ahead and get your room set up."

"Thanks," I murmured.

We went to work in separate rooms and made quick work of things. He leaned against the doorway of what would eventually be my bedroom as I unfolded the set of sheets I bought. Mine were with the movers, but when my bed got here, I would have another sheet set. I guess you couldn't have too many of those.

"Here." He held out a hand and helped me make the air mattress that had just finished filling.

I switched off the automatic pump and said, "Thanks."

"You got blankets, I hope."

I nodded. "I have a few. They're in the guest room with the rest of the stuff."

"I'll go look." He went out and I sighed. His presence was strange, but I would be lying if I said it wasn't welcome. Even after... well, maybe *especially* after... I squeezed my eyes shut and shook my head, banishing all thoughts of Ben back into the vault. That place in the dark recesses of your mind that you kept things you didn't want to ever see the light of day again. The things that hurt so much, you didn't think you would or could survive them, let alone survive them *again*.

I heard his approaching footsteps, and he came around the corner and up the hallway back to my room, clutching some folded blankets.

"Yes, those are it, thank you," I said and halfway through making the bed the rest of the way, a knock fell at the front door.

"I've got it," he said and went to gather the food. I finished up, stuffing pillows into their cases and flopping them down at the head of the mattress, straightening and sighing at the few totes marked 'mom's clothes' and 'mom's shoes' in Marc's scrawling teenaged-hurried printing.

I gave myself a moment to breathe, collecting myself, and standing firm against the rising tide of panic and 'what have I done?' before I went out into the hall and around into the dining room. I stopped at the doorway and opened it, calling up into Marc's room at the top of the stairs there, "Marc! Come down for dinner please!"

"Okay!" he called back, and I smiled to myself. No matter what, I loved that kid. Had and would always love my son more than life itself. Everything I did from here on out, I did with him in mind.

"He's a good kid," Jared remarked casually, unpacking two grocery takeout bags, and setting the containers of Chinese out on the six-foot folding table I'd bought. I figured, if anything, it could go out in the outdoor storage by the carport out back when my regular table came. I had no idea what use it might be in the future, but for now, it was a lifesaver.

"You drink?" Jared asked.

"What?" I asked.

"Do you drink?" he asked, and I nodded dumbly. It was out of left field a bit.

"Got a preference? Beer, wine cooler?" he asked.

"Um, I usually drink a Hefeweizen if it's beer at all," I said. He gave a nod.

"I think we've both earned it after a day like today. I'll be right back, just going to run to the gas station around the corner."

"Oh, okay," I said.

"Don't wait, dish up and have something to eat."

I nodded and he went out the front door. A moment later, I heard a motorcycle roar to life, the rumble of its engine fading as it pulled down the street. Marc bounded down the stairs behind me a second later.

"Alright! This stuff looks good!" he declared enthusiastically.

"Yeah, well, make sure there's enough left of everything for Jared. I know you and your hollow leg," I declared.

"I'm a growing boy!" he said with some protest, and I laughed.

"That you are," I agreed.

Jared returned quickly, just as Marc and I were settling into our meals. He came back in with a six pack of bottles, holding them up triumphantly. Out of his pocket, he pulled out a Mountain Mist and passed it to Marc. That made me smile.

"Hey, thanks," Mark declared, just before shoveling a spork full of fried rice into his mouth.

Dinner was a fairly quiet affair – there wasn't much talk. I think all of us were tired, and Marc? While he had what seemed to be boundless energy, he was laser focused on getting back upstairs to do whatever it was he was going to do.

"May I be excused?" he asked me, and I blinked a little surprised. Usually I just got a 'thanks Mom' before he jumped up from the table and disappeared.

"Sure," I said.

"Thanks, Mom!" He did just that, bounding to his feet and making strides with his long, lanky legs to the stairs. I swore by the sound of things, he took them two at a time.

I turned back and startled when I realized Jared's hazel eyes were fixed on me, twinkling with amusement.

"Sorry," I murmured, blushing.

"For what? You raised a good kid," he said.

I blushed a little harder.

"He *is* a good kid," I said, glowing with pride.

"Angry as hell at his father, though. Got a mighty big chip on his shoulder where that's concerned." I sighed.

"Speaking of concerns…" I murmured and smiled faintly.

"What's the story there, if you don't mind my asking?"

I sighed and felt my shoulders sag in almost defeat.

"Ben, Marc's father, and I were teenagers when we had him. I mean, we were both in college. Both of us having graduated early, but still – seventeen." I gave a lopsided smile and a one-shouldered shrug.

"Happens to the best of us," Jared said, shrugging one shoulder lightly. There was no judgment on his face at all.

"You have kids?" I asked, my curiosity getting the better of me.

"No. No kids, never been married… was engaged once," he admitted. "Didn't work out." He shrugged and put his hands down from where he had them steepled before him, leaning back in his chair and propping his hands on top of his thighs. He reached for his bottle on the edge of the table and was the picture of cool, calm, collected, and in control.

Heat unfurled in my belly, and I looked away, fixing my eyes on my plate.

"Anyway," I said. "Ben and I got married, we had Marc, and despite all the odds, we both graduated on time. I had a scholarship and grants that got me through most of the way, and Ben took student loans, but we both got our bachelor's in architecture. Ben was really great, and he got an offer from a firm in Georgia right away, but he would only accept if they looked at my designs too and, well, they liked us both and we moved across the country."

"Oh yeah? So, is this like coming home or whatever? I mean, are you from here?" he asked.

"Oh, sort of. Oregon originally, but my dad was tired of the income tax, so he and my mom retired here in Washington."

"Gotcha." Jared nodded thoughtfully. "I take it things didn't work out with Marc's dad?"

I smoothed my lips together, the vault doors in my mind groaning, fit to burst.

"I'd really rather not talk about it, if that's alright," I said unhappily.

"Hey, that's no problem," Jared said and sighed. "It's getting late," he said reluctantly. "See you sometime tomorrow morning?" he asked.

I nodded. "That would be great."

"Okay, try to have a good night," he said, getting to his feet. "And don't you worry about a thing. I'm sure everything is going to work out okay."

I pasted on a brave smile and despite not believing it, said, anyway, "Thank you."

"No problem," he said. "See you sometime tomorrow morning." He saw himself out.

I groaned and scrubbed my face with my hands, sighing out and staring at the wreckage of Chinese food cartons and paper plates across the table.

At least I'd remembered trash cans and trash bags at the store today.

6

*G*lass Jaw...

"You just met this chick," Mav said, taking a sip of whatever liquor he had in his glass.

"I did," I said, nodding. "At the same time, hello, Pot..." I raised my eyebrows at him and he smirked.

"Touché, brother. Touché," he said and sighed, but he was smiling.

"Colorado, huh?" he asked.

"Yup."

"I'll reach out to the boys out there and see what can be done. You got the info?" he asked.

I pulled my notepad out of my inside pocket and flipped to the page with the moving company's info and tore it out. I passed it to Mav who looked it over, his eyebrows going up.

"Really, now? Where did these fucktards learn customer service?"

"Dunno, but I advocate beating some fuckin' sense into that guy."

"I second that notion," he said. "I'll see what I can do." Mav was cool, too cool and I knew what that level of frosty meant. "You want direct confirmation?" he asked.

"It'd be nice," I agreed.

"Good deal." He dropped the leaf of paper from my notebook onto his desk beside his phone and looked me over appraisingly.

"Hope she's worth it, bro. Never known you to go out on a limb for a broad like this before."

I nodded. "I hope she is too," I said, thinking about Cadence. "I've got a gut feeling she is, though," I said.

He nodded.

"Always trust your gut."

"Somehow I thought you'd say that," I said grinning.

"Go on, get out of here. I think we got the rest of this shit handled."

I nodded. "Thanks, bro."

I got to my feet, and it took some effort. Fuck, I was tired.

The ride home from the club felt longer than usual and was filled with thoughts of the melancholy woman and the brave front she put on to the world. I think the only person on the planet wearier than me right this minute had to be her.

I could see it in her face, in every smooth line and curve of her body through clothes that probably fit a little looser than they had when she'd bought 'em. I knew buying a house was stressful, and I knew fuckin' Hilary made it exponentially more stressful than that – but there was something else there. I just couldn't put my finger on what it was.

I barely kicked off my boots before I flopped on my back onto my bed. I was too tired to fuck with anything else, but as I lay there, hands on my chest, staring at the ceiling, sleep eluded me. Instead, every time I closed my eyes, a pair of haunting green eyes so full of pain it'd like to break my own heart drifted up in front of my mind's eye.

Cadence Mitchell was an enigma; one I'd like to unravel if I could. Beautiful, tougher than she gave herself credit for, but withdrawn and sort of skittish. Except when it came to her boy – then she was a mama bear if I ever saw one. There was flint and steel in her eyes when I'd brought him up in casual conversation – mentioned the chip he had on his shoulder.

Eventually, my mind ran down, and I was able to sleep. Still, it felt like only the blink of an eye and my alarm was going off to get my ass up for another day.

WHEN I GOT to Cadence's place, I pulled down her back alley in my truck, the back loaded with what I needed to work under her fireplace down in her basement. She was coming out the back door, lookin' annoyed and harried – her boy dragging ass behind her, looking as morose as a teen his age could be.

I pulled to the end of the slight turn around, past her patch of back lawn and threw my truck into 'park,' popping the door so I could try to catch what she was saying to the kid.

"…if you wanted me to drive you, all you had to do was *ask,* Marc. You didn't have to go through this whole production of missing the bus. I wouldn't have been mad, honey."

"I didn't miss the bus on *purpose*, Mom. I swear, it was an accident!"

"Oh, Jared! Hi – um – let me let you in."

"It's okay. I can see you're in a hurry," I told her. "I have some stuff to unload and do out here. Just go and I can get in when you come back."

She gave me a look like I was saving her life.

"Hi, Jared," Marc said with a wave.

"Get in the car," Cadence said to her son sharply and I chuckled.

"See you after school, Marc."

"If I survive the ride," he said with a grin.

"Marc!" his mother barked as she got in on the driver's side.

He got in and she started the car. I could see her giving a classic mom lecture through the windshield as they pulled out of the driveway.

I chuckled and got to work hauling out boards and setting up my saw on the tailgate of my truck.

She returned, I don't know, probably around fifteen minutes later.

"I am so sorry!" she called out as soon as she got her door open. I laughed and shook my head.

"It's alright. I was a kid his age once too. I sort of know how it goes. I mean, I'm kind of surprised I remember back that far," I said, squinting in her direction for effect. "But I do."

"Well, I brought coffee... an apology? Peace offering? I didn't know what you liked, so I hope you don't mind – I just got a drip, but I have sugar packets here and there's some creamer in the house. I just got the basics yesterday but forgot the coffeemaker was with the movers."

I laughed and said, "Much appreciated, Ms. Mitchell. You moved to the land of coffee stands on every corner and a shop mid-block too, so you won't be lacking for caffeine any time soon."

"I can see that!" she said, eyes wide like she was a little overwhelmed by the caffeine offerings around here. She ducked back into her car to retrieve the coffees she'd brought.

"Can't beat the Pacific Northwest – Washington in particular – for a few things," I said as she walked toward me. She was gorgeous, drop-dead gorgeous, and she was still in her pajamas – a pair of vertically striped, blue-and-white, drawstring bottoms and a white tee that hugged the curves of her breasts. She wasn't wearing a bra, but she was a woman that was blessed with the ability to forgo one. Still, it was a chilly late spring morning, and I appreciated the stiff peaks her nipples made under the white cotton of the tee. My dick did too, rising to have a look of its own.

"Oh, yeah? What's that?" she asked, thankfully not noticing the bulge taking up residence in the front of my jeans which God's honest truth, the way my Johnson was situated, didn't feel that great.

"The coffee offerings, craft beer, apples, and some of the freshest and best damned salmon and seafood you could ever hope to put in your face," I answered, taking the offered paper cup with its plastic sippy lid.

She raised a deep chestnut and perfectly arced brow and said, "I hadn't considered those things. They all sound pretty good, actually."

"I know of several good places to go and indulge in any of them," I said casually.

"You'll have to let me know of a few," she said with a half-smile that bore some more of that sadness that sat on her slim shoulders. "Right now, I am going to be late for an online video meeting with my new firm, so if you don't mind, I can let you into the house and you can help yourself to whatever you need for your coffee in the kitchen?"

"Yes, ma'am. That's just fine by me."

"Please, for the last time, call me Cadence."

"Sure thing, Cadence," I said, tasting her name. I liked the way it felt in my mouth. If I had my way, I'd find out if she tasted just as sweet but there was plenty of time for that later.

"Like I said," she called over her shoulder, "just help yourself."

"I sure will," I assured her. She went straight for what would be her room and shut the door. By the time I finished stirring cream and a hint of sugar into my Sasquatch Coffee Stand coffee, her door had opened, and I listened to her move straight down the hall to what would be her office and that door shut.

I drank my brew and wondered how long I should give her before I started working downstairs. What had to be done was gonna get loud, and I didn't want to fuck up her meeting. I still had shit to do outside, but not a lot. So, to give her some time, I made some calls that needed to be made while I sipped my coffee, smiling to myself that she'd thought of me when she'd picked up her own.

7

*C*adence...

About twenty minutes after the meeting with my new boss online, a light rapping fell at what would be my new office door if I had anything more in here than my chair, my art cart, and my drafting table – which thank God, I at least had those things.

"Yes?" I called out curiously.

Jared poked his head in.

"Sorry to bother, I just wanted to make sure you were off your call before I started down there. It's gonna get loud."

"Oh, yes! Thank you for checking," I said and he nodded, then paused and looked me over.

"Everything alright?" he asked. I forced a smile and nodded.

"Oh, yes. My boss is being extremely accommodating," I said.

"Is that why when you say that, you look like you've just sucked on a lemon?" he asked with a chuckle.

I rolled my eyes and dropped my face into one of my palms.

"I feel so guilty!" I said honestly, before covering my mouth in dismay.

"How's that?" he asked curiously, leaning a shoulder up against the doorway, letting the door swing into the room.

I shook my head. It wasn't his problem. It was mine... but *Lord*, this new firm was being accommodating. I was supposed to be in the office, but they were letting me work from home, what with all the unmitigated chaos surrounding this move.

"It's cool," he said, pushing off the frame. "You don't have to get into it. Just thought it might be nice to have someone to vent to if you needed it."

I dropped my hand away from my mouth and a genuine smile took up residence there.

"Thank you," I said. "You've been very kind and accommodating, too."

"It's no problem," he said. "Believe me, I may not get all of it, but I've dealt with Hilary enough to get the gist of it all. You've got a long list left on that buyer's report of repairs and shit to do. You let me know, and maybe I could take some of them off your plate at a reasonable rate."

I stared at him for a long moment and relief washed over me.

"That would be really great," I said.

"Talk about it later?" he asked and lightly punched the doorjamb twice.

"Absolutely. I'm going to try and get some designs done, get ahead, you know?"

He nodded. "Sorry in advance for the noise," he said.

I waved him off. "It needs to get done," I said as kindly as I could make it.

"Yeah, it really does," he agreed. He slipped out of the doorway, leaving it vacant. I stared for a long time at the empty portal where he'd stood, eyes glazed and unfocused.

God, I needed to get it together!

With a sigh, I spun on my seat and stared at the top of my drafting table.

First things first, I needed my bond paper to draw out my plans and make the dream a reality.

"When did you last eat or take a break?" His voice was low and gentle from the doorway but still unexpected. I shot toward the roof and let out a yelp, pressing my hand to my chest. My heart thundered beneath it.

"Shit! Sorry, I thought you heard me coming!" he cried, and I turned around to find his posture mirroring mine, hand to his chest as he laughed, breathing a bit heavy from his startlement.

He was one seriously fine specimen of a man, *Jesus*.

My eyes drifted over him from his short cropped dark brown hair speckled with sawdust to his broad shoulders wrapped in its faded red tee, the sleeves hugging his muscular biceps. His body tapered down to narrow lean hips and powerful thighs pressed at the denim of butter soft, well-worn jeans.

I blushed faintly and swallowed hard, my eyes just a little bit wide as I asked, "What did you ask me?"

"I asked when you last ate anything was," he said, and that crooked grin made me blush that much harder. It, along with his smiling hazel eyes, said that he'd seen me checking him out and that he was pleased by it.

I was so not ready for any of *that* business.

"Last night at dinner, why?" I asked.

His brows crushed down in a frown.

"It's after noon. Come on. I know a place nearby that's good and you need to eat."

"I don't know..." I hedged, looking at the time. "Marc is going to be home from school soon."

"What time does he get home?" he asked.

"Around three o'clock. I really should be here."

"He's seventeen and that's over an hour from now. Come on. Let's get you some food and I promise I'll have you back here in a flash."

I hesitated just a moment longer, realizing my stomach was *not* happy with me, burning with that ravenous sensation that said I had gone way too long and then some between meals.

"Okay," I agreed and got up, sending a text to Marc, anyway, to let him know I might be out when he got home and asking if he was okay with that and to answer me between classes.

My phone went off a second later with an *it's fine mom* accompanied by an eye rolling emoji.

I smiled to myself and shook my head.

"Little shit," I muttered.

"What's that?" Jared asked, looking back over his shoulder at me.

"My son! Not you! Oh, my God."

He laughed at me and held out a hand to indicate I should go ahead of him into the dining room and head toward the back. I plucked my purse and keys off the dining room table.

"So how is it downstairs?" I asked as he opened the back door for me, which was sweet but not necessary.

I locked up behind us as he said, "All done for the most part."

"Really? That was fast."

"Wasn't a big job," he said as we went across the yard toward his truck. He opened his truck door for me, too – an ultra-modern RAM pickup, shiny and black.

"Watch your shins, there's a step that'll come down when I open the door." I nodded and he opened the door, a running board folding down from underneath the truck.

"Fancy," I said with a smile and stepped up into the clean cab.

He shut the door behind me with a smile.

"You like the house all gray like that?" he asked me when he got in.

I took a deep breath and let it out.

"No, not particularly. Get that enough around here as it is," I said, leaning forward to look up out of the windshield to the leaden-gray sky.

"True enough," he agreed, glancing too for a second as he started the truck. I blinked as the large panel lit up in the center and then *really* did a double take as he *twisted a dial* to select his gear.

"That's *crazy*," I muttered, and he laughed.

"Yeah, not gonna lie. I've turned up or down the volume a couple times by accident trying to put this thing in gear."

"It's a good thing you haven't fucked that up the other direction!" I declared.

"True story," he said and backed out of my driveway.

"You were saying about paint," I said, staring out the window.

49

"Yeah, maybe the movers taking a minute with your stuff is a blessing in disguise. Painting is a whole hell of a lot easier when there's no furniture in the way."

"That's true," I said. "So is cleaning." I gave him a little bit of side-eye on that one. His men had taped down a paper walkway on my floor all through from the basement out the front door, but my hardwoods were an absolute *mess*. They had tracked dirt from the basement all through the house, from the living room to the hall to what was now my bedroom and my office. I had yet to get a mop or broom to clean it up.

Jared laughed and had the grace to look a little embarrassed.

"Yeah, don't you worry about that. I've got it handled and the floor will be spotless before you know it."

"Thank you," I said with a tiny smile of my own.

"Technically, Hilary was supposed to give the place a good once-over before you moved in," he said, and I made a rude noise. He laughed and said, "Exactly."

That certainly wasn't going to happen. The woman was the epitome of cheap and lazy. I hadn't anticipated just how much work still needed to go into the house until I'd seen it in person. The photographs had been much kinder than the in-person reality of it. The paint job was shitty at best. Several closets didn't have knobs, let alone closet rods in them. I mean, I was handy, but it was *a lot* of little things that needed doing that honestly all added up to time I just did not have.

I worried my bottom lip between my teeth and tried to pay attention to where Jared was taking us, right up until he pulled us into the lot at an unassuming strip mall off the nearest main drag. He turned the dial on his dash to 'park' and turned off the truck, settling his fist on top of his thigh and turning in my direction.

"Spill," he said. "What's going on in there?"

I dropped my eyes to my phone in my hands, which rested on my purse in my lap – a modest canvas handbag with a clipped-on cross-body strap that spilled uselessly to the truck's floorboard.

"The house," I admitted.

"What about it?" he asked.

"The pictures were kind," I said, letting out a pent-up breath. "It's missing a lot of little things, and it all adds up time wise and I guess… I guess, it's all just a bit overwhelming."

He nodded and I smiled a bit ruefully.

"Thanks for listening to me bitch," I said after a moment of silence.

"Happy to help," he said. "Come on, let's eat, and we can make a game plan."

"Okay," I agreed.

We got out of his truck, and he led me across the lot to an inconspicuous little mom-and-pop Mexican restaurant.

"Really?" I asked as he opened the door for me.

"Best street tacos in the area," he said with a grin. "As authentic as you can get."

I smiled and said, "I guess we'll see."

He didn't wait for us to be seated, just picked a table, and slid into the booth. I slid in across from him and a moment later a woman appeared, a pad of paper in hand but no menus.

Jared rattled off some Spanish and she grinned. They bantered a moment and she laughed and nodded, wrote some things down, and he looked at me.

"Chicken, beef, or pork?"

"Um, beef."

"Shredded, ground, or steak?"

"Shredded please," I said.

He talked to the waitress some more and she left, returning a moment later with glasses of water, chips, and salsa.

"Okay," he said, looking me up and down, hands folded in front of him atop the table. "What's bugging you the most?" he asked. "Don't try and decide what needs prioritizing or any of that shit now. Just what's eating you about the house?"

"The lack of closet doorknobs, the fact that the kitchen cabinets and drawers don't have any knobs, and the lack of rods in the closets. I feel like I can't hang anything up or put anything away."

"All of those are easy fixes. After we eat, we'll swing by the hardware store and start getting some things."

I blinked and he cocked his head as if he were expecting an answer and I sort of jolted into the here and now and said without really thinking, "Okay."

He nodded as though satisfied with that and said, "Now, if it's alright with you, I'd like to ask..." he trailed off and my curiosity got the better of me. I nodded my assent for him to go ahead.

"What happened with Mr. Mitchell?"

I sighed and put my chin in my hand.

"That's a long story, and it doesn't have a happy ending," I said.

"We don't have anywhere to be," he said, holding open his hands and gesturing at the mostly empty restaurant around us.

"I suppose not," I said with a weak smile. "Where to begin?"

"Well, we went through pregnant, married, had kid, and we glossed over graduation," he said with a half-smile and I blushed.

"Careers," I said haltingly, both good. Really good, actually, his better than mine... but his required a lot of travel so we thought. I swallowed hard and said it out loud. "Ben died, suddenly... um." I cleared my throat, a lump taking up residence in it.

I took a deep breath and let it out.

"We thought he was traveling a lot for work, and it um... it turned out he had a whole other family that we didn't know about and a will, leaving everything to them."

"Oh, what?"

"Yeah." I nodded slowly. "That's pretty much the expression I wore, too."

"Holy shit," he said, his eyebrows reaching for his hairline. He picked up his glass of water and took several swallows and set it down, clearing his own throat. "So, uh, how did that all work out?"

"Not well, for either of us. I was Ben's legal wife, and so I, of course, contested the will, but it was legally binding and all of that so all I really got out of it was the small life insurance policy that was in my name. The rest? The house and everything else? Went to her and her kids... which considering I paid for half of it that was some bullshit, but you know." I gave a feeble shrug. "That's the south for you. Even dead, a man's word outweighs any of his wife's desires."

"Jesus, fuck."

"Honestly, I didn't want to fight anymore. I just wanted out what I put in. I got a fair bit so I could pack us up and move somewhere to start over."

I looked away, my cheeks heating with embarrassment. *Stupid, stupid, so stupid,* echoed through my mind. My mantra since everything had come to light.

"I can see why Marc is angry," Jared said soberly.

"Yeah." I nodded in agreement. "I just don't have it in me to be mad anymore. I'm just..." I shifted uncomfortably in my seat. "I'm just sad more than anything. Embarrassed."

He searched my face and asked, "What do you have to be embarrassed about?"

I sighed. "He was having his checks split between two bank accounts and handled the majority of the finances. I'll be paying some debts for a while. Embarrassed because we worked for the same firm and I guess... I guess they all knew. They had to."

"Jesus Christ, people suck," he said, and he looked about as queasy as I felt since this whole ordeal began.

"Right?" I asked and stared out into the dimly lit gloom of the restaurant with its colorful terracotta-edged booths with their cracked red-vinyl seats.

"I bet not one of them lent you a helping hand," he said, and I shook my head.

"Nope, it's just me and Marc against the world." I gave a small smile at that. "Of course, hindsight being twenty-twenty, it's just been me and Marc for a long time now."

"That ain't right," he said. He looked, I don't know... like he was angry on my behalf or something. The sentiment was appreciated. Aside from my parents, it honestly felt like I had no one in my corner, and even my parents... well, they may have been in my corner, but it was from afar. Always had been. They'd hated Ben and thought I'd made a terrible mistake marrying him and oh boy, they'd been right. I couldn't tell you how much I hated that.

I nibbled on a chip that I lightly dipped in the sauce-like salsa that'd been provided.

Jared looked like he was still processing, and it was all I could do not to squirm in my seat.

"To new beginnings," he said finally, holding out his water glass. I gave a watered-down smile and clicked my glass against his and wished I could share the clear firmness of his belief. I mean, I didn't hold out much hope for myself or my future. I felt damaged, and unlike my house, I felt as though I was beyond repair.

"To new beginnings," I murmured and had the grace to at least take a sip before I put my glass down.

8

*G*lass Jaw...

It was too bad a motherfucker could only die once. I had to reevaluate my initial impression of Cadence Mitchell after her revelation. I thought she'd been pretty before, maybe a little easily riled up or overwhelmed, but after that little bomb drop of hers, I quickly fucking realized that nothing could be further from the truth.

The woman across from me ran deep, incredibly so, and she had hidden recesses that I could probably only dream of.

It made her exponentially hotter, at least to my mind. There was honestly nothing sexier than a woman who could hold her own and keep her secrets. If she was this good at keeping her own, it meant if she had a mind to, she could keep a man's as well.

That was incredibly hot.

Likewise, I had to admit that her putting her trust in me like this? That was hot as well. I mean, clearly the situation with her dead husband caused her a lot of embarrassment, which it shouldn't. That shit was on him. But by the same token, I got it. I really did. It was the rest of the citizenry that got it twisted, not the likes of me. I'm sure she'd heard 'how could you not know?' more than a few times by now but she wouldn't hear it from me. She didn't know because he didn't *want* her to know, and that was usually how that kind of shit worked.

I knew, from personal experience, not to cheat on a woman – I wasn't scum. If I wanted to stray that fuckin' bad, shit was already over and I had the fucking decency to drop the axe and sever ties before I went and got my dick wet somewhere else. No, I meant I knew because of my ties with the club which were stronger than iron. You couldn't live this life and be completely honest with anyone but your brothers. Women, by default, played second fiddle – always. That was just the way it had to be, mostly for their own protection. Real men didn't drag their lady to hell with them.

As I looked at Cadence, her shoulders rounded forward and slightly hunched, the glint of hurt and the fear of being unjustly judged in her captivating green eyes, I hated for her that she'd put her chips all in with such a craven asshole. I bet she hadn't been touched in a while, and that was a damn shame. She was fucking gorgeous, curvaceous, all sleek sweeping lines that begged for the caress of a man's hands.

We were saved from an ensuing awkward silence by the arrival of our food. A few bites in, I turned the subject from personal to semiprofessional, talking about the house. She was bright and knew her shit and what needed prioritizing off her inspection report versus what was just a bunch of fucking penny-ante bullshit.

It just made her hotter to me, her intelligence. She was bright, and discerning, and holy fuck, she was the total package.

"Shit," she muttered, looking at her watch.

"Time to go?" I asked. We'd finished our meal a little while ago.

"Yeah, time flies when you're having fun, I guess," she said with a little laugh.

"Glad you're having fun," I said with a smile I couldn't suppress if I'd wanted to. She made it really hard to play it cool.

I paid. I wouldn't hear of her doing it, even for just her own meal. I told her it was my official 'welcome to Washington, I promise it doesn't suck here.' She'd laughed slightly, a tightness around her eyes that told me she was beyond worried she'd made some kind of horrible mistake in coming here to restart her and her son's lives, which inexplicably was a sort of kick in the 'nads.

It gave me the feeling that the whole process of getting across the country for her had been nothing but pitfalls and one big pain in the ass, all the opposition in the world coming from this corner of the planet. With Hilary McConnel in the mix, I wouldn't put it past anything that that was the case. If I was lucky, I would probably get the full meal deal on that and I was kind of eager to, to be honest. Couldn't fix it if you didn't know what was broken.

I opened the passenger door of my truck and warned her again to keep back and watch the runner board coming down. She smiled at me, a grateful little thing, and got in. I shut the door for her.

"Give your boy a call. We still have to stop at the hardware store," I reminded her.

"Oh, we can do it later," she said, and I raised an eyebrow.

"You gotta work tomorrow or can you rearrange a few things?" I asked.

"Tomorrow is Saturday," she said, and I nodded.

"I know it," I replied.

"I'm free," she said. "I guess."

I smiled.

"Good deal."

I took her back home. Marc was walking up the back alley to the back door of their place when we pulled up.

"Hey, Mom," he called as she stepped down from the cab of my truck.

"Hey, how was your first day?" she asked.

"It was okay," he said. "Hey, Jared."

"Hey," I answered genially. "I've got some cleanup down in the basement," I said. "Otherwise, I'm done." Cadence nodded and went to the back door, keying open both locks on the security door and then the back door to the house beyond it.

"Hey," I murmured, and she stopped and raised an eyebrow at me, a silent 'go on' and so I did. "Do me a favor," I told her. "When you leave the house, it's just an empty house with stuff in it. Stuff can be replaced. You and Marc can't. Just lock the deadbolt on one of these doors. When you're home? Yeah, lock all four – but when you're out, it takes too long to get in the house. You feel me?"

She paused and searched my face and finally nodded slowly. Marc said, "Way to freak us out."

"I don't mean to freak you out," I protested. "Just like to keep you both safe."

"Why?" Marc asked, shoving in the back door. "You don't even know us." He wasn't meaning to be rude. Nothing in the kid's tone telegraphed sarcasm or teen-attitude problem. He was just doing that thing teens did – thought to mouth, no filter in between.

Cadence gave him a slight glare behind the kid's back. One of those mommy looks of death that said she wasn't about to take him to task in front of company or whatever, but later? She'd verbally take a stripe out of his hide. I almost felt sorry for him... but you know how that goes. Never get between a mama and her cub.

"I'm sorry," she murmured at me, searching my face. I smiled at her gently.

"Don't be," I said simply. "No reason. He's just a kid being a kid." I gestured she should go ahead of me, and she stepped up into the house.

I followed suit, closing the security screen door. I went to close the inner door itself and Cadence called back over her shoulder, "Leave it open. It's nice out." I nodded and threw the lock on the security door, and she smiled and said, "Thank you for lunch."

"It was no problem," I said. "Welcome to the neighborhood."

"Thanks," she said and skirted into the kitchen and went back toward her office.

The basement door was directly across from the back door, and I went for it, smiling to myself when I heard her on the stairs overhead going up to Marc's room.

I knew that was right. She was gonna go talk to him about having a fuckin' filter.

Chuckling, I went down as she went up to finish my cleanup and to get out of their hair for tonight.

I found her in her office when I was through and ready to head out.

"Knock, knock," I called softly, and she looked up and back from her drafting table.

"Ready to leave?" she asked.

"Yeah." I nodded and stepped into the space holding out a couple of sheets off my yellow legal pad I kept around to make lists and write measurements.

"What's this?" she asked.

"Took the liberty of making a list for the hardware store," I said, clearing my throat. "The stuff on the first page is shit you really ought to get right now if you can afford it. I'm happy to work with you on cost when it comes to labor. Some of it I'm even willing to do for free if you can just wait for evening time or the weekend."

"Why would you do that?" she asked, frowning slightly.

I searched her skeptical expression and told the truth.

"You've been through it," I said, and her face drew down, closing off. "I think it's time someone helped you out some," I said.

"I can pay," she said, and it held an edge. She turned, her back stiff, pride radiating off her, swirling around her in a shroud of independence. *That was hot, too.*

"Never said you couldn't," I said. "I just said I wouldn't charge you."

She turned again, scowling slightly and I grinned. She couldn't hold it, and she giggled softly at me.

"We'll figure it out?" she asked, and I nodded.

"Sounds good. Just get what you can for now. My number's at the bottom of the second page. Call me when you've got some stuff for me, and I'll work out a time with you to come by."

"Sounds good," she agreed.

"Okay." I gave a nod. "Have a good night."

"Thanks," she said. "You, too."

I lightly punched the doorjamb a couple times and with one last lingering look at the smooth line of her neck and how it swept into her shoulder and down her back like a work of fucking art, I left.

My phone buzzed twice about ten minutes later and when I checked, it was a text from an unknown number.

Is there a hardware store you prefer, one over the other?

A second later another text came through.

It's Cadence, by the way. Sorry.

I grinned and waited until I was stopped at a light to text back. I shot her the name of the hardware place I knew was closest to her, the cross streets, and an assurance they should have everything she needed.

Thanks, we'll go tonight.

I grinned like a fuckin' moron.

That honestly suited me just fine. The sooner I could come back and get to know more about her, the better.

9

*C*adence...

    I sighed in frustration and rested my forehead against the cool stainless steel of the way-too-fancy refrigerator that had come with the house. Of course, the water wasn't hooked up. Why would it be? Just like the dishwasher wasn't properly anchored, though I suppose I should be grateful it didn't leak, and it at least seemed to be properly hooked up – it worked and worked well – even if it was just for cheap dollar-store dishes that Marc and I had bought until our stuff arrived.

"You okay, Mom?" he asked.

"What? Yeah, honey. I'm fine."

"What's the matter?"

"Fridge doesn't work for water or ice. It's no big deal, just have to figure out how to hook it up."

"Want me to YouTube it?" he asked eagerly, and I had to smile. I swear it was this kid's answer for everything, and nine times out of ten, it was miraculous the way the how-to videos laid everything out – but then again...

"With what tools, baby?" I asked.

"Oh, yeah..." He looked sheepish.

"They're with the movers," we said in unison and had to laugh, or I think I might cry.

That was pretty much the answer for 'Mom, where's *insert random object?*'

"Well, that sucks," he said, and I nodded. "Do we even have everything to make it work?" he asked, and I shrugged, shaking my head with a heavy sigh.

"I don't know," I said.

"Back to the hardware store?" he asked, and I nodded.

"Yup."

"What time is Jared supposed to get here?"

I sighed and asked, "What time is it?"

He looked at his phone.

"Ten o'clock."

"Shit," I said. "Any minute, now."

"Whoa, you better get in the shower," he said.

"What?" I asked, slightly alarmed and he grinned.

"When was the last time you took one?"

I had to think about it. That was problematic. This week had gone by way too fast. Last weekend had been multiple trips to the hardware store to stock the storage unit outside with things that needed to be accomplished, then we'd dove into trying to sort through the things we'd brought with us in the car and trailer – getting it all out of the guest room.

Then, the week had descended upon us with a bit of a vengeance. School, work, meetings for me and sports for Marc. His new school at least had a soccer program, which he absolutely loved and to my surprise, he had enthusiastically wanted to sign up for. His tryout had gone well – which shocked me. I mean, I knew he had played well with his friends back in Georgia, but I had no idea he'd had interest in playing for real through a program or his school.

That had led to a particularly soul-crushing conversation about how Marc hadn't wanted to bother me... knowing that his father wasn't around a whole lot, even when he had been alive, to help with anything yet how Ben had expected me to do all the things for him when it came to both my own work and arranging and executing dinner parties and a whole host of other things for him.

It made me angry now that I could look back and see with clarity that the things that I did for him were so that he could spend more time with his other family. It broke my heart, not just for me, but for Marc, in ways I couldn't describe. It hurt that all of what I did for Ben was also in a vain hope for more than a hurried 'thanks, babe' and a peck on the cheek.

God, it was depressing. I was so stupid. How could I have not known?

"Hold down the fort," I told Marc, not letting on that I was distressed if I could help it. "I'm getting showered, getting dressed, and we'll do what we can until Jared gets here, then we'll run to the hardware store.

"We gonna paint?" he asked, perking up.

I sighed. "We'll see. Depends on if Jared needs us for anything."

"K." Marc looked thoughtful, and I smiled.

"Love you, Bub," I said, drifting toward my bathroom.

"Love you, too, Mom. Save me some hot water."

Shit. I forgot to mention that to Jared.

"Jared shows up, you tell him about that, would you?"

"Yeah," he said.

Honestly, who sold a house with a shower that got no hot water to it? Apparently, Hillary McConnel did.

I showered and spent a little longer than I intended to under the hot spray, which was apparent when I heard the door to the bathroom open and Marc called in, "Mom, Jared's here!"

"Hey!" I heard from a little further out in the hall.

I rolled my eyes and called out, "Hi! Sorry! I'll be right out, I promise."

"Take your time," Jared called. "I'm going to look at the fridge and wait until you're done to look at Marc's shower."

I turned off the water and said, "I'm done! Fire when ready." I covered my face with my hands and silently groaned at how stupid that must have sounded.

"Sound's good," Jared called from the hall. I heard his retreating boot steps across the hardwoods.

"Wow," Marc muttered and shut the bathroom door.

"Little shit," I swore softly and pulled my towel off the curtain rod at the other end of the shower where it was safe from the spray.

This bathroom needed towel bars.

So did Marc's.

And bathroom furniture, like a hamper and maybe one of those cabinets that went over the toilet. It was a bigger bathroom than what we'd had in Georgia, so I actually had to go buy these things. It wasn't something that was with the frickin' movers, which don't even get me started down that road again.

I sighed. The list seemed insurmountable, and somewhere in there, I still had to get laundry done because the washer and dryer I'd purchased?

The dryer was being delivered this week, but the washer? Backordered for over a month, which of course they didn't tell me until *after* I'd purchased it.

By that point, I was just too frickin' tired to argue or try to go somewhere else. I had done all of our laundry before leaving Georgia, including bedding, and that was one of the things we had brought with us – all of our clothes in totes and suitcases. We'd been trying to cut down the number of totes and space in the moving truck, but it'd been futile. I'd still ended up over the space limit and had had to pay the movers over five grand more to get our stuff here. Only to, as you know, find out that they could essentially deliver it whenever they frickin' wanted to even though they'd said that it'd be here when we arrived.

I sighed and finished toweling off and wrapped the towel around me up under my armpits. I cracked the bathroom door and listened intently for where the boys were in the house before darting past the useless quarter bath between my bathroom and my bedroom. I really needed to do something more useful with that quarter bath, but with everything else wrong with the house at this point, it was quickly becoming a low priority.

Plus, I didn't know what I wanted to do with it yet. A pantry? A bigger closet? I didn't know. I shut myself in my room and curled my lip at the air mattress on the floor. I hated it. I had just turned thirty-five, had birthed a thirteen-pound baby – a fact I would *never* let Marc live down, and I was just feeling plain too old to be sleeping on an air mattress on the floor.

I glared at the bedroom closet that was also sans shelf or closet rod, which none of the closets had shelves or a rod either... *who sells a house without those details?* Thus, I was still rooting through wrinkled clothes in totes and suitcases, trying to find something suitable for the time being.

I was just pulling a sleeveless, army green tee over my head when a light rap fell on my bedroom door. I stepped to it, the thighs of my wrinkled but crisp fresh jeans swishing against each other in the quiet of my room and opened up my door expecting Marc but finding Jared instead. My cheeks heated in a blush, my hair hanging lank and uncombed around my face and leaving me feeling like a drowned rat.

"Oh, hi," I said, and he smiled at me, sweeping me from head to foot with those hazel eyes of his sparkling with... I don't know what, but it seemed delighted.

"Hi," he said, and I swallowed hard at the pitch and timber of his voice. The single word rich and husky skittered across my sense of hearing like it was sliding seductively across satin sheets.

I swallowed hard and didn't say anything, the words catching in my throat. His smile widened and he let me off easy by telling me, "Marc's shower is fixed."

"Oh yeah?" I asked, perking up a bit. "What was wrong with it?"

"Some damn fool installed the shower handle backwards," he said. "Had the temperature regulator turned all the way down. Easy fix. Won't cost you a thing."

I felt the breath rush out of me in relief and said, "Thank you."

"That outlet in his bathroom is a bit of a different story," he said frowning.

"What?" At the look on his face that bordered on anger, I whined a bit. "Nooo, don't tell me—"

"Yeah, I don't know what the fuck they were thinking but they've got a two-twenty running to that thing."

"I need an electrician?" I asked meekly.

"Nah, not necessarily," he said, rubbing the pad of his thumb against his full bottom lip, an unconscious gesture that had me pressing my thighs together just a little bit tighter.

"What do I do then?" I asked.

"You can get an adapter online. I'll show you what to get. They're not too bad, in the thirty-to-fifty-dollar range. That'll do yah until you decide to either hire an electrician, or you know, you can just deal with the adapter."

"It's not a fire hazard?" I asked.

"Not with the adapter, no. It's too much power and could spark or cause a fire if you plug anything into it without one, though."

"Okay, what's the other bad news?" I asked, rolling my eyes and he laughed.

"No other bad news, just need an adapter and a long enough hose for the fridge. That's easy enough. If I have the parts, I can do it. No plumber required."

I leaned against the doorjamb and nodded, lost in thought for the moment. Jared just stood there patiently. I looked up at him and his expression was kind.

"What else do I need?" I asked, finally. "From the hardware store. I can go get it."

He held up a piece of paper and said, "Got it all written down for you right here."

"Okay," I said, plucking the page from between his fingers.

"Go team," he said and held out a fist. I laughed and bumped it with my own.

He retreated down the hall. I sighed and called out, "Marc! You ready to go?"

We worked all day. As soon as I got back from the hardware store, Marc and I were given the go-ahead to paint the living room walls. Jared worked on things while we were gone, and the fridge once we had returned.

I breathed a sigh of relief when the shouting and general cursing ceased from the kitchen with a triumphant, "There we go! Now, that's what I'm talkin' about!"

Marc turned from the wall he was painting a wholesome vanilla and I faced him from the accent wall I was painting a soothing, light minty green around the fireplace, and we grinned at each other.

"Sounds like someone's victorious," I called out.

"You know it, baby!" Jared crowed from the kitchen, and I raised an eyebrow and felt myself flush vermillion at the endearment while Marc pointed and laughed at me mercilessly.

I rolled my eyes at my teenage son and turned back to my wall, smoothing paint over the drab gray with the roller.

I only wished erasing my sadness were so easy.

Dinner was a quick affair of ordered food, and I took a minute to leave the boys, laughing and talking at the six-foot folding table that served as our dining room table, taking my beer out the front door to lean on the front porch railing and just take a minute for myself.

I breathed out, the twilight settling in, darkness creeping sleepily out from between the houses and trees, out from under cars as the light began to fail and I let some of the tension from the day go.

"You okay?"

I startled and turned to where Jared leaned out the open doorway, hand gripping the frame stretching, his own bottle in a relaxed grip of his dangling hand.

God, he made everything look so nonchalant and *easy*... sexy, too... but I needed to not think about that last. I mean, I was *sure* he had to have a girlfriend. He was too nice and smokin' hot not to.

"Yeah, yeah." I harrumphed a chuckle and felt my lips quirk in a sort of smile. "I'm fine," I lied and thought to myself as I took a quick pull from the neck of my own bottle, *if fine means fucked up, insecure, neurotic, and emotional, then yeah, I'm just fuckin' peachy.*

"You can't lie to me," he said, and his voice had dropped, pitching low, the timber of it,,, I don't know. It was kind, warm, welcoming, and inviting.

I swallowed my mouthful of crisp beer around a sudden lump in my throat.

"You don't mind me saying..." he said, and I looked up and over at him, his expression slightly unsure and waiting for the invitation to complete his thought.

"Go on," I said, curiosity getting the better of me.

"You need to relax," he said and stepped out onto the porch, letting go of the doorframe and walking the few scant steps to join me at the railing.

I laughed a little and it sounded slightly bitter – a bitterness I tried to cover up by innocently asking, "And how do you propose I do that?"

He knocked his shoulder into mine and said, "I don't know, get laid or something."

I snorted and laughed, looking at him skeptically. "And are you offering your services to that effect?" I asked, quailing a little on the inside at either answer he was about to give me – yes or no – both seemed to have anxieties attached to them.

He shrugged, trying to hide his pleased look. Playing it cool, he said, "It probably wouldn't take much persuading."

"Oh, my God," I uttered and blushing so bright I thought I might become a bug zapper, I leaned my forearms against the railing and rocked back and forth on my feet.

"Hope I'm not making you uncomfortable," he said and cleared his throat. I shook my head, kind of speechless.

"No," I said. "Trust me, it's not you, it's me…"

He nodded slowly and we lapsed into silence for a time before he said, "Look, no pressure, but I'd really like to take you out and get to know you a little better."

"Yeah?" I asked, hardly able to believe my ears. He straightened and turned to me, leaning a hip against the railing. He looked at me, his eyes narrowing slightly.

"Why do I get the feeling you don't think very highly of yourself?" he asked, and I straightened and mirrored his stance, leaning a hip against the railing and raising an eyebrow. I took a pull off of my beer with a little shrug.

Truth be told, his question hit a little close to home. I didn't think very highly of myself. Why should I, after everything?

He looked me over and the sincerity in his eyes, on his face, kind of stole my breath. He gave a little nod as though he'd made his mind up about something and an almost determination steeled his gaze.

"Alright," he said.

I frowned slightly, a bit jittery, and asked, "Alright what?"

"Well, as you know, I'm pretty good at building things," he said. I nodded carefully, unsure where he was going with this. "You lay the designs and the rules and let's do this," he said, sweeping out an arm.

"Do what?" I asked, brow furrowing in confusion.

"Rebuild that broken self-esteem of yours."

I felt my eyes widen. He raised an eyebrow and patiently waited me out to say something – anything. The problem was, what exactly did you fucking say to something like that? *Holy shit!*

"I don't know what to say," I finally admitted softly, and he lightly took my hand that was hanging by my side, lining his palm to the back of my hand and curling his fingers between mine. I stared down at our hands and swallowed hard, suddenly scared – but not of him. No, I was scared of *me* and of the potential of opening up the Pandora's box of pain I had buried deep inside of me.

"Say 'yes,'" he said with a little shrug. "Say you'll let me take you out and show you some things."

"Some things?" I asked, meeting his eyes.

"Around here." He shrugged one shoulder and the sincerity in his eyes when he said, "How beautiful I think you are," touched me soul deep. He raised our joined hands and planted a kiss softly in the center of my palm.

I shivered and it had absolutely nothing to do with being chilled by the deepening night. No, in fact, it was quite pleasant out here.

I swallowed hard, speechless.

"All you have to do is say 'yes,'" he murmured and *God*, did it sound so tempting.

"Alright," I whispered and the smile that graced his lips was other-worldly.

"Is that a 'yes?'" he asked, and I nodded carefully.

"That's a 'yes,'" I whispered. He took a step forward and before I was ready, or before I knew what was happening, his lips were descending toward mine.

I think I plucked up every bit of bravery I had in the moment and turned my face up to his rather than look away. I closed my eyes and his lips brushed mine so softly, so carefully, and suddenly it was a sensation like falling though I stood so very solid and so very still.

The kiss was chaste, gentle, and soft. My heart pounded the inside of the cage of my ribs as he brushed his lips across mine, back and forth in the barest of touches. So careful of me, so slow, so... *safe.* He didn't rush me and was playing it safe for my comfort.

"Hmm." He hummed his pleasure and searched my face, which I could only stare wide-eyed and surprised, as much at him as I was at *myself.*

"I'll be back tomorrow, okay?" he asked softly, and he let me go, my hand suddenly suspended without the support of his behind it. I made an uncertain strangled noise and nodded a little too quickly.

"Goodnight," he said with a smirk. He disappeared back through my front door, the hollow tread of his booted feet against my hardwood floors retreating through the house.

Holy shit... had that really just happened?

I looked down at the half empty beer in my hand with the nervously peeled label and swore at myself.

"Jesus, *fuck*, Cadence. What is wrong with you?" I whispered as I closed my eyes.

Wasn't that the question of the ages?

10

*G*lass Jaw...

"Where the fuck you been all day?" Mav asked me as I dropped onto the barstool next to his. I didn't hide the fact I had to adjust myself in my pants. Fuck, I was *still* hard almost an hour later, the tingling memory of her soft lips lingering against my own, that soft whimper of need she probably hadn't even known she'd let out echoing in my ears on a repeated loop in my brain and *fuck*.

"Oh, man... I am so fucked," I said with a savage grin. "I've got it *bad* for the widow Mitchell."

Mav's eyebrows went up.

"Oh, yeah?" he asked.

"Oh, yeah."

He leaned back some and caught Ms. Momma Kat's eye and jerked his head in my direction. Momma Kat grinned, gave him a chin lift and set off to pour me something good.

"So, what happened?" he asked.

I told him all about it.

"Oh, man… this woman? She is fucking *beautiful*," I said. "All soft lines and sweeping curves, big doe eyes and the longest, softest-looking sleek-brown hair. Definitely the softest fucking lips I've ever put against mine and I swear to fucking God, I can still taste her."

I closed my eyes and leaned back on my seat and just relished the recent memory of her for a split second. When I opened my eyes, Mav's indigo ones were sparkling, his bottom lip caught between his teeth as his shoulders shook in silent laughter at me.

"I know, bro. Believe me, I know how ridiculous I look right now, but I can't muster up any fucks to give."

"I've never seen you like this over a piece of ass," Mav declared, and I shook my head.

"I've never felt like this about a woman before, but man, Cadence? This isn't that," I said. "This goes way beyond a hit-it or quit-it sort of scenario. She's not the type, man. This is a woman you take your time with, a woman you spoil and the kind you marry."

Mav was laughing at me so hard tears were leaking out of the corners of his eyes by this point, but I didn't give a fuck. He could laugh all he wanted. If there was such a thing as love at first sight, I think I'd found it. Cupid shot his shot, and that arrow went right up my mother-fucking asshole.

I said as much, too, and Mav damn near fell out of his seat he was cuttin' up so hard.

"I'm happy for you," he said between wheezing gasps. "When you gonna bring her around?" he asked.

"In due time, brother. In due time. I'm just gonna take my time and enjoy this if you don't mind."

He shook his head and said, "No, bro. I don't mind at all." I nodded once and took the drink from Momma Kat that she served me.

"That's the good shit," she said with a wink. "Since it looks like we're celebratin' and all."

"That we are, Momma. That we are," I said, raising the glass. "To love at first sight."

"Aww," she said, leaning her chin on her fist. "I love, love," she declared with a whimsical sigh and I sipped and grinned.

This really was the good shit, top shelf, the best.

"I never had much use for it," I declared. "Until maybe now."

"I can't wait to meet her," Mav said, looking at me speculatively.

"Sooner rather than later, I hope," I declared and winked at Momma who pushed back into a standing position and lumbered up the bar to fix something for one of the other boys.

"Don't wanna overwhelm her?" Mav asked. I nodded and got into some of the nitty-gritty.

"She's pretty fragile," I declared, and he frowned.

"How's that?"

"Single mom, seventeen-year-old boy. Her husband died suddenly, and pop goes the weasel. Turned out he had a whole other family with this side chick."

Mav's eyebrows shot up into his hairline. "No shit?"

I nodded, "She's tough, real tough. Moved her and her boy clear across the country by herself and it's been one minor disaster after the next, after the next, after the next, and she just keeps taking the pressure like a champ. Refuses to fall the fuck apart, but yeah. She's got more baggage than the overhead compartment of a full flight on a 747."

"This is so not your thing," Mav declared, polishing off what was in his glass as his ol' lady sauntered up and leaned an arm on his shoulder, his arm automatically going around her trim waist.

"Could say the same about you at one point," I pointed out with a raised eyebrow, and he grinned.

"What are we talking about?" Marisol asked. "Or is it club business?" She rolled her eyes at that last and I grinned and hid it behind my glass as Mav smacked her on her jeans-clad ass and squeezed a good handful of it. Marisol yipped slightly and let out a throaty moan as he manhandled her, shivering a little at his side.

"Watch it," Mav warned but none of the affection left his tone. Marisol's grin was suppressed into a cheeky smirk as she looked over at her man.

"Nah, not club business," I said, letting her off the hook. "Personal, though, and I'm not ready to share with the whole-ass club. Just my best buddy here."

"Gotcha." Marisol nodded her understanding and whispered something in Mav's ear.

"Sorry, bro, duty calls," Mav declared, and I grinned as he got up, hauling Marisol up against his body and devouring her from the mouth down.

"No worries, bro, I get it," I said. "Hopefully I'll be in the same place soon."

"Right on," Mav said. "I hope for your sake that you are too." He punched me lightly in the shoulder and I watched them go, slightly staggering into each other as they moved up the hall to Mav's office.

God, man... it would be nice.

THE NEXT MORNING, out of the blue, my burner started ringing like a mofo, shattering the peace of an otherwise idyllic Sunday fucking morning where I got to fucking sleep in for a change.

"What?" I growled into the line.

"This Glass Jaw?" an unfamiliar voice on the other end demanded almost hostilely.

"Yeah," I said. "What's up? What you waking me up for?"

"Shit, sorry, man. I keep forgettin' the fuckin' time difference." The voice lightened up. "This is Trap with the Rocky Mountain chapter."

"Oh, shit." I sat up. "What can I do for you, Trap?"

"Nothin' brother, it's what I've done for *you*. We got our hands on that asswipe for you. Your lady's shit should be getting loaded on a truck. I got fellas with the Atlanta chapter at the warehouse right now, supervising."

"Oh, yeah?" I said impressed. "Right on! Thank you much, brother."

"How's she doin'?" Trap asked.

"Not too bad," I said. "Stressed, but wouldn't you be?"

"Fuck no. I'd be pissed and fuckin' some motherfuckers up myself," he said laughing.

"Yeah, well, priorities, man," I said, laughing myself.

"No doubt. Anyway, her shit should be there this week. Just thought you should know. Took us a while to track this weaselly little fuck down. Busted out all his teeth for you. Talkin' to a lady like that." I heard the dude spit.

"Good deal," I said. "Hopefully, lesson fuckin' learned."

"Oh, I'm sure of it," Trap said.

"I sure do appreciate it," I said.

"That's what family's for, ain't it?" Trap asked.

"Sure fuckin' is. You need anything, you don't hesitate."

"I'll keep it in mind. Don't have much going on out that way, though."

"Thanks for calling," I said.

"No problem. Keep the shiny side up, brother."

"Same to ya, now," I declared.

The line went dead, and I smiled to myself. Good deal.

I went back to bed and slept like a fuckin' baby 'til about noon.

11

—————

*C*adence...

The Lana Del Rey song playing through my phone was interrupted by a call, my ringtone blaring out into my office and startling me. Thankfully, my pencil tip wasn't making contact with the paper when it happened. I set the implement of my craft down and picked up my phone.

Movers flashed across the screen before dissolving and the number followed by *Colorado* took its place.

I steeled myself, taking a deep breath and answered.

"Hello?" I let the breath out in a silent, measured count.

"Ms. Mitchell?" an unfamiliar man's voice filtered across the line.

"Yes?"

"Don Walters with your moving company," he said.

"Yes?" I repeated carefully.

"Just wanted to let you know that your belongings are going to be there tomorrow or the next day. Trying to find out what works best for you, ma'am."

"Uh, are you serious?" I asked a little stunned.

"Yes, Ma'am."

"Tomorrow!" I practically cried. "Tomorrow is perfect."

"Tomorrow it is. Thank you, Ma'am."

"Thank *you*," I said. I was desperate to have my things and not even caring at this point. Okay, well, maybe I cared a lot, but I didn't want to rock the boat. I just wanted our things. After that frightful conversation with one of their operators the day that our things were *supposed* to be here, I was honestly afraid I would never see them again.

"Yes, Ma'am," he said and hung up the phone.

I sat at my desk, cheeks a little flushed on the verge of crying with relief when it struck me – I just had to share the good news. I called Jared without even thinking in my excitement.

"Hey, what's up?" he asked.

I squealed, yes, *squealed* like an excited teenager, and told him the good news.

"The movers are coming tomorrow with our things!"

"Ha ha! That's great," he said. "Want me to see if I can maybe come by?"

"That would be great," I said. "But you've already done so much. I don't want to take you away from your work. I feel like I have so much already."

"Cady, baby, in case you haven't noticed – I *enjoy* the time I get to spend with you, and I'd like to do more of it if you'll let me."

I quieted and went still.

"You really mean that, don't you?" I asked softly. I could almost hear him smile over the line.

"Yeah, I do. Wouldn't say it if I didn't," he answered.

"Okay," I said, nodding to myself.

"Okay," he said. "I'll see what I can do."

"Okay." I smiled and blushed, and that effervescent feeling in the pit of my stomach started up anew.

"I've got to go for right now. I'll see you soon," he said.

"Alright, bye for now," I said.

"Bye for now," he said and hung up.

I set my phone down and stared at it for a long moment before giggling insanely.

The back door opened, and Marc called out, "Hey, Mom!"

"In the office, baby!" I called back and he came to find me.

"What's up?" I asked.

"Nothing," he said, then frowned slightly. "What's up with you?"

I grinned. "The movers are coming with our things."

"Oh yeah?" He looked as surprised about it as I felt.

"Yep."

"When?"

"Tomorrow."

He frowned then. "I'm going to be at school."

"That's alright. We'll figure it out," I said.

"But that's not fair – wait, who's 'we?'" he asked, sharp and perceptive as ever.

"Jared's going to try and come over to help."

He straightened up and looked relieved. He said, "Oh, nice!"

"Is it?" I asked, eyeing my son.

"Yeah, he's cool. I like him."

I stared at my son for a heartbeat too long and he rolled his eyes. "Get it, Mom," he said, and I felt my eyes widen, and the blush that overtook me was a furious one. Marc burst out laughing and I spun on my chair and faced my drafting table.

"Out!" I cried. "Get out! You little shit!" This of course just made him laugh even harder, all the way down the hall and up the stairs. I could still hear him howling through the ceiling as I dropped my face into my hands and sighed.

I was so not ready. He was not allowed to be this grown up!

Good Lord, have mercy, I thought.

～

THE ARRIVAL of the moving truck was heralded by the roar of motorcycles – not the sound one expects – so when the knock fell at my front door, I was confused at first. When I opened my door, my confusion only deepened.

"Cadence Mitchell?" The biker stood tall, his iron-gray and dark, long hair pulled back tight, yet still frizzed in a static crackle around his head backlit by the morning sun as it was. His gear was road worn and dirty, his face prematurely wrinkled and sun damaged, a pair of wraparound black sunglasses reflecting me back at myself.

"Yes?" I asked, intimidated.

"Your stuff's here," he said. "You want we should bring it up through here?" He looked down the stairs to my narrow front porch and I swallowed hard, looking past him to the moving truck on the street. The driver leaned out his window, another biker standing on the ground below him, his arms crossed over his chest.

"Oh, um, it would be easier to bring in through the back," I said. "There's an access alley off of Bader Street, just there." I pointed past my neighbor's house at the corner, and he followed my pointing finger.

He smiled at me and with a polite nod, said, "I got 'cha." He turned and gestured, yelling instructions at the driver. I paled as my eyes roved his back and the faded colors of the big patches there.

The Sacred Hearts...

I listened to enough true crime podcasts to know there were *a lot* of unsolved cases attributed to them. Some of them stomach-churningly brutal. Others weren't unsolved at all and there were members of The Sacred Hearts scattered throughout the prison system all over the U.S. and even Canada. Maybe even a few other countries.

Holy fuck! What were they doing here?

My answer rode up, pulling to a smooth stop at the curb and I felt myself blanch all over again.

Jared looked... okay, he looked really good all decked out in black leather but still, when he said he belonged to a motorcycle club, I had never imagined that it was The *Sacred Hearts!*

"Hey," he said breathlessly after jogging up the walk and taking my front porch steps two at a time.

I leaned back and pulled my front door shut so Marc wouldn't hear. Jared's face sort of closed off when I turned back.

"What's all this?" I asked, carefully defensive, more than a little scared.

You knew it was too good to be true, that derisive voice whispered from the back of my mind.

"What?" he asked, and he looked like he was confused but not surprised.

"The Sacred Hearts?" I asked and shifted nervously.

He smiled and it would have been endearing if my nerves weren't running wild, anxiety fizzing thoroughly and with great speed through my entire body with a vibration that set me to feeling like I was on a whole other plane of existence.

"I told you I was in a club," he said.

"But *The Sacred Hearts?*" I asked, the bitter taste of fear coating the inside of my mouth.

He reached out and I stood my ground. I would not flinch. Marc was just inside, and I had to reevaluate a few things. I didn't know if I wanted me and my son anywhere near the level of criminal activity associated with Jared's so-called *club.*

Holy Shit...

"Yeah, The Sacred Hearts," he said evenly. "Why? Is that a problem?" He sounded almost... I don't know, hurt?

"I..." I closed my mouth and took a deep breath. "I've got to say, I don't know, Jared." I crossed my arms over my stomach and bit my lips together, surprised to find *I* was hurting, disappointment weighting my heart like a stone. "They – you have quite the reputation."

"We do," he said, nodding his in understanding. "I don't know what you've heard," he said. "But your stuff needs to be set up, so do you think we can table this just for right now? You could let me help you, and we can discuss it after the movers and my brothers are gone?"

"What did you do?" I asked. "I mean, why are they here with my things like this? Where are they even from?"

"They're from Atlanta," he said. "Tracked your things down to the warehouse there and set it up to get it here sooner."

I frowned. "Why would they do that?" I asked.

"Because I asked them to," he said, and he rubbed his chin.

"Just like that?" I asked, confused.

"Just like that," he said, and his hazel eyes searched my face. "Maybe hear me out?" he asked.

I chewed my upper lip as my thoughts raced through the possibilities and he smiled at me. It held an edge of sadness and its own sort of disappointment.

"Maybe consider we aren't all as bad as the headlines make us out to be?"

"I definitely have questions," I relented softly, and he lost a bit of the smile but nodded.

"I'll see what I can do to get you answers," he said and raised a hand to touch me. I let him, because ever since that kiss, it seemed like it was all I wanted now... even with this little revelation.

Part of me rationalized that Ben, by all appearances, had been the perfect man – hardworking, a provider, if not the best father due to what we all thought was his being a bit of a workaholic – but Ben had been anything but, now hadn't he?

And yet, here Jared stood, clearly all-in with what society had branded a criminal organization, but he had done more for me and for Marc in the last two or three weeks than Ben had in *years*. My heart was already mourning the possibility of losing out on that because goddamn it... Jared was *present*.

Fuck.

"We'll talk," I said softly as his fingers drifted lightly against the side of my neck and his thumb caressed my jaw as though he were memorizing its line.

"That's all I ask," he whispered, stepping just a little bit closer. "Just hear me out."

I nodded and dropped my eyes, both of us jumping as my teenager thumped against the inside of the door and springing apart before it opened.

"Mom," he said. "There's a biker at the back door and the movers are – oh, hey, Jared. That explains that. Never mind!" He pulled back into the house and shut the door. Jared and I exchanged a look and both laughed a bit nervously, but the tension of the moment before sort of released and began to drain away.

"Let's go put your house together," he said gently, and I nodded.

"Okay."

He reached past me and opened the door for me. I slipped through, Jared following right behind me.

"Yo, you Glass Jaw?" the biker in my kitchen, who was the one who'd met me at the front door, asked and I looked back over my shoulder at Jared. I felt my brow crush down even as an eyebrow went up.

"You two don't actually *know* each other?" I asked and the biker in my kitchen grinned.

"Explain later, babe," Jared said, and he lifted his chin in the direction of the other man. "Yeah, I'm Glass Jaw."

"Right on. I'm Slugger and the brother out there getting the movers going is Miner."

"Good to meet you, brother," Jared declared and held out an arm. They grasped each other's forearms and pulled each other into a manly hug. I smiled politely, very much on the outside of whatever greeting ritual was going on and trying my best to hide my confusion amidst the white chaos bubbling about to fill my empty house with boxes and blanket-wrapped furniture.

"This is my lady, Cadence," Jared said, and I stepped up and shook Slugger's hand. I tried not to be as intimidated as I was by his sheer size. The man was as broad as he was tall, bearded, and had long hair. Your quintessential bedraggled biker, I guess you would say.

"Right on," he repeated. "Nice to meet you, Cadence."

"Nice to meet you, too," I said, Jared's introduction ringing in my head. *My lady, Cadence.*

I was slightly unnerved at how much I liked the fact that he wasn't afraid to 'claim' me so-to-speak.

God, my marriage had been so broken... so, so, broken. Ben forgot to even introduce me by name half of the time. Usually just keeping it at *'this is my wife.'*

"We're ready to get started when you are, Cadence. You just point and we'll shoot," Slugger said, and I nodded.

"Okay, thank you."

The outdoor storage unit off the back porch had been cleared out, thanks to Jared. So that's where I chose to stage the boxes for now.

Furniture wise, we started with the dining room, which is when I discovered that a good bit of my furniture maybe wouldn't be arriving in one piece.

"Yeah, when we got to the warehouse, these were like this as they were being loaded onto the truck," Miner said.

He was tall and lanky, and resembled the pirate from the *Pirates of the Caribbean* movies with the wooden eye, except he most certainly had both of his – a watery blue and red rimmed. I was a bit nervous about him. I couldn't tell if he suffered from allergies or if there was some sort of illegal drug use at play.

I got my answer an hour or two later when he asked me, "You wouldn't happen to have any antihistamines I could bum off of you, would you? Something up here is straight *murdering* my face."

I felt instant guilt, just add me being a judgmental basket case even after these two men rode along with my belongings all the way from *Georgia.*

"Sure." I turned to my son. "Marc, honey, since you're going inside, get under my sink in my bathroom and grab the box of allergy medicine for me, please?"

"Sure thing, Mom!" he called from the opposite end of one of my living room display cases.

"And a bottle of water if we still have one in the fridge!" I called a little louder.

"Got it, babe!" Jared yelled back from the back step.

"Oh, God. Thank you so much," Miner said, sniffing hard.

"It's no problem. I wished you would've said something sooner," I told him. "You look absolutely miserable."

He laughed a little and waved me off, and went back for the next dolly of plastic totes to roll into the storage shed.

The truck's driver came over with paperwork and he looked more than a little nervous.

"You, uh, got a minute to go over this with me?" he asked.

"Of course," I said, while the two movers he'd brought with him, the three bikers, and my son toiled away, unloading and setting things up inside the house.

I appreciated Marc so much then, as he took the weight off of me having to direct where everything was supposed to go. He knew, and he directed with aplomb. He was such a good kid, so much more confident than me. Definitely the best parts of me and his dad both. I was so proud of him.

"We're supposed to charge a seventy-five-foot fee," the driver said, and Slugger cleared his throat from nearby. "But on account as you've got your own help with you, I'm just going to go ahead and waive that for you," he said.

"Thank you," I said, and I knew my smile was a bit brittle, but I'd already been massively overcharged up for every roll of tape that they'd used to wrap moving blankets around my furniture when they came to pick my belongings … to the tune of over five hundred dollars.

To now have a bunch of my dining room chairs broken and my grandfather's rocking chair that he'd rocked *me* in as a baby broken as well? I was trying not to cry about that one. That was definitely the most upsetting, seeing as it had traversed the country to Georgia via the freaking *mail* the first time and had come through unscathed.

I listened patiently to the driver as he explained how to go about making a claim with the moving company for any broken or destroyed items. Something I was on the fence about doing after being cursed out and screamed at on the phone by Boston Joey.

"Thank you," I finally said quietly but politely when the transport driver was through with his spiel.

"It's no problem, pretty lady. I'm happy to help," he said, and I nodded.

It only took the five men and my son an hour and a half to unload a lifetime of belongings from the back of the truck. With assurances that the bikers and my boy could and would take it from there, they sent the two boys and the truck driver on their way.

"It's your time to shine," Jared declared, grinning at me. "Show us where you want this stuff and how you want it set up."

I nodded and said, "Let's do it."

It took a considerable amount of time to set up the living room, bedrooms, and find all the totes for the kitchen.

Jared had bid farewell to Slugger and Miner, giving them directions to the club and telling them they'd be set up with a place for however long they chose to stay.

Once the furniture was set and things were manageable between just me and Marc. Jared, of course, stayed and continued to work alongside me and my son.

By the time all the furniture was in place, the area rugs laid, the beds made, and the dining table clothed, etc., I was ready to throw in the towel.

"Hey, Marc," Jared called over to my son, straightening from where he set down a tote or two of Marc's things from the storage outside.

"Yeah?" Marc asked.

"You mind if I take your mom out for a bit?" he asked and I blinked, surprised and even a little touched that he would ask my son for permission and include him like that. It was... sweet.

"Yeah, go ahead. She needs to get out of the house."

I frowned at my kid. "Hey!"

"It's true," he said, rolling his eyes.

I sighed.

"Fine, you're not wrong." I gave Jared a look like, *and we do need to talk...* He nodded and what I said out loud was, "Can I at least get a shower and a clean change of clothes first?"

"Absolutely," he said back. "Brought some clean shit of my own. You mind if I go after you?"

"Sure." I nodded.

"Good deal. You go first."

I nodded and more than slightly dreading the conversation ahead, I went in and found some clean things to wear and took a hot shower to wash the sweat and grime of the day down the drain.

Jared went next, and Marc came down from upstairs while I settled at the kitchen counter on one of the tall kitchen stools to look over the paperwork the driver had given me.

"Hey, Mom?" Marc asked as he closed the fridge, one of his sports drinks in his hand.

"Yeah, baby?" I asked.

"For what it's worth… I really like Jared. You should give him a chance," he said, wandering back to the doorway at the bottom of his stairs.

"Yeah?" I asked.

"I know you, I'm your kid," he said. "I know you don't like the biker stuff, but he's been really good to us, and I like him."

I pursed my lips and considered what my son said to me.

"You're a good kid, you know that?" I asked.

He grinned. "That's because you gave birth to a legend," he said, blowing on his fingernails and polishing them against the shoulder of his tee shirt.

I laughed, shook my head and said, "And there you go, ruining the moment."

"Love you, Mom." He tossed the frosty bottle in the air and caught it, disappearing up his stairs.

"Love you, too, kid," I murmured and sighed.

I heard the water in my shower cut off a moment later and sighed again, feeling like it was time to face the proverbial music.

12

*G*lass Jaw...

I had that low-level thrum I got from the ride going through me as I opened the bathroom door, a bag of my sweaty shit dangling from one hand. The vibration going through me didn't have shit to do with my bike, though. It had everything to do with the solemn woman sitting at her kitchen counter, the struggle in her expression setting hope and fear at war with each other in the center of my body.

I could see it written all over her, this desperate need to make good choices and everything about her citizen upbringing screaming at her to run in the opposite direction from the big bad biker.

Only problem? This wolf had her scent, and I wasn't about to give up without a fight. Everything in me screamed to pin this gorgeous creature against the nearest wall and to kiss every one of her doubts about whether this was wrong or right away.

Except that wasn't how things worked anymore and my baser instincts needed to sit bitch until the time was right and that time certainly wasn't right now.

"Hey," I said, and she looked up from the pink legal-sized slip of carbon copy paper in her hands.

"Hey," she echoed back softly.

I stood feet apart from where she sat and we just looked at each other, roaming one another from head to foot, just drinking each other in with our eyes, and I had to say she was better than a cold beer for my parched soul. Sweet, ripe, those green eyes cut right through me.

"Let me take you for a ride?" I asked, my voice a little rougher than I meant for it to be – but shit, the things this woman did to me.

"Excuse me?" she asked, those green eyes widening.

I cleared my throat and felt a rush of something like embarrassment, except I didn't let myself get embarrassed.

"On the bike, you dirty girl."

"Oh!" She blushed and somehow blanched at the same time, looking slightly stricken and I laughed.

"Is it safe?" she asked, looking worried and I knew her first thought was for the boy upstairs.

"Ain't no place safer when it comes to me. You ever ridden before?" I asked.

She shook her head mutely.

"First time for everything," I said and held a hand out to her. She stared at it for just a moment and then reached out, meeting me half-way, taking it and slipping to her feet.

I smiled and led her through the archway into the living room and to the front door, stopping at where she'd stashed her jackets and the like in the entry closet once I'd hung a rod in there for her.

I pulled down a jean jacket, the most rugged thing she had, and handed it to her.

She put it on without any argument and called out, "Marc!"

"Yeah?" His voice came faint from above us, filtering down the stairs across from us.

"I'm leaving!" she called.

"K!" he called back, and she rolled her eyes.

I laughed slightly and opened the front door. With my hand to the small of her back, I guided her through.

My Harley sat at the curb, flat black skin, chrome gleaming under the sun which was getting a little low in the afternoon sky.

"Where are we going?" she asked, moving her phone with its little silicone wallet attachment to the case from her back jean's pocket to the pocket of her denim jacket.

"Thought it might be nice to go down by the water," I said, stashing my shit back into one of my dusty leather saddlebags. I buckled it closed and stood back up. "You sure you're good to do this right now?" I asked and she looked up at me, her green gaze going a bit flinty like she had something to prove. I think maybe she did, but certainly not to me.

"I'm good," she said, and I smiled. She was soft with a core of steel to her, and I liked that about her. I liked that a lot.

"Okay, this is what I need from you..." I ran her through the safety shit, pulled a spare helmet out of the saddlebag on the opposite side of my bike and helped her put it on.

I got on the front of my bike, sticking the key in the ignition, and giving it a twist, thumbing the ignition switch and revving the engine if for nothing else than for the fact that I loved that purr, loved to roar my pride and joy out when I gave her a little throttle on startup.

I turned and gestured for Cadence to get on, the buzzing of my nerves turning to butterflies taking flight at the prospect of having her on the back of my ride.

She settled on behind me and wrapped her arms around my chest. Without thinking, I reached behind me and gave her ass a slight squeeze, pulling her to indicate she should get closer, and she did, sliding along the seat and pressing up against me and aw, yeah... that was the stuff right there. I checked to make sure her feet were on the passenger foot pegs and she wasn't going to melt the soles of her Tennie's on the exhaust pipe by accident and then with a turn of the handlebars, a grip of the clutch, and a twist of the throttle, I pulled us smoothly away from the curb and glided us up the street, leaving her house behind us.

I kept it to surface streets and a decent cruising speed, rolling us up out of Federal Way and North Tacoma, along Pacific Highway toward Saltwater State Park and Des Moines. I wasn't sure where I was going to wind up taking us, but it wasn't about the destination at the moment. It was about the journey and making sure she had a good time.

I wound up cutting left and dropping down onto First, sliding at a sedate pace along the stretch of boulevard that bordered the sound along Redondo Beach, past Salty's. Cadence squinted out over the water, and I smiled to myself, thinking about stopping someplace to get her some sunglasses for those delicate, lightly colored eyes of hers. My own were on my face, lenses dark, retrieved from the deep recesses of one of my inside jacket pockets.

We slid along the beach in the clean salty air and climbed up the other side, making the turn to head down past the school toward the final turns down into Des Moines where there were more shops and places to eat that were a lot less pretentious than Salty's. I ended up parking the bike on the street in the block between Des Moines' main drag and the marina. I tapped the outside of Cadence's thigh, and it took her a second, but finally she realized and leaped up for me.

I backed the bike against the curb and cut the engine. By the time I had my lid off and hanging off one of the bars, Cadence was handing me her own.

I nodded and hung it opposite mine.

"I recognize this place from when I was a kid, but it's a lot different," she said. "Way more crowded."

I nodded. "Yeah, things have changed in the Pacific Northwest in the last twenty years or so. Shit, in the last *ten*. It's not the same place it used to be. Population is *booming*."

Her lips twisted back and forth, and she nodded. "We'd come up this way from Oregon on family vacations – go to Seattle and the aquarium; the Pike Place Market," she said. "We'd stay in cheap motels or hotels near the airport."

"Ah." I nodded. "That's just up that way," I said and pointed. I took her hand in mine lightly, turning to stroll, just picking a direction.

"I… I feel like I reacted badly this morning and I'm a little embarrassed now," she confessed.

"Aw, yeah?" I asked.

"Yeah," she said, eyes fixed on where she was stepping.

"Don't be," I said, shrugging it off. "I know the club has a rep among you citizens. It's not completely unwarranted, either. Like anything else, the club is made up of people and this life? It can attract some rough characters."

"That's putting it a bit mildly," she murmured.

I laughed a little. "Just what have you heard?" I asked.

"I told you," she said, looking slightly uncomfortable. "I listen to true crime podcasts. Mostly when I work."

"A lot of gruesome shit?" I asked.

She laughed a bit nervously and almost shyly.

"You could say that," she agreed.

"Let me guess. You listened to some shit about the cartel wars?"

"The ones in the south," she said, nodding. "Kentucky and the like."

I nodded in understanding.

"It really wasn't that long ago when you think about it," she said gently.

I shook my head. "No, only like fifteen, sixteen years ago," I said.

"When it started. But the skin-walker murders were sometime into the start of things... then there were the more recent gang wars out that way," she said.

Shit, I thought to myself, but out loud I asked, "Just what kind of podcast are you listening to?"

"It's called *Oblique*. It's on all the major streaming services," she said, and I stopped and looked at her, tipping her chin so she would look at me.

"You know, I'm impressed by you," I said. "By a lot."

"Me?" she asked, her eyes widening.

"Yes, you."

"Why?" she asked.

"Clearly, whatever you've heard has you scared shitless of the patch on my back," I said. "But you're still here," I said softly, touching her chin with my thumb, grazing the soft skin in a line back along her jaw toward her ear.

She held her breath as she looked up at me then finally blurted, her voice low and struggling to suppress her need, "Please kiss me again."

"Yeah?" I asked, stepping gently and carefully into her space.

"Yeah," she said, her voice both hoarse and breathy all at once.

I lowered my mouth to hers carefully, slow and controlled and she let me, tipping her chin up, her eyes slipping shut at the last second to enhance her sense of touch as my lips met hers.

I wasn't so chaste this time, pressing my mouth to hers, parting my lips, hers following suit in this beautifully sweet echo to my movements – an even sweeter submission to my will to have her in my arms. I drew her close, slipping my tongue past her lips, between her teeth, desperate to taste her if it was only ever going to be this once – which *ha!* I sincerely doubted this was anything like an end before we'd even begun.

"Mm!" The sound was *grateful* almost, as she nestled closer to me in my arms, one hand on my waist, the other against the leather over my chest as my arm passed behind her, locking around her back and holding her tight, hauling her up against my body which I kept unyielding.

The kiss turned into a wild thing – deepening, passionate – until we both stood in the sunshine beating down on us, tearing away breathless from one another. The heat of that dying afternoon light was something, but it didn't hold a matchstick to the fire ignited in my blood.

"Does that mean you think this could work?" I asked between breaths.

"What?" she asked dazed.

"Me taking you out on dates, taking things as fast or as slow as you want to, but there being a potential for an *us*. You think it could be a thing with me being in the club and all?" I asked.

"That depends…" she murmured.

"On?" I asked.

"Do you kill people?" she asked me, and I choked on a laugh.

I shook my head. "I've never killed anyone," I said. "I've been arrested," I said honestly. "A few times for stupid shit when I was younger. Fighting, possession of marijuana with intent to sell – which I wasn't – and nothing ever harder than some weed. I've been in a fare few fights, but nothing any more serious than your average dick-measuring contest... but murder?" I shook my head. "No. I'm clean. Don't even have a criminal record."

"Can you say the same for everyone in your club?" she asked.

"You mean the club as a whole or just the guys here in the local chapters?" I asked.

She rolled her eyes slightly and said with a small smile, "Obviously you can't for the club as a whole, or my podcasts wouldn't have anything to talk about." I laughed a bit and just enjoyed holding her, feeling better and better about shit as we talked. "No, I mean locally," she said. "Anyone that might come in contact with me and my son."

"Ah." I nodded. "No, I can't necessarily say the same for all my brothers," I told her and at the light in her eyes dimming slightly with dismay, I tried to head that shit off at the pass. "But," I said. "What I can tell you is we don't go around advertising that shit or making a thing out of it. We've all made our mistakes, babe. Some of us harder core than others, but that's the thing, the whole point of the club as a whole," I said, rocking her back and forth slightly in my arms.

"What's that?" she asked curiously.

"What's done is done," I said with a shrug. "It's in the past. We bury that shit and move on. That's the point. We accept each other, black marks, dirt, and pasts and all and we try our best to help each other from making the same shit-ass mistakes. We're a rolling brotherhood, a chosen family when most of our blood relatives or society has given up on us and told us to kick rocks. We're there for each other, and bad reputation aside, we try not to judge."

She looked thoughtful and I couldn't help but feel a bitter resentment for whatever podcast she'd been listening to which damn sure didn't tell the whole truth. Hell, they never did. Those things were geared toward law enforcement being some sort of righteous paladins or some shit.

You'd never hear any LEOs talk us up for any of the *good* shit we did. Bet the dweebs telling their horror stories didn't have shit to say about the charity toy drives or the anti-bullying protection services we provided for kids or any of that.

No, they only focused on the horror show resulting from the retribution we'd had on some dead cartel thugs that had come at us first. I wondered if they'd covered the fact that those happy bastards had gunned down the mother chapter's president's ol' lady and several brothers in cold blood over something that prez hadn't even done. Or the fact that they had damn near taken out his son, too. What? Were we supposed to let that shit stand?

Would anyone if it was *their* family?

"You've been so good to me and Marc since we arrived," she said finally, snapping me out of my deepening rage spiral. I cut that shit off at the knees and focused on her.

"Seems like you guys needed a break from all the bullshit. Just one person to be fucking *nice*," I said.

"Thank you for being that person," she said, folding into my arms further. I smiled down at her.

"I live to serve," I said with a cheeky-ass grin and a raised eyebrow, and she laughed.

"You and Marc both, ruining the moment."

"Ah, no," I said in all seriousness. "I'm very much enjoying the moment." I rocked her gently.

"Me too." She let the confession slide easy from her lips and I smiled.

"Well then," I said, turning and taking her hand in mine to continue our stroll. "Let's just see where it takes us, real easy like."

"Okay," she agreed and the last of whatever weight or fear that I bore that she'd rabbit on me melted away, lifting off my soul. She seemed lighter too.

"I'm starving, how about you?" I asked, hooking an arm over her shoulders, and pulling her into my side.

"I could eat," she said, nodding. "I could *really* use a drink."

"God, yeah. A beer sounds really fucking good," I said.

"Doesn't it just?" she asked, and I turned us at the next block, away from the water and toward the strip and Wall Eye's Chowder House. They had good shit and a decent selection of beer.

13

*C*adence...

Dinner was nice, and the air felt clean and clear, both literally and figuratively as we strolled back down toward the water. We sat on a bench, watching some eagles up high, perched on some dead branches sticking up above the tree canopy.

We chatted, although not about the club. There was no more of that. No, we talked about each other and the things that shaped us into the people we were. Some childhood, some not, some about interests and how we got into doing the things we each did for a living.

It was nice, and I swear, Jared was the easiest man to talk to. It was effortless, and I didn't feel like I should expect some off-handed remark that would and could hurt or even devastate me. He just wasn't... I don't know. He wasn't oblivious, for one, and he didn't seem casually cruel or even intentionally so for that matter. He seemed genuinely interested in what I had to say, in learning about me, and overall, it was *incredibly sexy*.

I think the sexiest thing of all was the fact that he wasn't hyper focused *on sex*. He was focused on me as a whole, and not just my tits and ass. It was so easy to tell with guys, you know? Not that I had tried to date after my husband's death and my life had exploded so spectacularly into the mess that I was *still* trying to clean up. Still, there had been guys. Some from work who'd never given off predator vibes before that certainly had turned out to be absolute creeps.

For real, who tries to corner and make a move on a widow at her husband's wake? Especially knowing what a scumbag the husband was just after said widow found out for herself? That was another reason why I made the decision to come home to my mom and my stepdad and start things over here. Some of the attention from ill-meaning potential suitors back in Georgia had been stomach churning and had gotten to the point I had just wanted *away* from it.

Even Marc hadn't been immune, one of them trying to recruit my baby to his cause of winning me over.

I was a proud momma bear on that one. Not only had Marc shut him down with aplomb, he'd turned the guy in to me and had told me what had happened so I could have my own go at him.

You would think all of that would have left a bitter taste in my mouth where Jared was concerned, but nope, he didn't give off that kind of vibe at all. Was he interested in me? Yes, but none of it had felt half as superficial. With Jared, I felt gorgeous, beautiful, and not just because of my looks. I felt like he appreciated things way beyond them. He engaged me and challenged me on an intellectual level. I could tell he appreciated me as much for my intelligence as he did for what I had always been told was a pretty face, but honestly didn't understand that.

My father hadn't ever let me get by on my looks and when I had tried as a teenage girl, realizing that they could be used as an almost form of social currency – Lord had he and my mom been disappointed in me. It'd been soul crushing and it'd needed to be. I had never tried a stunt like that again. They had, in fact, raised me better than that. Unfortunately for me, I was already pregnant but fortunately, or so I had thought, Ben was a stand-up boy and wanted to be a father. The rest as they say was history.

"You ready to get back?" Jared asked softly as dusk was beginning to settle and I sighed.

"No, but yes," I answered. "This has been nice."

He smiled at me in the growing dark and nodded. "Yeah, it has."

I held my breath, wishing he would kiss me again, and not exactly confident or brave enough to make the first move. Plenty of rejected first moves when it had come to Ben left me on uneven footing. Plus, it had been a *really* long time since I had done the whole trying to date or be intimate with anyone other than my husband thing so... yeah. There was that.

Whew.

I didn't know how I managed to do this to myself; be so comfortable with him one moment and a complete nervous wreck the next, but I guess it was just my own personal superpower or something. As far as superpowers went, I felt gypped.

We stared at each other for several heartbeats, each of us, I think, waiting for the other to make a move and I sort of just blurted out, "If you're waiting for me to kiss you, I'm sort of bad at making the first move – it's just not my thing. I mean, I think it used to be but things with Ben and time... I am so sorry I am like this insecure neurotic mess and are you really sure you want—"

He shut up my insane anxiety fueled babbling by covering my mouth with his, kissing me fiercely and almost possessively. That last part wasn't uncomfortable in the slightest. No, not at all. It was powerful, and beautiful, and made me positively melt. All the tension and worry caught on the light wind off the water and tore off from around me to float away.

His lips were warm against mine, kissing me with a near-bruising force that felt so good, as though his kiss alone could silence my fears and drive the worry right out of me. I only wished exorcising my demons could be so easy, but God... seventeen years of nothing but lies and liars surrounding me, my trust was so far eroded I didn't know if I had much left. I couldn't in good conscience, expect any man – especially not a man like Jared – to be patient with me while I still floundered, struggling to get my fucking shit together.

Still, while he held me like this, kissed me like this, all of that just sort of fell away and left me floating in this pleasant void that felt so calm and so safe, the sensation a ridiculously addictive one.

When Jared broke the kiss, he smiled gently and ordered me, voice rough and husky with desire, "Stop overthinking things, baby. You're fine."

I swallowed, speechless, and nodded slowly.

His smile grew and he said, "I'll remind you as often as I need to until it takes." I smiled because the way he said it didn't sound demanding or impatient or exasperated in the slightest. It sounded like a gentle promise.

I nodded, my hair shifting against my face where it was trapped beneath his hand and I just couldn't seem to remember when he'd captured my face between them, but I liked it. I liked it so much. It was different but in all the right ways. The good ways.

"Come on, let's get you home." He let me go, fingers trailing in a touch, down my denim-clad arm to slip gently along my palm, grasping my fingertips with his as he stood and drew me to my feet. He wound those same fingers between my own and I leaned into him, hugging his leather-clad arm as we walked, a slow lover's stroll out of the park and back in the direction of his motorcycle.

The temperature was dropping, and I was a bit chilled by the time we reached my house. It was unusual going to the front door when I was so used to entering the house through the back. He walked with me, to my door and I took my keys from my jeans pocket. He stopped me after I'd unlocked the door and I looked up at him.

"You have your choice," he said softly.

"Choice?" I asked, staring up into his eyes which held such a light in them.

"You can either have me kiss you goodnight and leave you here at your door like it's the fifties or some shit…" he said and then paused.

"Or?" I asked, cautiously, my curiosity eating me alive.

He leaned in and put his lips near my ear and said, "Or, I kiss you like I'm putting the breath of life back into you, you wrap your legs around my waist, and I carry you to your bedroom and really give you the ride of your life. I mean, rock your world until you can't walk straight for days afterwards."

Holy shit.

"I'll take option two, please," I said, my voice a bit high and breathy in excitement and anticipation rushing through me and forcing the nervousness and even a bit of dread so far out of the way, so far down, the latter drowned completely in my desire for what he was offering.

"You sure?" he asked, and I could tell, this was my last stop to get off this train before it took off and whisked me to destinations unknown.

"I'm sure," I said, and it was all the permission he seemed to want or need before turning the intensity up to a thousand. His mouth came crashing down over mine and he pulled me by my hips into the front of his body even as he stepped forward and fetched my back up hard against the siding by my front door.

I couldn't help myself, I moaned into his mouth, and he swallowed it, swallowed *me* whole. His tongue glided against mine, his body pressing hard to my front, the siding digging in at my back as his hands swept down my body, one going to my hip, the other continuing on, sliding over the denim over the outside of my thigh. He bent slightly, never tearing his mouth from mine, and dug his fingers insistently at the back of my knee.

I raised it, pressed safely between him and the wall, and allowed him to take me off balance in that security. He stepped in, grinding against me, showing me without words just how excited he was to be here.

Though my eyes were closed, I felt them roll to the back of my head as a certain thrill swept through me at the hard, hot contact of his throbbing cock against me, even through the multiple layers of our clothes.

I moaned again with an almost desperation when he pressed into me harder, my arms going unbidden around his neck and shoulders, pushing my fingers through the back of his close-cropped hair, sable soft and bristling between them as I pulled his mouth against mine and kissed him back with every bit of fervent passion that he kissed me with. He growled against my lips, and somehow, his other arm found its way between my back and the house. He pulled me closer to him, his other hand raising my knee even higher over his hip as he made good on the second part of his promise and lifted me clean off my feet.

I wrapped my legs around him and didn't feel an ounce of fear that he would drop me or anything like that. He lifted me easily and pressed us together where it counted, and I wanted to die all over again.

God, how long had it been?

Too long.

He reached next to us, supporting me against the house, and twisted the knob, pushing the front door inward on smoothly oiled hinges, which at least there was that.

I tore my mouth from his and murmured, "Marc—"

"He's old enough," Jared growled. "He hears anything, he'll keep it to himself."

I smirked.

"You don't know my kid."

He grinned and reached up with his mouth and ordered, "Hold on to me," as I lowered mine to meet his. I held on to him, and he backed me away from the wall and propelled us both forward through my front door, carelessly kicking it shut behind us. He carried me bodily through the house and into my room, kicking that door shut behind us too before tossing me down on the bed.

I bounced laughing and halfway sat up, his hands pushing the denim jacket I hadn't worn since high school off of my shoulders and halfway down my arms, trapping them at my sides. He climbed over me, putting one knee to the edge of the bed near my hip and smiling down at me. He murmured playfully, "I've got you now."

I felt my breath rush from my lungs and asked, "Now what are you going to do?"

His playful expression sobered some and grew very solemn and very serious all of a sudden.

"Whatever I want," he answered. You would think such words said in such a way would chill me to the very bone but it had exactly the opposite effect. I felt my body heat from the inside out by several degrees, as though his rough voice and murmured promises cranked my thermostat.

"Why does that sound so hot coming from you?" I asked as he leaned in close.

"Because I'm me?" he asked, and his voice held an edge of teasing to it that made me smile.

"I've certainly never met anyone quite like you." I whispered the confession.

"And you never will," he said. "I'm one of a kind, baby."

Now that, I could believe. I said as much and he grinned at me, his mouth the barest inch from my own as he leaned over me, my arms still trapped.

"You nervous?" he asked.

I blinked stupidly for a moment and confessed, "Yes."

"Mm." He leaned past my lips and his own tickling the hair by my ear, his breath sliding down the side of my neck in a warm, tingling rush. He said, "Don't be nervous."

I rolled my eyes at first in exasperation, but then his lips caressed the lobe of my ear and a second later, his teeth, hard edged and sharp, skimmed the side of my neck and my eyes rolled back for an entirely different reason. I shuddered, the rippling sensation of light airy tingles radiating from the erogenous zones he plied with expert effect in a tingling rush over my shoulder. It went down my arm, and across my back beneath my jacket, under my thin and well-fitted tee, and even beneath the constriction of my bra beneath that.

So many layers, too many layers did he cut through with that one, light, barely there graze of his teeth and I almost couldn't deal with how my body responded.

You'd like to think I was some kind of virgin sitting here!

I didn't have long to allow my nerves to take over and shut me down. Jared's lips were working along my jawline and capturing mine again. Every time he kissed me like this, my God, I just… I just couldn't hold on to a single thought, a single worry or care and it was so instantly *addictive*.

He backed off and let me sit up, taking my jacket from me and letting it fall to the floor. With my hands suddenly free, I could reach for him, and I did, eagerly, catching his face between my hands, the stubble along his jaw rough against my palms as he came in for another kiss, which I offered up to him more than willingly.

His tongue swept against mine, sure and true, and I melted into his embrace. He advanced on me, personal space a thing of the past, thrusting a thigh between my legs and up against me, our jeans separating us still, but damn. Just the feel of his muscular thigh against me there, where honestly, no one had gone for what felt like *ages* was so hot. I felt as though my panties were going to catch fire at any moment.

His hands swept down my body to the hem of my tee and obediently and without any thought, I raised my arms and let him sweep it up off over my head. He threw it down on my bedroom floor, his hands going to my hips as he leaned back and took me in. His eyes roving over my chest in its pushup bra, his gaze sparkled with appreciation.

"Look at you," he breathed, and it was the same sort of awe and reverence reserved for discovering some ancient treasure, not for the likes of *me*.

The effect his words and his tone caused me to practically *glow*, and effervescence I hadn't felt for a very long time swept through me to the point I felt lighter than air as I shoved his jacket with its leather vest over it back off of his shoulders.

He tossed his jacket and the vest on top of my dresser behind him and without my prompting, grabbed the back of his tee between his shoulders and hauled it over his head in that way that guys just *did* and holy smokes was it hot. Watching his muscles flex was a treat and I bit my bottom lip as he dropped the tee to my floor and practically dove in for another kiss.

We lay back in a tangle of limbs, tongues twisting around one another, lips pressed, hands wandering over exposed skin, pressing and massaging. His hands delved beneath me from where he lay over the top of me and with a snap of his fingers, my bra came unhooked. I laughed as the band practically sighed with relief around me and he swept everything efficiently from my arms, almost magically making the elastic and lace disappear.

It was immediately replaced with the warmth of his skin as he hitched my thighs higher around his hips and pressed our lower halves together. I could feel him hot, an iron rod through our jeans as he pressed me into the rumpled covers of my bed, his mouth stealing my enthusiastic cry of surrender. He echoed the sentiment with a satisfied *mm,* as though tasting the sound and finding it delectable.

He let his hands glide over my skin, his touch warm and firm, sweeping over my body, memorizing every plane, every curve, every goosebump, scar, or imperfection by touch, learning me by braille, the effect intimate and so pure.

I likewise let my hands wander over his hard body; the muscle carved from hard work rather than time spent at the gym, over knobs and hard ridges of muscle and bone, his body so hot, so warm beneath my touch. I loved that. It made me want to press more of myself against him.

He leaned into me, his capable hands pressed behind my knees, bending me in half, the position leaving me vulnerable and feeling exposed despite the fact I was still clothed from the waist down. He leaned up and let my legs down, his hands going for my waistband, and I watched him curiously.

He watched me right back as his hands moved, unfastening things, unzipping others. Finally, slipping shoes and socks off my feet, he peeled me out of my jeans and panties beneath in one fluid motion, dropping them to the floor and kneeling over me, sweeping with those intense hazel eyes.

I covered my chest out of – well, I don't really know why, and he frowned slightly.

"Don't you ever cover those perfect tits of yours when we're alone like this," he ordered, and I immediately dropped my arms to my sides. "That's a good girl," he said and went for his belt.

Holy shit.

He shucked himself out of his own jeans and the tightly clinging boxer briefs beneath them efficiently and I all but held my breath. He was… he was definitely more well-endowed than I was used to but considering I had ever only been with my husband, that wasn't saying much.

He kneeled at the edge of the bed and smoothed his hands up and down the tops of my thighs before hooking his arms beneath my knees. I yelped in surprise as he dragged me bodily toward him, leaving my butt hanging slightly over the edge of the mattress.

"What are you doing?" I asked breathless with a mixture of anticipation and uncertainty.

"Having my dessert," he said, and he literally hooked my knees over his powerful shoulders and without any more preamble, thrust his tongue against my sex, teasing my pussy lips apart and suckling over my clit.

"Ohhh, God!" My voice was strangled with surprise and I lay back and let him do whatever he wanted.

He chuckled deeply and my hips jerked slightly at the tickling sensation the vibrations from that laugh sent through me.

He worked me expertly and nearly had me coming before he ever even slipped a finger inside of me.

"Oh!" I arched, gripping fistfuls of the blankets and sheets beside my hips and he hummed in satisfaction against me, adding a second finger to the first, meeting no resistance, gliding through my wetness and *Lord* I was wet. I was wetter than I could ever remember being. I panted as he felt around inside me, and I let out a strangled cry when he touched something particularly sensitive. Pleasure rippled out from that place, and he stared up my body, watching my face as he swished his finger over the spot again to make sure. I was only vaguely aware of my eyes rolling into the back of my head as I panted. With another devious chuckle, he had lowered his mouth to my body once more.

Oh, God! The feel of his mouth on my clit, tongue gently teasing, as his fingers swept over that spot inside me... it was almost too much. No, it *was* way too much! Before I knew it, I was caught in a riptide of pleasure that swept me out from the safety of the shore and dragged me under mercilessly, sweeping me down and spinning me until I didn't know up from down or what was touching me inside from the outside. I cried out, panting, gasping as though I couldn't get my breath, drowning in whatever he was doing to me.

The bubbles swept against my skin, goosebumps rising on my skin in their wake. I couldn't identify if I was hot or chilled and I shuddered and shook as though a very real current ran through me. I experienced a complete loss of control as he refused to stop, refused to let me up, even though I frantically slapped and then *pushed* against his shoulders. Just when I thought it would never end and when I was on the verge of complete panic, he let up, chuckling with this smug, self-satisfaction as he wiped the back of his hand over his mouth and chin, rubbing my essence away.

I lay back, limp and panting, overloaded, as he rose.

"You on birth control?" he asked.

What?

I nodded dumbly, and he smiled.

"You want me to put a condom on?"

My mind flashed briefly to how quickly and expertly he had released my bra without looking, and only one-handed, and I had the presence of mind – just barely – to nod again.

He turned back to his jacket on the dresser and rooted in a pocket, pulling out a silver foil square and tearing it open with his teeth.

He watched me watch him with a heated gaze as he rolled the latex over his considerable girth and down his equally considerable length.

"Get up on the bed," he ordered, and I pushed myself back up onto the mattress where he would have enough room to join me. He moved over me like a panther – movement controlled, eyes fixed on me in a gaze that was equal parts predatory and victorious, and I have to say, nothing about either of those things exactly turned me off. Quite the opposite was in effect, actually. My lady parts tingled with anticipation as he laid me flat and nudged my thighs apart with his knees.

He kissed me hot and heavy as he settled over the top of me, and I silently sighed out in blissful surrender.

It had been too long... far too long, and I felt as though I had *wasted* so much time trying to make things work. In hindsight, I had been the only one trying.

"Stop that," he ordered briskly.

"Stop what?" I asked, confused.

"Thinking about him when you're with me," he said. "No offense, darlin', but he treated you like shit and I'm not about that. Let his ghost go and join the land of the living."

He smoothed my hair back from my face and his expression was one of tenderness. I nodded, tears pricking the backs of my eyes at how deftly he dealt with the situation, efficiently laying my memories down and picking up the good. He wasn't being hurtful, he wasn't trying to be a dick, he was just... I don't know what, but there wasn't any malice or selfishness in how he spoke. He communicated as much without words as he did with them.

"I'm sorry," I murmured, and he smiled and shook his head.

"Nothing to be sorry about," he whispered and kissed me sweetly.

I closed my eyes and let myself go then – let a lot of things go – and just sank into the moment with relief.

God, I didn't deserve this. I didn't deserve a man as strong and as *present* as Jared was in the moment.

His body moved against mine and I whimpered slightly. If he only knew how much I wanted him to be inside me at this very moment. How much I wanted to feel good. How much I wanted *him* to feel good.

He slipped inside me, startling me at first, my hips giving a little jerk of surprise. He put a hand to my hip and stilled, meeting my eyes with his, silently checking with me. With a slight nod from me, he slid in against me a little further and oh, *God;* it was pure fucking nirvana.

He hummed out in purest pleasure and lifted my leg over his hip, thrusting in just a little bit deeper, and I clapped my hands over my mouth to keep from crying out too loudly. He chuckled then and rolled his hips *just so* against mine, and I swear my eyes rolled into the back of my head.

We fell into this glorious rhythm that evoked feelings and sensations in me that I don't think I had ever felt before. It was somewhere between floating down a pure river of bliss and flying on little air currents of ecstasy.

I wrapped my legs around his waist and my arms around him too as he thrust deep, carefully and slowly. He bowed his head and grabbed fistfuls of my hair, tipping my head back and demanded in a low, sexy, dirty tone, "You like that? Hm?"

"Yeah." My voice was breathy and high, almost unrecognizable.

"You want me to give you this dick?" he asked. "You want me to come back here and fill you up like this once a week?" he demanded.

Holy shit. Ben had never talked to me like that, and it was so... so hot.

"Yes!" I gasped and clung to him harder.

"You want me to fuck you like this every time?"

"Mm-hm!"

"Yeah?" he asked.

"Yeah!"

He turned up the volume to his pace, thrusting both harder and faster and I lived for it. He grinned, pulling my head back, but it didn't hurt. No, I don't know how he had his hold on it, but it didn't hurt at all. It just didn't allow for me to go anywhere. I felt wholly at his mercy and goddamnit, I was overjoyed to be there because as wild, on the edge, and just plain deliciously dirty as Jared fucking me felt? It also felt *safe.*

I knew in my very bones, by the look in his eyes, that he had me, that I wasn't going anywhere, and by the same token, he wasn't going to let anything bad happen to me. He was in perfect control, and I was pleased to let him have it. To not be the decision maker for once. To cede control and to just let things happen and to just *be* for the time being.

God, it felt so fucking good, so damn... *cathartic.*

14

*G*lass Jaw...

I can't even describe how good she felt wrapped around my cock. Shit, wrapped around *all of me*. How her legs wound around my waist, how her arms went around my neck and shoulders. She twined around me like some kind of kinky, flowering vine and I carefully and sweetly pushed my luck to see how far down the rabbit hole her submissiveness went.

I tangled my hands in the back of all that rich, long, mahogany hair of hers, the strands like fucking silk against my palms and between my fingers. I got snug and tight up against her scalp and fisted her long locks, not pulling per se, but definitely locking shit in place so I had the control. She gave this throaty moan of surrender and I almost nutted right then and there. It was everything I had in me not to blow my load too soon.

"You like that?" I asked her, my voice raw with need, with how much I desired her.

"Mm!" It took her a second to form a coherent thought and I definitely liked that – the effect I had on her when she finally made up her mind and went with *yes*, her hum of appreciation sweet as she went, "Mm-hm!"

"Yeah?" I demanded. I wanted this shit clear as day, black and white, no gray area.

"Yeah!" she cried.

I plunged deep and deeper still into her sweet wet heat and reveled in it, in her, fully. She was all softness and silk under me, and I gathered her to me like a treasured living flame.

The way she moved underneath me was intoxicating – the way she arched into me, the way she held onto me, the way when I hit and rode over that sweet spot her nails dug into my arms slightly.

I was just beginning to unlock all of her secrets, one by one – which angle worked best, pace, rhythm, how deep, how long, how slow, how fast, how short on the stroke – experimenting to find the right combination of things to make her come. I wanted to bring her to that pinnacle screaming, then I wanted to go and do it again and again until she was too exhausted and satisfied to do anything other than come for me, sighing.

I wanted all her secrets. I wanted to test every position and see what pleasures I could bring her, and I was dead serious that we weren't leaving this bed until I had thoroughly rocked her fucking world, tilting it on an axis she'd never even dreamed possible.

I started slow, gave myself somewhere to go, and I loved how just *talking to her* evoked such clear and positive responses.

I had a thing for talking dirty and I think my girl liked it which just turned me on all the more.

"You like that dick, don't you, baby?" I asked her.

"Yes!" she gasped.

I met those green eyes of hers and asked her, "You want I should come fill up your tight little pussy on the regular? Hm?"

"Yes," she half-gasped, half-cried as I moved my hips into a better angle to glide over that slightly rougher patch on her pussy's roof. The one they still argued to death didn't really do anything or that it even existed. I was here to tell any motherfucker different and that it was a lame fucking cop-out. That was how you could tell a man from a boy, by how well they pleased their woman… and I wasn't no boy. I had no cause to be any kind of lazy in this department.

I drove into her at a slow and steady pace, talking dirty, working her up, and then I changed things up ever so slightly. I bowed over her arching body and slid an arm under her lower back, over her butt, deepening the arch of her body and thrusting her pelvis down on my cock, changing the angle and where I stroked. I thrust my hips, rutting deep, and the head of my cock worked some magic because she gasped, shuddering, her hands going to my shoulders and pressing slightly as she tried to grow used to the intensity of these new sensations.

Jesus fuck, had nobody ever properly fucked this woman? It was a rhetorical question, as clearly no one had if *that* was all it took to send her voice into the rising and falling cry of surprise that was swiftly and keenly drowned in her pleasure.

God, she was so fucking wet. I was slid in tight and so fucking deep. I gritted my teeth and tried to slow my roll, or this was going to be a short first time and I didn't want that. I wanted to go for hours with her. I wanted to bend her and make her come so hard I nearly broke her, but it looked like I might be setting the bar a little low.

"*Fuck!*" My balls tightened, and my cock jerked inside her. She moaned, holding on to me tight.

The only saving grace to the entire scenario? I felt her pussy tightening rhythmically around my shaft as a light orgasm swept through her at the same time and *goddamn* did that pussy milk me fuckin' dry.

"Shit! Oh, fuck!" I cried and fisted her hair in my free hand, pulling her head back, playing my lips along the long, lean line of her throat.

She let out a devastated shuddering gasp at the attention and her nails dug into my shoulders. I thought I was done, but my cock gave one more strong and throbbing pulse and I swear to God, shot a fuckin' blank. There wasn't anything left to shoot.

I panted a moment, letting my heart slow, even as hers fluttered against the cage of her ribs like a butterfly trapped in a killing jar.

"Holy crap," she muttered, and I grinned and sat up just a little to look down into her dazed expression, those green eyes just a little bit wide. I was *not* going down inside her, my cock just as rigid as when we'd begun.

Score.

"Gimme just a minute to swap out the condom and we'll go some more," I muttered between gasping breaths.

"Wait, what?" she asked and looked at me like I was some sort of alien being.

I unthreaded my hand from her hair and used it to slap her ass – well, low on her hip toward her ass.

"Did I fucking stutter?" I asked her. She laughed and I grinned, shuddering as I pulled out of her.

Yeah, I was sure of it. I was good for an immediate round two.

I LAY in the dark of Cadence's room and stared sightlessly into it. She was snug against my side, breathing deep and even, her head on my shoulder, the warmth of her breath rushing over my chest in even intervals as I massaged the base of her skull with one hand, the other resting on my stomach, fingers twining with hers.

It was nice. Too nice. I mean, I had no desire whatsoever to be anywhere but here. This was heaven, bliss, the purest nirvana lying here like this beneath her warm, sated body as she cuddled me close.

So, what was bothering me so much?

Why couldn't I sleep?

Cadence whimpered slightly in her sleep and nestled closer. I held her tighter and tried to glimpse her sleeping face. There was just enough light from her curtain-shrouded bedroom window to glimpse the highlights – the curve of the apple of her cheek, a dark winging brow, the depth of the hollow beneath her high cheekbone made deeper still by the shadows in the room.

God, she was so fucking beautiful, so giving of herself... I think that's when it hit me that this went way beyond simple lust for me. Yeah, I lusted after her, and I lusted after her *hard,* but I really *liked* her. Like, it would fucking hurt if she woke up in the morning and told me to fuck off. I didn't think she would do that, but... fuck me, I *hoped* she wouldn't do that.

I rubbed my lips together and sighed out, closing my eyes, and just trying to memorize the feel of her against my body.

She'd had so much rotten shit happen to her. How did I know she wasn't afraid of the same thing? What reason did she have to trust me?

She didn't. I held her just a little tighter still and absently pressed a kiss to her forehead. She stirred slightly and I stilled, feeling like a heel if I did something stupid like woke her up.

"What's wrong?" she whispered into the dark and I felt her chin raise, her hair slide against my chest as she looked up at me or tried to. I didn't know how much detail she could pick out but at the same time, I had been able to pick out enough and the window was technically at her back while I faced it.

"Nothing, baby," I lied a little too easily. "Go back to sleep."

"Not until you tell me what's wrong," she murmured. She disentangled her fingers from mine and raised her hand to trail fingertips down the scruff on my cheek.

I sighed and finally fessed up.

"I'm not sure I'm good enough for you," I said.

She pushed herself up and demanded, "Why would you say that?"

I smiled faintly and nodding, said, "Not sure that you realize, but I don't think anyone is."

I think she was smiling faintly at me. I couldn't tell now that her back was to the window and all light had fled her fair face.

She made a rude noise and said, "Whatever!" I could hear her rolling her eyes at me even if I couldn't see it. She snuggled back into my side, and I held her close.

"You don't have to lay it on so thick, you know," she said on a yawn. "You've already got me."

I laughed. "Now who is flattering who?" I asked, even though I was secretly tickled by her words.

"I'm not!" she said and slapped my chest lightly. I gathered that hand with my free one and grazed her fingertips with my lips. She sighed contentedly and man – what I wouldn't give to make her make that sound some more. Shit, I had every intention of it. She was just too sweet, and I was smitten.

I had no idea what it was that was going on in my head. I'd honestly never felt this way about a woman before. I hate to call it, but I was a real manwhore, I guess. I just didn't do the whole relationship thing beyond a few months. Lately, I was even worse than that, preferring to just hit it and quit it. But not here, not with her. Cadence was like the perfect drug or some shit. I'd only had a taste and I was already hooked.

"Steady as she goes, baby," I murmured absently, more to myself than to Cadence. "We got nothing but time to figure it all out."

"Is..." she hesitated, and I waited her out. "Is it weird or bad that I really like the sound of that?" she asked.

I palmed the back of her head and massaged her scalp through her thick mass of unbelievably soft hair and spoke my heart, which I was finding incredibly easy around her which was another really new thing. "Not at all, sweetheart. Not at all."

15

*C*adence...

I woke to the smell of pancakes and masculine laughter in the kitchen. I didn't want to get up. I was lying comfortably on my stomach, which I almost never did, and the sheets and blankets were pooled at my waist. My feet were warm, and my back was cool. Everything was just sort of the perfect temperature, leading to a whole lot of just wanting to bask in the morning afterglow of all that we'd done the night before.

I felt my lips curl in a smile even as my pussy gave a throbbing, slightly but deliciously used ache.

God, he was so hot, I thought to myself and hummed in satisfaction at the images of him in my kitchen that I conjured in my mind.

In my version, he was shirtless and barefoot, jeans zipped but unbuttoned, that tantalizing happy trail leading from his belly button into the top of his pants.

It'd been a long time and my imagination seemed happy to make up for lost time. I guess it wasn't quite as atrophied as I thought it'd been.

Speaking of being creative... Jared had taken me through positions I had no name for last night and woo boy; did I honestly want more of that.

I slid my arms beneath me to try and push my way up at the sound of heavy tread on my hardwood floors coming this way. I peeked at my open doorway to make sure it was Jared and not my son coming up the hall and nearly swallowed my tongue.

He wasn't barefoot, but he *was* shirtless, and that top button on his jeans was most definitely undone.

Holy shit, this man was sex personified.

He grinned at me carelessly and I was *instantly* wet.

"Hey, baby," he murmured, sitting on the edge of the bed and holding out the steaming mug in his hand.

"Hey," I murmured, blushing shyly now that we were in the light of day because *had that really been me last night?*

He smiled and let me turn and sit up, only handing me the cup when I was situated, the sheet over my breasts and the pillows piled behind my back.

"Good morning," he murmured seductively and my mug in my hands, he leaned in for a kiss.

His lips were soft, the scruff of his fresh growth a rough contrast, and he kissed me like he meant it which made me smile. I kissed him back, despite worrying about the potential hazard and turnoff my morning breath could be.

He tasted of rich coffee and clean male and smelled just as delicious. There was no better scent or aphrodisiac in the world, at least to me, than the scent of clean and freshly showered male. Just something about it.

"Made use of the shower, I see," I murmured when he leaned back.

"Mm-hm." He nodded. "Hope you don't mind."

"Not at all! Smells like you took over the kitchen, too."

"Sort of. I started the coffee. Marc is the one that fired up the griddle."

"Aw, yeah?" I asked, sipping my coffee.

"Yeah, hooked a brother up with how you like your coffee with that fancy creamer shit you got in the fridge, too."

I laughed and coffee almost came out of my nose which led to me swallowing wrong and half-choking.

"Ah shit!" Jared took my mug and set it aside on the dresser, sitting up and snatching a random dish towel out of his back pocket to mop the sputtered coffee off my chest while I half-choked and half-laughed.

"You okay?" he demanded warily while I sputtered some more and all I could do was nod and wave him off.

He grinned at me, and I laughed a little. When he was sure that I could handle it without killing myself, he handed my coffee back to me.

"Sorry," I muttered, and he chuckled, bowing his head, and shaking it.

"I'm the one who should be sorry. I'm the one that made you choke."

"It's fine, *I'm fine*, really!" I declared.

"Not how I want to be defined as a 'lady killer,'" he said with a wink. "You're gonna have to get with the program there, buddy."

I laughed after safely swallowing my mouthful of coffee this time and asked, "You think I have time for a quick tactical shower before my man-child out there is done making a mess?"

"I think you got time for more than just a quick PTA."

"PTA?" I asked frowning. "What's the Parent Teacher Association have to do with me showering?"

He grinned a little wider and said, "Different worlds, baby."

"Then what's PTA in yours?" I asked, arching a brow.

He got to his feet and said with a wink, "Pussy, Tits, and Ass."

I almost choked on my coffee a second time to a track of his laughter as he left the room and drifted up the hallway.

I rolled my eyes and finished getting my caffeine fix before I got up myself and rushed to close the bedroom door before Marc did anything crazy like came around the corner. With a long-suffering sigh at the tongue-in-cheek prospect that I may have just adopted a *second* man-child, I fetched down my satin robe off the hook I mounted on the back of my closet door and slipped into it, liberating my long hair out from against my back and the robe's collar.

I paused with my hand on the bedroom doorknob and breathed out, my heart hammering against my ribs.

I had never been with *anyone* except Marc's father, and I really didn't know how my son would feel. But the rational part of my mind told me if my kid was out there flipping pancakes that he likely didn't mind. *On the flip side*, though, the mommy part of my brain that was terrified of fucking up and scarring my child for life was in full hysterical meltdown in its corner.

I did what I always did in these situations where I was afraid of failing as a mother. I asked my daddy for help. I closed my eyes and sent up a little prayer that he guide me on yet another one and with a smile, thought he would honestly be laughing at his adult daughter were he here right now and, in the end, that's what gave me the bravery to open the damn door and slip down the hall to my bathroom.

I could have *lived* under that shower's spray for *hours*. I was maybe a little sorer than the satisfied kind. Although I was more than satisfied for the time being, last night had also woken a ravenous hunger in me and I was a little afraid that Jared would be the only one to feed it. I mean, I had *never* met anyone quite like him and though it was a strong word, I positively *loved* how he had held me last night.

I felt like Alice tumbling end over end into wonderland and damned if even this morning, I felt as though I were still falling.

Fast. Too fast... keep it to yourself, I thought to myself.

I jumped when a knock fell at the bathroom door.

"Yeah?" I called out.

"Mom, breakfast!" my son called through the door.

"Be right out!" I called back and I rushed through the rest of my shower.

It struck me I only had a year or so more of interrupted showers and my boy calling out 'Mom' before he would be off to college. That was the one thing I carved out of the fight over my dead husband's assets. A future for our son – his firstborn.

Ugh.

I slammed the door on those thoughts. I didn't want to think about how easily and thoroughly I'd allowed myself to be duped. How all of the looks and giggles behind hands at the watercooler now made sense. I hated myself for allowing this shit to happen to us, not just to me but to Marc. I hated it so much.

I shut off the water and dried off, wrapping my hair up in my towel and re-donning my robe. I opened the bathroom door and took the few steps to peek around the hall wall into the dining room and kitchen.

"Getting dressed, two minutes, I promise," I said and smiled at how at home Jared looked on one of the kitchen stools and how equally comfortable Marc looked with his stack of pancakes on a plate next to the griddle as he flipped another with pride.

I dipped back into the bedroom and dressed swiftly in clean jeans and a fresh camisole and button-down plaid-pattern blouse. I skipped socks and shoes for now and rejoined the boys with my coffee cup in hand. Jared immediately got up, took my cup for me, and went over to refill it.

"Aw, you guys are positively *spoiling* me this morning," I declared.

"You've earned it," my kid said nonchalantly with a one-shouldered shrug. He set a stack of pancakes in front of me with the syrup and the jar of peanut butter. I smiled at him with a mixture of pride and gratitude.

"How did I get so lucky as a mom?" I asked him.

He shrugged all blasé but what came out of his mouth was anything but.

"You gave birth to a legend," he said, and I laughed. I couldn't exactly say he was wrong, but I had to completely admit my bias.

"So, what have you all got going on today?" Jared asked. "Any big plans?"

Marc and I exchanged a look and both sort of shrugged in unison.

"Just unpacking and putting the house together," I said.

"Kitchen is almost done," Marc said. "I mean, I tried. You'll probably move everything around, but I did what you told me about the spices and the dishes." He gave a shrug and I smiled at him.

"I bet you did great," I said, and he smiled at me.

The smile turned into one of his cheeky grins and he said, "I wouldn't say that until you've gone through it."

I vowed right then and there, that no matter how he had set up the kitchen, I wouldn't move a thing. I didn't care. Some things were more important than whether I felt the coffee cups were in a good spot in relation to the coffee maker or whatever.

"Need a hand with anything? I might be able to come back this afternoon," Jared said and I turned and smiled at him, too.

Oh... I thought... I pasted on a smile and said, "No, you've already done so much..." I could see Marc nearly choke out of the corner of my eye where he stood opposite me and Jared at the counter, eating his breakfast. I knew it was because he was dying to say some smartass and probably totally inappropriate comment and I wasn't about to encourage it even though I was sort of burning with curiosity because when my kid *did* pop off? I was usually too busy laughing to reprimand him with any sort of parental authority.

I had more than a few parenting fails versus wins in this regard.

"Alright, then. I'm going to have a look at getting a few more things on that inspection report accomplished, maybe head home and look through my private stash for parts and pieces. I would stick around, but something came up with the club that I've gotta be there to handle."

"Alright." I nodded, a little sad to see him go, but I knew I would see him again, and soon. At least I hoped. I know it was likely just my history with Ben, but I couldn't shake the feeling this was some sort of excuse to leave.

We finished eating, and he slipped off his stool and paused, a hand on my shoulder to lean down and kiss me.

Marc immediately made himself scarce, ducking around the corner and going up the stairs to his room.

I sighed happily against Jared's lips, and he drew back slightly.

"I'll see you soon," he murmured, and I had to smile. It sounded like a promise.

"I'll see you soon," I repeated back to him. He smiled back at me before drawing back and heading around into my room to finish getting dressed.

I started cleaning up the kitchen. It was only fair since Marc had cooked. He had a knack for the kitchen and cooked with me on the regular. Now that he was getting older, there were times he came out with recipes and fairly infrequently like this, even cooked all by himself.

I was still working on getting him to do his own laundry. I think that had less to do with laziness, or lack of know-how on his part, and more to do with even though he was as independent as he was, still liking his mom to do certain things for him.

I seriously didn't know how I had lucked out so hard as to have a kid as great as Marc.

Jared came back into the kitchen as I was rinsing dishes and loading them into the dishwasher and stole one last kiss before leaving.

"I'll see you around, gorgeous," he murmured, then lest I become too complacent at his sweetness to me, he slapped me on the ass. I jumped, letting out a yip that dissolved on a laugh.

A moment later, the front door opened and closed. A few seconds after that, I heard my son come down the stairs. He entered the kitchen and I glanced back over my shoulder.

"You alright?" I asked curiously.

"Yeah. Why wouldn't I be?" he asked.

I pursed my lips and steeled myself for the hard talk.

"I haven't ever really been with anyone but your father," I said quietly, dumping the water off the plate in my hands and lowering it into the bottom rack of the dishwasher.

"Mom, he was never really around. Let's face it. You haven't really been with anyone in a long time."

"Marc—" I didn't want him to be so *angry* with his dad.

"Mom, no, it's okay. Like, it's totally cool. I like Jared." He shrugged. "I just want you to be happy."

I shut off the water and turned around, leaning back against the sink.

"Have I really been so very *un*happy?" I asked.

He went to the fridge and got out one of his bottles of sports drink, rolling it back and forth between his hands.

"You haven't exactly been happy for a real long time," he said. He sounded like he felt guilty for even saying it. "I know you put on a brave face for me all the time, but I'm old enough now. You don't have to."

I sighed. "I'm the adult, and you're still my child," I said. "My very, and sometimes annoyingly, *perceptive* child."

I crossed my arms over my stomach; a subconscious movement to hold my hurt in, I think. I felt like this wasn't exactly one of my finer parenting moments here. Marc shouldn't have known. I felt like a bit of a failure for not hiding it better.

He gave me a reckless grin and tossed his sports drink in the air with some spin and caught it, backing out of the kitchen toward the bottom of the stairs.

"Like I said, most moms don't give birth to legends."

I rolled my eyes and he laughed at me and went up the stairs.

"I'm sure I'm not the only mother to give birth to such a smartass," I muttered under my breath, but I was smiling. I finished washing and putting things away, opening cupboards to find where Marc had stashed things, apparently the day before while I had been out.

Again, I felt a surge of pride at what an excellent kid he was. Even if I did have to argue with him about his room starting to stink and getting it cleaned up on occasion. Such was the life of a boy mom.

I spent the rest of the day unpacking and with Marc's help, getting certain furniture pieces into their final position so that the rest of the unpacking could commence. I tried to focus on the living room the most, getting it ninety percent of the way unpacked and set up. I called it quits that evening and with a sigh, went out on the back patio and dropped into one of the lounge chairs out there.

I chewed my bottom lip and stared at my phone's empty screen, void of any notifications. I sighed and worried vaguely that Jared might be done. That I'd put out and he'd won the prize and there wasn't anything left there… I mean, irrational much? Sure, but, agh God!

It was so frustrating. The years of disinterest, the touches shrugged off, the affection waved away and the excuses. My God, the excuses… *I'm busy. Not right now. I have a headache, babe. I just don't feel like it right now.*

I thought it was me. I'd thought it was me for so long and I carried that secret pain and burden that it was *me*. The stretch marks, and even after they'd faded, the fact that my figure wasn't as taut, wasn't as toned, thinking I was maybe too needy… that maybe my looks were fading… plucking the one or two gray hairs, trying anything to get him to look at me like he used to. Blond? Nope. Red? Nope. Getting back in shape? Nope. Sexier clothes? No, and when he threw a fit and demanded to know if I was cheating?

God, that had been devastating in a way I can't even explain and to find out he *was?*

Whew, there had to be an entire 747 overhead compartment bin full of baggage and anxiety I had to unpack but Lord, it was all mine to unpack. It wasn't Jared's problem and fuck if I didn't want to come across as too needy.

So, I sat, and I stared at the blinking cursor on my phone, and I warred with myself on should I, or shouldn't I text? Should I, or shouldn't I call?

I mean, he hadn't texted or called me, so was it over? Just like that? I wanted to reach out, to know, and I was literally sitting here driving myself *crazy* overthinking all of this but…

My phone buzzed in my hands, and I jumped and let out a yelp.

"Mom?" Marc called from inside the house, the security door closed, but the back door beyond it standing open. It was a nice mild day, and as such, I was letting the house air out a bit.

"It's fine, I'm okay!" I called but here was my kid, coming out the back.

"What was that?" he asked, the ghost of a grin on his face. I looked at his handsome face, so like his father's, with his father's brown eyes and my thick mane of chestnut hair, although definitely cut shorter in a style more appropriate for a boy.

"I'm just overthinking things in my classic style and my phone went off and startled me," I confessed.

He laughed at me a little and sat down, spooning some of the cereal he'd poured himself into his mouth.

"Is it Jared?" he asked around his mouthful.

I looked and shook my head. "It's Evelyn," I said.

He rolled his eyes slightly at the mention of my best friend's name back in Georgia.

"I don't want to be around for *that* conversation," he said, getting up and going back inside.

"I love you!" I called at his back.

"Love you, too!" he called after the security door slammed shut. I winced. I'd never been a fan of loud noises.

I called Evelyn, because her text was pretty much a *Girl, when are you going to call me?*

"I was wondering when you were going to get your bony ass on the phone with me!" she crowed by way of greeting when she answered.

I laughed and shook my head. "It's been busy around here," I told her.

"Aw, yeah?" she asked. "What's going on now?"

"Well." I sighed to buy myself some time. I didn't know where to start. "The movers finally showed up yesterday," I said finally.

"Oh, yeah? How'd that go?" she asked.

"They broke a bunch of my shit," I said, making a disgusted noise.

"Oh, no! Girl! I'm so sorry, on top of everything else."

"Yeah." I nodded. "I know, but you know what? It's not the end of the world. They're just things. Marc and I made it here safe, and we have a sound roof over our heads and..." I hesitated, unsure of what *exactly* to tell her about Jared. I mean, she knew about him. We'd texted, but...

"Bitch, you better *spill*," she demanded when I was silent too long.

"The handy guy," I said.

"Mm-hm, the hot one?"

"Yes." I drew out the word and she chuckled a little.

"Uh-huh, and what about tall, dark, and handsome?"

"He uh... he maybe stayed the night last night."

I had to hold the phone away from my ear at her excited and deafening squeal she let out on the other end of the line. Okay, she was *way* too excited.

"Okay, tell me *everything*. I need *all* the delicious dirty details."

I rolled my eyes, but her excitement was sort of infectious. I put all my doubts and fears aside for the moment and reveled in the memories of my wild night.

I told her everything, and I could just picture her on the other end with her big glass of red wine and a bowl of popcorn, hanging on my every word.

"Right, that sounds *amazing*, but you didn't sound happy when I answered the phone. So, come on, tell me, what else happened?" she asked.

"Nothing. I just haven't heard from him the rest of the day and you know me—"

"Overthinking every little minute detail to absolute goddamn death and letting your insecurities run rampant?" she asked, and I gave a sardonic laugh.

"You know me so well," I said flatly.

"Girl, we have *talked* about this!"

"I know, I know!" I groaned.

"Don't make me put my therapist's hat on," she said, and I smiled to myself. Try as she might, Evelyn, my friend, my best friend, the shrink, couldn't always help herself. She tried valiantly not to head shrink her friends but sometimes… I couldn't say it upset me. Well, it did sometimes, but most of the time I found her wisdom incredibly insightful and needed.

"You're right." I sighed and confessed, "My insecurities are eating me alive right now and God, Evy, I don't know. It's like when I'm with him the stupid things sleep. They raise their ugly heads every once in a while, but he just… he just always seems to know what to say or when to change the subject and talking to him is so *easy* and—"

"Now that's what I'm talking about!" she crowed triumphantly.

"What?" I asked with a little laugh.

"You listening to yourself right now? When you talk about him, girl, you sound *happy*."

"I am!" I put my hand to my forehead and rubbed at the headache that was forming there. "But I can't help it. The 'what-if's' are out and in full force."

"Well, your 'what-if's' are almost always usually a *what the fuck* and you need to push past 'em, baby."

"I know, I know, and I wish it was just that easy but—"

"But what? What are you gonna tell me that I'm not gonna like?" she demanded.

I blinked and said abruptly, "Evy, I'm going to have to call you back. He's here."

"Tall dark and handsome?" she asked.

"Yeah."

"What do you mean he's there?"

"I mean, he literally just pulled up," I said, having to raise my voice over the chug of his motorcycle's engine as he pulled to the end of my drive in the part where you pulled past everything and could put it in reverse to back down the drive.

Instead of backing into the driveway itself and blocking my car in, he just heeled down his stand and leaned the bike onto it.

"Well, if that isn't just the best way to tell your insecurities they can take their lies and shove it," she said, and I could hear her smile.

I laughed and as Jared strode down the drive, said, "I'll talk to you soon."

"Bye," she sang out.

"Bye." I hung up.

"Hey," he said, and I stood up as he finished crossing the distance between us.

"Hey," I said back, and he swept me up against him with an arm around my waist and kissed me soundly.

"Hmm," I hummed in peace against his mouth.

"You okay?" he asked against my lips and I nodded, struck dumb for a moment by his kiss. "Didn't hear from you all day. I started to get a little bit worried."

I closed my eyes as he rested his forehead against mine and just enjoyed being held close for a moment.

"Yeah, I'm fine," I said and swallowed hard.

"Liar," he said, and he was smiling, grinning hard. His voice held some mischievous teasing to it.

I rolled my eyes as I pulled my head back from his and said lightly, "Didn't want you to get sick of me."

I'd meant it to be silly, a little joke, but it definitely didn't strike him as funny. His smile flattened and his expression became serious. He shook his head.

"I didn't want to be too overbearing or overwhelming or whatever, but, babe, I don't think I'd ever get sick of you. Please, don't ever think that."

He dipped his head to capture my gaze with his when I stopped looking at him and I blinked once in surprise at the sincerity in them. He asked, "K?" I realized he needed to hear me say it.

"Okay," I whispered.

"Promise me." He wasn't asking.

"I promise."

He nodded carefully after searching out my eyes for a moment.

"Okay."

"What are you even doing here?" I asked with a slight laugh.

"Like I said, I hadn't heard from you all day and I was on my way home and passing by. I just had this urge to see if everything was alright, so I dipped at your exit and here I am."

"Oh…" I murmured; happy he was here.

"I'm not overstepping, am I?" he asked, and I smiled and shook my head.

I did the brave thing then and took a deep breath. "When I hadn't heard from you, I guess I started overthinking things," I confessed.

He frowned slightly. "What do you mean?"

I drew in a shuddering breath and said, "I thought maybe I was… um, like a hit it and quit it or—"

He grabbed my chin lightly and stared me in the eyes, his hazel ones full of fire as he shook his head.

"I wouldn't do that to you," he said, and his voice was clipped. He dragged his phone out of his pocket, unlocked it, and put the screen in front of my face.

He had texted me, like three times throughout the day, asking how things were going with the unpacking, asking if I was doing alright, and finally, letting me know he was getting a little worried.

I frowned and opened my phone and showed him none of those texts had been received.

"Technology, gotta love it," he said sardonically, and I smiled. "So, we good?" he asked.

I nodded. "Of course!"

"Restart your phone for me," he said, and I did. We waited for it to cycle through its startup screen then waited for a time after that. Still nothing.

He sighed and restarted his phone and almost as soon as it restarted, it started buzzing in his hand with alerts and text messages from other people. A moment later, all three of his texts came through on my phone.

"I guess it wasn't really you, it was me," he said with a wink, and I laughed.

"Gotta be anywhere in a big hurry now?" I asked.

"Can't say that I do. Just need to get ready for work tomorrow."

"Hungry?" I asked.

"I could eat. Are you on the menu?" he asked, grabbing my ass playfully and I laughed.

"Chicken. Chicken is what's for dinner."

"Count me in," he said with a smile.

"Okay, great."

16

*G*lass Jaw...

    I woke up to a text that morning from Mav.

Major got himself picked up on a drunk and disorderly down in Tacoma last night. You're closer. Bail him out, please? Club's got it.

Shit. I was supposed to spend the day here, but fuck if duty didn't call.

I showered, made coffee while the kid started up breakfast. He'd made some progress on his mom's kitchen while I'd had her out yesterday afternoon and I appreciated that. He was a good kid.

I hated leaving like this. It felt abrupt, and I didn't like that, but things were also still new and club first... damnit.

I would make it up to her. Wasn't sure how, but I would.

After a swift goodbye and a lame excuse, I rode down to the Pierce County jail and posted the modest bond on fuckin' Major.

"Wanna tell me what the fuck happened?" I demanded. My brother looked rough, the neck of his faded black tee stretched and torn, but with the way he had the sleeves cut out that could have been a before or after.

"Motherfucker called me a nigger. I couldn't let that disrespect stand. I was *about* to knock his fuckin' teeth down his throat but the cops showed up and arrested my ass for all the yelling."

"What motherfucker would this be?" I asked.

"Fuckin' bouncer. Some Aryan Nation yahoo fuckin' weirdo," he said.

"You know where you left your bike?"

"Shit, man. They probably towed it. It's back over on Pearl Street," he said.

"Where the fuck were you? Hell's Temple?"

"Naw, that new fuckin' club. Didn't know the girl I was with had a daddy and brother who were a couple of racist fucks."

I laughed to myself. "I was wondering when you were gonna say pussy had something to do with it."

"Man!" He made a tsking noise. Wasn't the first time he had chased some white tail that was just trying to stick it to her racist daddy by sucking some big black cock.

"You're lucky the pigs just arrested your ass and didn't fuckin' kill you," I said. "Come on. Let's see if we get lucky and find your bike."

"Shit, you ride here?" he asked.

"Yup and you're sittin' bitch. Nut to butt, honey."

"Man, fuck you!" He laughed. Neither one of us were homophobic pieces of shit but we knew plenty of guys that would balk at being thought of as gay.

We rode out to where his bike should have been parked on the street, but he was right, looked like it'd been towed.

"Fuckin' A, man," he swore and called the number on the nearby sign to find out where it was and how much it was gonna cost to get it out of impound. I sat on my bike nearby and waited on him.

"Almost seven hundred dollars?... What?... What?... *What?* Man, you fuckin' blood sucking assholes are something else. You had my bike less than four hours and you wanna charge me six-hundred-and-eighty-nine dollars to get that shit out?"

I gave a low whistle. Bail may have been on the club, but this? This was all him.

"You better not have fucked any of my shit up." He swore into the phone and then demanded, "Aight, where am I goin'?"

I put the address into my GPS and checked out the route. I knew where it was. It was on South Tacoma Way just a few streets down from this wholesale place I got some of my construction supply shit from.

I sat by while he handled his shit, and while he griped and grumbled about it, he did it with sort of a smile. I mean, it wasn't the lot attendant's fault his shit got towed, it was his dumbass fault for parking on the street like that.

"You good?" I asked as the gate rumbled open so he could go in and retrieve his shit.

"We'll see in a minute," he said.

I waited, and a few minutes later his bike fired up and he carefully came out over the gravel on it.

"Alright, club?" he called over the chug of his engine and I nodded. I fired up my bike and we rode together back up I-5 to Rat City and the club, dipping off at state route 518 and taking it all the way into Burien.

Mav was waiting outside the club with a few other guys and handed Major a joint when he got off his bike on the side of the clubhouse building.

Major took it and took a hit off it. Mav said, "Come on and fill us all in on what the fuck happened."

Major nodded and handed the joint back, holding his breath and the fragrant smoke in as we all stepped around the front of the building to where some of the rest of the guys were piled sitting on the picnic tables and benches out front with their morning beers.

"Calling service?" Deacon asked and Mav chuckled and shook his head.

"Naw, no sense in dragging everyone else in here yet. You want to do this in my office or is out here cool?" Mav asked.

"Out here's cool. I didn't do nothin' wrong, man."

"From what I gathered, the only thing he fucked up on is he may have been tryin' to stick his dick in some crazy," I said when Mav looked past him at me.

Squatch and Nine laughed at that.

"Fill us in," Mav ordered, and Major did.

"Said he'd hooked up with this chick through a couple of mutual soldier buddies from his time in the Army down around JBLM." That was Joint Base Lewis-McChord. "Said he and she had hit it off some, and he was sorta lookin' to hit it but hadn't gotten there yet. She and some of her hoochie-ass friends wanted to hit a bar down on Pearl and he hadn't really been feelin' it, but he wanted to tap that ass so he'd knuckled under and taken her.

"Said they'd been knockin' back drinks and were having a good time when her brother comes in and starts chewin' the girl's ass and he told us, 'Not gonna lie, like at first I was like 'hoooo, shit! She gotta boyfriend!' then I asked her who *is* this dude? Right? And this motherfucker turned on *me* and said 'I'm her brother, you stupid ass nigger!' and I ain't about that so I told him to get his honky ass outside he gonna talk to a brother like that. Then he's all callin' me *boy* and we go outside and I tell him this *boy* is gonna whoop that ass, and the cops show up. This fucker keeps screamin' at me and I just kept taunting him back. The next thing my ass knows, *I'm* the one bent over the back of the fuckin' car, bracelets goin' on me."

"Anything happen to this *pendejo?*" Mav asked and I secreted a smile. Marisol was rubbing off on his lily-white ass and giving his language some color.

"Naw, they let *him* go, even though girly was tellin' 'em that he started it. A bunch of other people in the crowd, too."

"You're lucky you didn't get your ass beat," Squatch said.

"Nah, too many phones out, cameras rolling," Major said. "I wasn't resisting or nothing. I was drunk, yeah, but I wasn't that stupid."

I met a sideways look from him and saw it plain on his face, he'd been legit pissing himself he'd been so scared, but we all knew it. We didn't need to tear him down further by refusing to take what he had to say at face value. It was enough that we all fuckin' knew.

"Alright, we'll bring it up at our next church meetin' but the best thing you can do right now is lie low, stay outta Pierce for a minute, and build back your capital for the next set of fines and shit. We'll send the club lawyer with you to your court date."

Major nodded. "Appreciate it."

"No worries," Mav declared.

"Don't think either the girl or her brother are gettin' off the hook, either."

"Oh, hell no, the fuck they aren't," Major glowered. "I know the drill. Bide our time."

"That's right." Mav nodded and leaned back, passing me the joint. I took a hit.

I would be getting my shot in on Billy bumfuck racist myself just for interrupting my time with Cadence.

I texted her throughout the day and checked in on her but didn't get a response, which worried me.

I hung around the club and my bros for a few hours and changed the oil on my bike over at the boneyard since the lift was free and made it easier. When I got my baby back on the ground and checked my phone for the millionth time, my third and last text still gone unanswered more than an hour later, I decided that was it. I was swinging by Cadence's place on the way home – which wasn't *really* on the way but fucking whatever.

I was glad that I did stop. I felt like a shitbird that it was my phone causing the problem and I damn sure would be getting with my service provider to find out exactly *what the fuck*. But honestly, all of it just sort of just drained away or turned to so much white noise the second I had Cadence back in my arms.

I wished like hell I could stay, but I knew she and I both needed a little breathing room. We could be too much of a good thing and I wanted to nurture this ember between us. I didn't want shit to flame out and fade away. I wanted something with this woman that would burn brightly and for all eternity, but I definitely didn't want to move too fast, nor did I *ever* want her to think I was apathetic or that she wasn't enough.

Once again, as I stood there on her back patio with her, I wanted to kill her fucking ex a second time over. She was riddled with a guilt that wasn't her burden to carry, holding up the weight of his infidelity and all the bullshit that came with it – the anxiety, the shame, people's sniggering and their judgments. Even from almost three thousand miles away, I could see it weighing her spirit and I wanted so bad to untangle the gordian knot of pain she was wrapped in and set her fucking free. I followed her into the house, and she stopped in her kitchen. She went to the sink, and I waited her out as she cut open a package with a whole chicken in it.

"I feel so dumb now, jumping to conclusions like that," she said as she shook, *yes shook* the guts out of her chicken into the garbage disposal.

"It's fine," I said, shoulders shaking from the laughter I was trying to suppress and failing at it. "Just, *what* are you *doing?*"

She grinned at me sheepishly. "Shaking the innards out, why?"

"I've never seen *anyone* do shit that way."

"I don't like to touch them!" she cried. "They're slimy and gross! I've always done it this way."

"Oh, my God! Here, let me." I went over to her and the sink and took the whole chicken – still mostly in its wrapper – from her hands. Like, legit, she sliced open the package over the chicken's ass and literally held on to the thing with both hands like you pick up a cat or a baby and shook the shit out of it, trying to dislodge the guts. It had to be some of the funniest shit I'd ever seen.

I gutted the damn thing, peeled the wrapper off, and asked her, "Where do you want it?"

"Back down in the skillet," she said, pointing to a cast-iron skillet standing by.

I laid the chicken in it and turned back to the sink to wash my hands.

"You're too cute," I said over my shoulder.

She blushed faintly and I noticed that about her – that she wasn't used to compliments or praise and she soaked that shit up like a sponge.

Being who I was and where I came from, I knew a thousand and more little ways to destroy a human spirit. It wasn't always the kicks or punches that hurt the most, but the well-placed unkind words or worse yet, using a person up. The never saying thank you, taking advantage of them over and over when all they wanted was just a little recognition.

It was the truly good people who just kept on going despite it all and Cadence was one of the good ones. I could see that, and I just honestly didn't know why anyone from her life before couldn't.

I hadn't had the best upbringing. Had spent several years as a teen in and out of foster care. Dad in prison, mom so far gone on her drug habit that there wasn't any alternative. Aunts and uncles were maxed out with their own brood of kids, grandparents too infirm to handle a hellion of a teenage boy with anger issues.

For a long time, all that boy had wanted was to be loved, but finally that boy had decided *fuck it*, that it wasn't ever going to happen.

It was sometime in my twenties when I'd found something close enough in the brotherhood of the club. Spent years getting us on lock and where we needed to be so that we could just coast with this regular thing. Took me just as long to build my own business, working my way up from working for other guys in the contracting, building, and remodeling business to owning my own company and doing for myself.

I was sitting flush now, and that was good – no it was *great* and all, but something was and had always been sort of missing. Hooking up had satisfied the physical needs, but there was still some of that wounded boy in there, buried deep, and I think it was high time to give myself the deeper connection I'd so desperately craved all those years ago.

I dried my hands off on a kitchen towel and leaned my ass up against the sink counter's edge and watched Cadence work. Her oven preheating the temperature, ticking up on the display and nearly there as she poured liquids and seasonings over the chicken.

"How long is this supposed to take?" I asked her, hooking one of her belt loops with my finger and towing her into my arms once the oven door was shut.

"Hold on, let me set the timer." she said lightly. I let her punch buttons and she told me, "It takes a couple of hours, but I need to baste it at the one-hour mark.

"A couple hours?" I asked, and then teasingly I pulled her the rest of the way against me and said, "Oh, no... whatever shall we do to fill the time?"

She chuckled, kissed me, and said, "Mm, that's dessert. I still have sides to prepare."

"Oh, God!" I rolled my eyes and let her go with a sweet whack on the ass.

She laughed and got out some potatoes. She'd stocked her kitchen with food even if she didn't have anything to really cook with and the preparation on her part had paid off. She'd gotten a lot done today by the looks of the living room.

I wandered back around the kitchen counter and retook my seat on the stool I'd vacated to help her out.

"Looks like you got the living room done today."

"Almost," she said, rinsing a golden potato at the sink and peeling it.

"What's missing?" I asked, raising an eyebrow.

"Just some art on the walls is all," she said smiling. "You should go have a look in the display cabinets. That's my life's work in there."

Now that piqued my curiosity.

"Well, I don't mind if I do," I declared and got up from the counter to let her work in peace for a minute.

I tell you what, I was not prepared.

The cabinets had all framed photos of completed buildings next to framed schematics and concept drawings and the *models*... They were impressive, not overly large, probably the biggest one was the size of both my hands put together at the base, but whoa, were they insanely detailed!

The only thing that smacked me harder than anything else was knowing that Cadence had designed every one of them and there had to be more than half a dozen in there. I stopped and took the time to count... eight. There were eight in total, and these buildings were put up all over the world.

I gave a low whistle as Marc came bounding down the stairs.

"Oh, yeah, huh? Pretty awesome, right?"

"You're telling me," I agreed.

He pointed to the one, third down on the shelf in front of me and said, "That one's my favorite."

I bent at the waist and looked. It was pretty cool. It looked like something sleek, black, made entirely out of glass, and like it belonged in *Blade Runner* or some other futuristic flick.

"Where's that one at?" I asked.

"Beijing, I think."

"China?"

"Oh, yeah. Mom's got buildings on every continent except Antarctica," he said.

"What?" I asked and Marc beamed.

"I think it secretly pissed my dad off," he said in a low whisper. "He was still missing Russia."

I nodded and thought to myself, *of course it pissed him off*. Sounded like the dude's ego seriously knew no bounds.

"Hey, Mom, when's dinner?" Marc asked, going into the kitchen while I eyed Cadence's accomplishments some more.

I didn't listen to them; I was a little too engrossed here. The way she'd displayed these pieces showed how proud she was of them, and they were all something worthy of being proud of.

Damn. I didn't realize—

"You're awfully quiet in there," she called, and I went back into the kitchen. She'd finished up the potatoes and was trimming off the ends to some asparagus.

"Awestruck is more like it," I said honestly. "Those are some damn fine achievements. I didn't know I was hooked up with such a badass."

She blushed prettily and she honestly looked like she was downright giddy.

"It's nice to hear someone say that instead of telling me not to let my ego get out of control," she said and bit her bottom lip.

I pulled her to me and kissed her temple. "After what I just saw in there, you're allowed to have an ego."

"Should I make up some squash, too, or do you think potatoes and asparagus is going to be enough?" she asked.

"I think that'll be plenty," I said. "How much time we got until you need to be back in here?"

She glanced at the timer and said, "About forty-five minutes."

"Mm, plenty of time." I swept her up into my arms and she half fell into them, shrieking with surprise. I carried her swiftly, laughing, into the bedroom with every intention of having a little dessert first.

17

*C*adence...

He carried me into the bedroom, and it was strange. I didn't feel like I was a small girl by any stretch of the imagination, but he carried me and tossed me on the bed, pulling me across it toward him like I weighed nothing at all. I mean, it took some effort on his part, but it was as though he didn't mind it, and not once did he make any kind of disparaging comment even in a joking manner about it.

I was grateful. There were points in our relationship where Ben had been cruel and now, I didn't know if it was unconscious or not. There was no way to know, and I wrestled with that and so much more.

"What are you going to do to me?" I asked playfully, biting my bottom lip as he unfastened my jeans and gave me a wicked grin in return.

"Gonna make you come, so you better be quiet," he murmured, pulling both my jeans and my panties beneath off in one smooth motion.

I giggled when he kissed my stomach. Giggles that turned into unbridled laughter when he blew a raspberry against it. He laughed because of my laughter and dragged me back to the edge of the mattress, parting my legs and folding me in half, exposing my pussy. His strong hands were on the backs of my thighs behind my knees as he licked a wet line from my opening to my clit.

I let my head fall back to the bed and moaned, clutching the covers to either side of my hips, knowing I needed to hold on because when Jared got started, he was *relentless* in the pursuit of my orgasm.

I jumped slightly when he slipped a finger inside me all the way to his base knuckle, and gasped and shuddered when he stroked over that spot inside me.

"Oh, God!" I gasped.

I could hear the grin in his voice when he said, "Don't forget to be quiet."

Oh, that dirty, dirty, mother—

I didn't have the chance to finish the thought because his tongue was back on me, teasing my clit while he assailed my G-spot with the pad of his finger. He was oh, so, gentle about it. One time with me and he already knew what I liked. Not too hard, not too fast, just the one finger felt so nice, so good. I panted and tried to keep my voice out of things as he teased me slowly, holding off just that hair to bring me up slowly.

It was like those movies where they're on a river, and they're slowly heading toward the cliff with the roar and pummeling waterfall, about to plunge over the side and to their deaths. Everything building slowly, the music, the mood, everything tense, the characters not realizing the danger at first, then all too soon, overtly aware, but it's too late. My resolve, much like their boat, breaking up in the current, both my hands clapped over my mouth as I plunged over the side into that shining fall, trying not to scream, my voice muffled to a whimper as he held me down and took me way past comfortable, outside of my scope of control, as he just kept on assaulting every one of my senses with the pure bright fire of his attentions. Tongue lapping at me lazily, finger slowing inside of me as my wetness grew, and I clenched rhythmically around it in my loss of control, my body on maximum overdrive until all I could do was close my eyes and lay limp beneath him, shuddering and shaking involuntarily with sweet little aftershocks.

I panted and he wiped his mouth with the back of his hand, coming up to lay next to me, propping his head on his hand with a smug look of satisfaction. His other hand he placed on my pussy, stroking me gently, plunging a finger through my slick, wet folds and teasing my opening, slipping it inside of me, pressing the heel of his hand against my clit.

I panted, gasping for breath as he smiled serenely, an almost shit-eating grin, and with some force behind the massage, shook his hand, pressing, these little shock waves rippling through me.

"Shhhh..." My hands flew from where I'd wrapped them around his wrist and went back to my mouth, clapping over it to muffle my cries. I didn't *think* Marc could hear me from upstairs, but I didn't want to take that chance. He was a teenager, yes, but as far as I knew, he wasn't sexually active yet, and he *really* didn't need to hear his *mom!*

Jared chuckled, made me come *again*, but this time eased off when I grew overwhelmed.

Thank God...

"Mmm, mm-hm..." he hummed in satisfied appreciation, leaning way over to kiss me lightly. I tried to deepen the kiss and he pulled back and asked, "You sure? I just went down on you."

"Shut up and fucking kiss me," I breathed, and he laughed, but obliged me.

A moment later, I was vaguely aware of the oven timer going off.

I'd completely lost all sense of time.

Christ, he was intense!

18

Glass Jaw...

The following weekend after leaving Cadence's was _rough_. We had a border run to make, and I was on deck. We headed up to the old bootlegger's inn we used, and shit wasn't good, man.

There was some heat over the border, and we only got half our usual supply. I was on the phone with Mav, trying to figure out logistics because there were people who _needed_ these drugs. Who were counting on us, _but fuck_, they knew the risks and shit like this some-times happened. Sometimes, there just wasn't any avoiding it.

"Right, so half the usual stock of insulin and maybe a third of what we usually get for the blood pressure meds," I said as Deacon handed me a scrap of paper with the figures. "Looks like we're also off on the numbers for the seizure medicine."

"Sad to fuckin' say that last one isn't too bad now that one kid didn't make it," Mav said. "So we're alright on what we _do_ have in that regard.

"Which kid?" I asked.

"That eighteen-year-old. It wasn't his epilepsy that took him out, suicide, I guess. Just couldn't handle the bullshit his classmates were giving him."

"Fuck, that's rough," I said.

"Tell me about it. He was a good kid."

"We got any overstock hidden to make up for the shortages?" I asked.

"Yeah, some, not enough to fully make up for it but it'll hurt less. I don't know what we're gonna do if it's like this next month," he said.

I nodded. "So how does this play?" I asked him.

"Make your usual drop, then get your ass to the stash house and pull the rest of what's needed and head south to the Oregon boys. I'll have some of them meet you in Washougal."

And that's what fucked me up. The additional miles on the prescription train screwed me right out of seeing Cadence for dinner tonight. *Fuck me.*

"Got it," I told him. "Just gotta disappoint my lady, first."

"Whoa, whoa, whoa, *your lady* now, is it?" he asked laughing, and I rolled my eyes.

"Shut up."

I hung up on his laughing ass.

I sighed and the guys were looking at me expectantly.

"Gimme a second," I said and pulled out my regular phone.

I thought about it and shook my head.

"We ride for the drop, but I gotta stop at the rest area and make a call, so let's mount up and get the fuck out of here," I said to a round of nodding heads.

We did just that, the ride a hard one. We had to stagger our departure times, trying not to tip off the cops we were up to anything nefarious, which we weren't – not when you considered the fact that the American healthcare system was a million times more nefarious in its dealings than we could ever fucking hope to be.

Yeah. I said it. What of it? It's the truth, isn't it?

I knew plenty of guys, that if it weren't for the fact that we had our own doctor inside the club by way of Eulogy, they would have just gone untreated and would have *died*. Same with a lot of the fuckin' people we brought these drugs to. Were we making a profit off of them? Yeah, a handsome one, *but* we were also taking all the risk to get them where they needed to be, *and* these folks were getting them dirt-fucking cheap by comparison. Hell, some of them even by virtue of having insurance couldn't afford the sky-high drug costs *and* eat.

Lifesaving shit. Not just the insulin they needed, but epi pens, seizure medication, some psych meds and most of all, heart meds, not just cholesterol-lowering drugs, but blood pressure medications and yeah, even some pain meds. Low-grade stuff like Tylenol 3 – the shit with codeine which none of us could figure out why that shit was outlawed down here except to pave the way to push the harder shit.

We were even delivering much needed *cancer*-fighting drugs to some patients that couldn't otherwise afford 'em.

It was fucked up. A cryin' shame. Yet the fuckin' bureaucrats just kept on letting it happen.

It wasn't profitable enough to have a healthy populace, I guess.

When we stopped at the rest area along the highway, I powered up my main phone and called down to Cadence.

"Hey, you," she answered me warmly. "How's the job going?"

"Like absolute fuckin' garbage," I growled.

"Oh, no!"

"Yeah, I'm really sorry, baby, but I don't think I can make dinner tonight."

"Aw, that's okay," she said, although I could hear the disappointment in her voice.

"No, it's not. I'd much rather be spending my evening with you."

"Ah, a raincheck," she said. She was being so fucking nice about it. I knew in the back of my mind, she had to be wondering and I knew with the front of my head that it wasn't my issue, and I didn't have to worry about it or sweat it, but fuck, I did.

I'd told a little white lie and had said I was up near the Canadian border, pulling volunteer work for today. The big lie was that it was on a Habitat for Humanity project. She'd believed me, and I had some pictures of some volunteer work I had done with some of the club brothers the summer before that would fly if she asked me, but I didn't want to go there if I could help it.

I just wanted to keep her clean and sin free, even if what we were doing was technically on the side of the angels.

"I promise," I said. "I'll see you around."

"Okay, be safe and have fun," she replied, and I chuckled.

"Will do."

We ended the call and after Tic got back from taking a piss, we rode on. It was gonna be a long fuckin' day into the evening, and I wasn't looking forward to any of it.

We swung down to the Steven's Pass drop point, made the exchange of what we had and then made south for the Renton stash house. We picked up more supply there and hit 405 to the I-5 interchange, heading south.

The whole way down past Cadence's exit, my heart hammered in my chest that I was going to get caught. That for whatever reason, she and

Marc would be on the freeway and the jig, as they say, would be up.

I lucked out. My phone remained still in my pocket, my earbuds silent, no notifications, no calls from her specific ringtones and notification sounds. I'd set hers special so I wouldn't miss a thing.

We pulled in at River's place as the sun began to set. Yeah, he was a brother that lived in Western Washington, but geographically speaking, he was way closer to the Western Oregon chapter, and thus one of theirs. He was also their VP, so that said something about the dude and his commitment to the club.

He came out front to meet us, his dog Champ, a neurotic border collie, leaning against his legs and whining like a son of a bitch with excitement over the people in his yard.

"Hey, Riv, how's it going?" I asked.

"Good, good. Eulogy's on his way here with a couple of others. Should be here any minute. Got the grill fired up out back and some cold ones on standby around the firepit. You fellas go ahead."

Tic and Deac nodded and went down the path along the side of the house.

"What's up?" I asked cautiously.

"Word on the street is we're all under watch."

"Oh yeah?" I asked.

"It's the big time, now."

"Fibbies?" I asked. Our term for the FBI.

"And the DEA."

"Motherfucker."

"Yeah," he said. "I'm thinkin' one of the disgraced boys in Eastern Washington maybe has a loose pair of lips."

"I'll get it to Mav," I said. "Anybody else hold the theory?"

"Only the whole damn Western Oregon chapter, maybe some of the boys in Eastern Oregon."

I threw back my head and said, "Fuuuuuck me!"

"Not my type," River said dryly, his blue eyes sparkling as he laughed behind his dark, van dyke beard.

I rolled my eyes.

"Thanks for the heads up," I said. "We were wondering why the supply was running a little low."

"That might be why. We need to watch our fuckin' asses. This international shit's gonna get us on the radar with the Department of Homeland Security. Might be time to change some shit up."

I nodded. "Might be."

"Come on," he said. "Let's get you a beer and something to eat."

"What's on the menu?" I asked.

"Meat," he said with a shrug. "What else?"

"You sarcastic motherfucker," I said laughing and followed the vice president for the Western Oregon chapter into his backyard, his black-and-white dog trotting by his master's side.

"I hear you got a lady friend," he said, pulling out a grapefruit Hefeweizen from the cooler and handing it over. I popped the top with the bottle opener on my keys.

"That's putting it mildly," I said, looking out over the pink sky, deepening to shades of purple over the hills that stretched forever. We were so close to the Washington/Oregon border that the majority of those hills weren't even in this state. They were Oregon side, across the Columbia River basin.

River's place was a whole lot of meadow sloping down into deep woods. He used to raise goats down here, like Fenris, only on a much smaller scale, but he'd given that up. He still kept up a pretty healthy vegetable garden, but that was about it now. The pastures he'd used for his goats weren't going fallow. He was working on some crops. Had his grower's permit and was getting into the legal marijuana trade as a supplier of some quality green.

It was just one more medicinal product we traded in. Big pharma didn't corner that market... yet.

"What's her name?" he asked.

"Cadence," I answered.

"Nice name. What's her story. How'd you guys meet?"

"Man, what's with the third degree?" I asked laughing.

He shrugged and said, "Never figured you for the type to settle down but the word's going around you're serious about this one."

"I am," I said, nodding. "But it's also *really* new, bro."

"How new?"

"Like just a few weeks, new."

"Yeah, the way it's getting talked about and making the rounds, I thought it's been going on for months or something."

"Jesus fuck, for a bunch of fuckin' bikers, these sons of a bitches sure do like to gossip like a bunch a little old ladies at the fuckin' hair salon."

River threw back his head and laughed, and I mean laughed and laughed, clapping me on the back of the shoulder. I hadn't thought it was *that* funny, but fuck if I knew.

"So, you bringing her?" he asked.

"Bringing her *where?*" I asked.

"Long Beach ride!" he cried. "Next week."

Oh, shit... was it?

"Fuck, I don't know, man. I have to ask her and her kid."

"Whoa, kid? How old?"

"Seventeen, so old enough," I said laughing.

"Shit, okay. Give me a fuckin' heart attack. If you said like eight, nine, or ten, I was gonna be like, 'who are you and what have you done with Glass?' because that shit just wouldn't be right."

We wandered over to the firepit and I shook my head.

"Man, why you gotta make me out to be some kind of pedo?" I demanded.

River roared with laughter again and we heard a call from up by the house. Two more of the Western Oregon chapter was headed down. Eulogy and it looked like R.B. which was short for Rat Bastard.

"Hey!" I called out.

"Sup?" R.B. called back. He was a fuckin' brute. A real rat bastard in the ring, which is how he got his name.

"Nada, just grilling Glass Jaw over his new lady," River said with a wicked grin.

"What's that now?" R.B. asked, putting a hand behind his ear like he needed it fuckin' repeated.

"You heard me! Seems like Glass is finally starting to settle down."

"I wouldn't count on that!" Tic called from behind us at the fire as Eulogy and R.B. helped themselves to a beer each.

We all wandered en masse toward the fire.

"Why you say that?" Eulogy asked.

"He ain't even brought her around the clubhouse." Tic snorted.

"You know, you're right," Deacon said and looked me up and down. "Although, I think you got it twisted, brother. The fact he *hasn't* brought her around tells me just how serious things are."

"Ha, ha," I said dryly.

"I'm being serious!" Deac said with a grin.

I knew he was, and he was right. I just wanted to keep her to myself just a little bit longer before these jackals ran her off.

"Maybe I'm just biding my time," I said, taking a pull off of my beer.

"Dude, you really are serious about this one. What's the deal?" R.B. asked.

"Leave him alone," Eulogy said and gave me a nod, the look he gave me placid and understanding.

"Yeah," I said. "Fuck off, and I mean *all* the way off."

I was sick of talking about it, especially because it meant I couldn't stop thinking about her and I wanted to be there instead of here.

"Drink more, talk less. Let me throw some meat on the grill and then you can be too busy to talk because my meats in your mouth."

We all laughed at that one and River got to grilling. Thankfully, the subject changed and went back to the problem at hand – getting these drugs into the hands of the people that needed them.

19

adence...

"Come with me," he said, hands on my hips. "Marc, too."

"Me, at a biker rally?" I asked, skeptically.

"You, me, and Marc, at the beach, which also happens to be hosting a biker rally, yeah."

"I don't know," I said laughing. "I can't picture it."

"Aspen's driving Marisol's little brother and can drive you and Marc. Or just Marc, and you can ride with me for at least part of the way."

"Wait, there are other kids?" I asked. I hadn't expected that.

"With us? Just Marisol's little brother. He just turned eleven, but there are other teens whose parents belong to the other chapters."

"Just how many are at this thing?" I asked, starting to do some of the math in my head. I mean, it would really be nice to get out of the house for a weekend and do something as a family.

"Mom, I totally want to go." I jumped slightly, and Jared laughed.

"Jesus, Marc! How long have you been standing there?" I asked, hand pressed to my chest. "You nearly gave me a heart attack!"

"Sorry," he said sheepishly. "And long enough to hear beach, biker rally, and other kids my age which is enough for me. I really want to go."

I chewed my bottom lip and nodded.

"Okay," I said, nodding and caving in to Jared's charismatic smile.

"Okay?" he asked.

"Okay," I affirmed, and he smacked the biggest kiss on my lips. I sucked in a breath at the unexpectedness of it and he pulled back.

"Will you ride with me for part of the way?" he asked.

I nodded. "If it's okay with Marc."

"Are you kidding me, Mom?" he asked grinning. "Who's the adult and who's the child right now?" he asked.

I looked at him and didn't know how to say in front of Jared that I knew I was the only parent he had left, and I wanted to take his feelings into account.

"Give us a minute?" I asked Jared gently.

"Yeah." He nodded. I glimpsed the knowledge in his hazel eyes. He knew what I was thinking. Then again, we'd talked about it before. "I'll be out on the front porch. Gonna make a call."

"Okay, thanks," I said.

When the door shut, Marc looked uncertain.

"Am I in trouble?" he asked. "Did I say something wrong?"

I smiled and shook my head and held out my arms.

"What?" he asked and drifted over and hugged his mama like I wanted.

"I know it's not likely something you actively think about," I said. "But I am keenly aware that I am the only parent that you have left." I pulled back and looked at him, giving his shoulders a squeeze. "Riding motorcycles can be dangerous."

"Oh," he said and, to his credit, looked like he was really thinking this one through.

He finally shook his head as though banishing a thought and said, "You've ridden with Jared before, and everything's been fine."

I nodded. "I know, but that's only been local little trips, nothing at freeway speeds, honey, and nothing longer than twenty or so minutes from the house. Long Beach is something like *four hours* away if I remember correctly, and it's mostly freeway speeds of sixty to seventy and then winding highways of fifty to fifty-five."

He thought about it, and then said, "Jared only wants you to ride part of the way, right?" I nodded. "Then can it be the later end where the speeds are a little slower and there's not as much traffic?"

I nodded and touched the side of my boy's face. Was I a little sorry about bringing this to his attention? Yes, a little, but I thought it was more important to keep safety in the forefront of my boy's mind.

"I love you," I told him, and he smiled.

"I love you, too, Mom."

"Go get Jared for me?" I asked.

He nodded and went over to the front door and poked his head out. Jared looked up, his phone pressed to his ear.

"Yeah, go ahead and throw a Karen Tax on that," he said. "This shit is redic."

I smiled and could only imagine what a 'Karen Tax' meant.

"Uh, huh... yeah, man, I gotta go... Okay, cool. Bye."

He hung up the phone and came back inside, and I leaned a hip against the back of our recliner.

"Everything cool?" he asked as Marc shut the door behind him.

"Yeah, but what's a Karen Tax?" Marc asked.

Jared grinned. "It's when the cost of a job goes up, sometimes exponentially, when the homeowner is being an absolute Karen."

"You literally charge people extra just for putting up with them?" I asked, eyebrows raised.

"Damn straight," he said, and Marc laughed.

"That's cool."

"So, you guys are still coming, right?" Jared asked, and I smiled.

"Yes, but Marc has some rules."

"Mom!" Marc looked a little mortified and Jared nodded in understanding.

"No, sounds legit. Let's hear 'em."

"Uh, just if my mom rides with you, can it be later on the highway at slower speeds and where there's less traffic?" he asked.

Jared looked thoughtful and nodded slowly. "Sounds perfectly reasonable," he said. "Can you maybe do something for me?" he asked.

"What's that?" Marc asked.

"On Saturday night, we ask the teens to sort of be Camp Counselors to the younger ones. S'mores, scary stories by a campfire in the trailer park we stay in – which is not exactly like it sounds! You'll just have to see on that, but it's so us adults can hit one of the bars in town and cut loose just a little bit."

Marc looked to me, and I nodded. He was a responsible kid.

"Yeah, sure, okay."

"And there you have it. First lesson learned about club life. We take care of each other." Jared winked at the both of us and Marc and I smiled at each other.

"One last thing before this adventure," Jared said. "I need to know your sizes, both of you."

Whatever could that be for? I thought.

IT TURNED out it was for tee shirts, or so I thought at first. Fun shirts that said things like *Support Crew* and *Hang Around in Training*, which I had no idea what that second one meant but Jared had advised me and Marc that since we were so new, to try and not ask too many questions – that it would make us look like citizens and if we did have any lingering questions, to try and quietly ask him or Aspen or one of the other Western Washington chapter's ol' ladies.

The clubhouse wasn't in what appeared to be the best neighborhood, but Jared assured me, my car would be safely parked in the club's parking lot over the weekend.

"Do you have cameras?" I asked, looking around, and some of the guys had laughed at me for asking. I didn't want to sound stupid anymore, so I didn't say much after that. To be honest, it was all more than a little overwhelming.

I liked Aspen. She was sweet and cool as a cucumber amidst the barely controlled chaos that was getting everyone in order, vehicles packed, and everyone on the road outside the clubhouse.

Approaching her forties, she was blond and had light green eyes, slightly lighter than my own. She was the ol' lady of a big brother they called Fenris, who looked like he had just stepped out of being an extra on that History Channel show, *Vikings*.

There was only one man bigger, an inch or two taller than Fenris and just as rough looking with his long brown hair and brown beard and that was a brother named Dump Truck. We'd been advised *not* to ask how anyone had come about their nickname, which I guess the club called them *road names*, because I guess it was deeply personal information sometimes. I could respect that, even if I couldn't fully understand it.

Jared *had* told us about his road name, Glass Jaw. It was a boxing term, he said – which I had known that, even if Marc didn't. He said all it took was one fight where he'd been tapped *just right* and he had gone down like a ton of bricks. The name had stuck and while it was a bit of a mouthful, most of the other guys just called him 'Glass.'

I didn't know if I would ever get used to that, but I could try.

Marc took to it like a fish to water. I think he had it a bit easier than me, since all of his friends on his video games had different nicknames they called gamer tags. All of them self-chosen, unlike the biker's road names which I guess were bestowed upon them when they got their vests. Or so Aspen filled me in.

It was a lot of vocabulary to learn in a short amount of time, but somehow, we managed.

Marc was honestly a big help in that regard, keeping me straight on the lingo.

I didn't know what to expect, but I guess I expected something... I don't know... *smaller?* I mean, not as many people.

There was Jared, and then Maverick, Dump Truck, Fenris, a bitter blond man with super curly hair pulled into a short ponytail they called Tic-Tac, and a man that I recognized that had been on Jared's crew in my basement they called Mace. Squatch, who looked like a Sasquatch as mean as that sounded, so not a big stretch of the imagination as to how he got his road name, and a tall, almost willowy black man with gorgeous ebony skin tone, a charismatic smile, and pencil thin dreadlocks they called Major. Unfortunately, Major absolutely reeked of marijuana to the point it almost gave me a headache, but then again, weed and I had never really gotten along the few times I had tried it. All it did was make me feel like I had a gnome with hammers pounding on my brain and good Lord, the sleepiness. One hit and I could sleep for *days*.

After I had been introduced to Major, Jared had swept me along to introduce me to Deacon. He was a suave-looking older gentleman, maybe fifties but could even be sixties, who looked good for his age. A silver fox, I think most women would call him. He was a kind man and had that suave look to him although he was completely gentlemanly and respectful.

Finally, there was Nine, Cipher, and Blackjack, and a bigger man called Derry to round out the rest of the crew.

The women were a whole other story. Aside from Aspen, there was Kestrel who everyone called Little Bird and who was paired with Dump Truck, which I just could not fathom how that worked out, but it did, and you could just see how positively in love with each other they were.

It made me smile, but it also made my heart ache just a little, and that voice in the back of my mind whispered *that was supposed to be me.* Jealousy was a bitch, but I shoved that bitch down just in time to meet Marisol who looked a little young to be with Maverick, but I reserved judgment. I mean, who was I to throw stones at anyone?

Then there was Dahlia who didn't really seem to belong to or be with anyone but who sort of naturally gravitated toward Tic of all people. She was a fiery one, like Marisol, and I got the impression she and Marisol maybe didn't always get along.

Finally, there was a quiet, almost who I would describe as a hippy chick with a very decidedly modern flair that everyone called Raven, although I couldn't be sure if that was her real name or not. She was with Mace.

Marisol was introducing her little brother Mateo to Marc since they would be riding in the back seat with each other in Aspen's SUV which looked pretty new.

"About fuckin' time he got here," Jared muttered, and a final brother pulled up on a bike with a person riding his back tire in a box truck.

"Who's that?" I asked curiously.

"Used to call him Sauley when he was a prospect," Glass said. "Some still fuck up and do. He's only been patched a few months. Now he goes by the road name of Fish."

I shaded my eyes and asked without thinking, "Why Fish?"

"Careful with that," Jared cautioned.

"Oh, sorry."

He smiled at me, winked and said, "A few months before he became a full member, he got a job at the Market at one of the fish stands and kept coming around reeking of it. So, he got Fish."

"Who is that behind him in the truck?" I asked.

"That'd be Dipshit."

"I'm sorry?"

"New prospect. If you don't want to call him Dipshit, call him 'Prospect.' That will do just fine."

"I cannot *even* pretend to understand your ways," I said laughing. *Who called someone Dipshit?*

"Yeah, well, he comes by the name honestly. He is kind of a dipshit."

"He barely looks eighteen!" I said.

"He's eighteen, started hanging around about six months ago, just became a prospect last week. He's one of Deacon's project kids. Deac is sponsoring him. Good kid for the most part, likes to get into fights but can't blame him. He grew up rough. In and out of foster care, dad's a drunk, mom's an addict. The kind of kid society gives up on before he's even had a chance just because his parents are who they are. He's still figuring it out."

I chewed my bottom lip and said, "He's not much older than Marc."

"True," Jared said. "Like I said, though. You can't blame a kid like him for having the rep of a bad seed. He doesn't know any better and he ain't got the type of parents to show him." He lifted a shoulder in a shrug and asked, "How is he supposed to know?" I looked up at him and Jared's eyes were shuttered. "Schools are just interested in maintaining the status quo, and it sucks learning by being in trouble literally constantly. Gets to a point where you're like 'fuck it, I can't do anything right' and it's even further downhill from there."

"You sound like you speak from experience," I said softly.

"Guilty," he said. He looked back over at Fish and… the prospect.

"Some of us kids slipped through the cracks." He huffed a bitter laugh. "Society likes to think we've turned our backs on them but when it comes to a lot of the guys standing here," he shook his head, "kids like me, and Dipshit over there? Who really turned their back on who?"

Hm.

It was food for thought and something my thoughts chewed on for almost the entire ride down through Olympia and beyond.

The towns started to grow sparse, and we stopped for lunch after turning off of the main highway. It was there that Jared grabbed my hand and lifted his chin at Marc to hold up before we went into the burger place that was completely old-world mom-and-pop and like it had never left the fifties.

"Marc, you good if your mom rides with me the rest of the way?" he asked.

Marc grinned. "Yeah, I kinda want to see this."

I rolled my eyes at my kid.

"Okay, but first you're gonna have to change," he said to me, and I blinked in confusion.

"Into *what?*" I asked, taken aback.

"Prospect!" Jared shouted and I winced. It was better than shouting out *Dipshit* but still...

The prospect came jogging up from the box truck and handed Jared two stuffed bags marked with the Harley-Davidson logo.

"The real reason I needed your sizes."

"C'mon, Mamma. I'm here to help." I jumped slightly at the voice behind me and turned to see Dahlia grinning. She was dressed to match the joint we were invading, all sexy and cool, fifties pinup bombshell.

"Go on, let Dahlia get you taken care of."

"Yeah, Mom," Marc said, grinning at me stupidly. "I know what you like. Jared and I will order for you."

"Gee thanks, kid." I shot Marc a look like *et tu* and followed Dahlia to the ladies' room.

So, I didn't have to take anything off but my shoes, really. Thank goodness for that. My sneakers were swapped for a pair of knee-high boots that laced in the front *and* the back, but thankfully had a zipper up the inside of the leg. Those were easy enough. What wasn't easy, at least not on first glance, were the thick leather chaps she helped me into. They were plain, but butter soft and fit me almost like a second skin.

Next came the leather jacket which fit me like a dream and was beautifully embroidered with hummingbirds at the lapel and on the sleeve here and there amidst embossed flowering skulls. I didn't know how they had done it, but the leather was permanently raised with the pattern, and it was actually stunning.

"Okay, hold still," Dahlia said when I looked at myself in the mirror, speechless. She went to gather my hair and I ducked slightly away.

"What are you doing?" I asked. I had always been super particular about my hair.

"Trust me, darlin', you're gonna want this in a sheathed pony or a braid or you'll be so snarled and knotted up you might never pick all the tangles out."

"Oh," I murmured and let her do what she needed to. She pulled my hair into a long ponytail and took this long piece of leather and wrapped it around it, snapping snaps all along the joining length until it was snuggly protected in a leather sheath like the rest of me.

"There you go, all done," she said.

"Thanks," I said, blushing faintly.

"Don't worry, honey, we've all been there," Aspen said, coming out of one of the bathroom stalls and beaming at me.

I smiled back at her and stepped aside so she could wash her hands.

"They're gonna go nuts when you step out there. You look just like one of us," Dahlia declared, and she looked proud of herself.

She wasn't kidding when she said they were going to go nuts. Wolf whistles, shouts, cheering, and applause left me blushing fiercely and feeling about three inches tall with their looming attention and scrutiny.

I was so not used to being the center of attention. I sort of slunk back to Jared's side and sat down between him and Marc who was laughing at my expense.

"Remember," I told him. "I gave birth to you. I can take you out."

That, of course, just made my kid laugh harder.

~

THE RIDE into the little town of Long Beach was beautiful. Despite the cooler air coming off the water and the wind from the bike itself as we traveled along, it was *hot* under all this thick black leather with the sun mercilessly beating down from a cloudless sky. We slowed, rumbling through the little town's streets, passing bars and restaurants, a little touristy oddity museum, and an old-fashioned ice cream parlor.

We went further, the water on our right, sliding past a distillery and across from it one of the tallest buildings in town. Fancy and rich, a hotel or time-share condo by the look of it.

It was interesting to me. I vaguely remembered some things and others were so new. That was the thing about it, though. You could clearly see the divide between old and new. Most of the houses and buildings were salt worn and dilapidated, while others were newly restored and gleamed softly in the summer sun with new paint.

It was vibrant traveling along in the line of motorcycles, the vibrations thrumming through me like a second heartbeat as we joined the traffic jam of other bikers cruising the main boulevard through Long Beach to its outer edges.

The bikes all congregated at a strange little motel and campground full of antique travel trailers, all kitted out in their little permanent fixed parking places. I hopped off the bike with a smile at Jared's urging as he backed into the rows of motorcycles along the street out front of the place which was charming and unique. Each travel trailer gleamed, some freshly painted, some just their stainless-steel selves in their little bubble forms. Each one parked, each little plot decorated in a different sort of landscape.

This one surrounded by potted cactuses, that one surrounded by rocks that weren't native to the Pacific Northwest, but maybe somewhere like Moab. The oranges and reds stood out starkly among the conifer trees soaring against the sky throughout the little RV park.

There was a great lodge off to one side with communal facilities such as bathrooms and a picnic shelter in the center of the expansive park.

I couldn't see how far it went, but clearly it was the only place that was big enough to host all five chapters that Jared had said were coming.

Tents were already being pitched throughout the camp spaces scattered among the trailers, and I could now see why Jared hadn't bothered to even try to describe the place. I mean, I could hardly describe it myself.

Marc bounded up to me just as Jared heeled down the kickstand on his motorcycle and leaned the heavy machine onto it.

"Mom! Check this place out!"

"I know!" I cried grinning. We were about a block down from the nearest beach access, an easy walking distance.

"Aspen told me to check with you and Jared before I went out and found a place for my tent," he said.

"You can honestly pick anywhere but I'd get too it quick if I were you, before all the good ones are gone," Jared called.

"I'd rather you stay close to where we're staying but I don't know where that's going to be," I hedged.

"Aw!" Marc's grin didn't diminish.

"Babe," Jared called, pulling a pack from one of his saddlebags. "It don't matter where he goes in this zoo – he's gonna be safe as safe can be, I can promise you that. It's a different way of life out here to begin with. Not like the city."

I chewed my bottom lip but at Jared's easy smile and the gently chiding look he gave me, I finally nodded.

"Go," I told Marc, and he bounced on his feet and dashed off into the trees, his tall and gangly frame ducking between trailers.

"Where *are* we staying?" I asked.

"One of the trailers. They're reserved for chapter council, officers and the like and older members after that who don't do ground sleeping so well anymore."

I nodded and he came to me, holding out his hand. I took it and wandered into the bustling chaos with him, following him down the drive to the lodge and drifting in his wake like a shadow while he greeted other men and connected with Maverick who gave him a key on a diamond-shaped plastic tag.

"Thanks, man," he said.

Maverick grinned at me. "How you doing over there, Little Mermaid?" he asked me and I frowned slightly.

"Little Mermaid?" I asked.

Maverick's grin grew.

"Way you're looking around and clinging to Glass's hand there, you remind me of the Little Mermaid – all excitement and awkward like you just stepped out of the sea for the first time and you're trying to take in all the things."

I felt myself blush. "I definitely feel like it's a whole new world," I said, and Marisol laughed.

"That's Aladdin," she said, and I shrugged.

"It all blurs together after a while," I said laughing.

"Come on, baby. Let's grab your stuff out of the back of Aspen's cage and find our crash pad."

"Sounds good," I murmured and waved goodbye to Maverick and Marisol as Jared led me away with a gentle tug on our entwined hands. They were smiling and Maverick lifted a hand back in my direction to wave us off.

We stopped at Aspen's car in the small parking lot and retrieved my little rolling carryon out of the back. Jared insisted on carrying it for me as we made our way through the scattered trees and plots along the gravel trails and across little wooden foot bridges built over ditches and gulches.

There was a big circular clearing, also gravel, with a big firepit at its center, surrounded by low, split-log benches that was utterly charming.

"Kids'll have a great time around the campfire tonight. Perfect weather for it," Jared said, and I smiled.

"Got enough fixings for s'mores?" I asked and he chuckled.

"Always."

20

*G*lass Jaw...

There was a post outside each trailer door with house numbers nailed to them. Artful, not too bad. We wandered through the camp and park and found the post with the matching number to the tag on our key.

We had a little airstream tucked back into the trees, some flowering pots set up on stone pedestals around it, and lavender by the steps leading to the front door. Pinwheels spun in the light breeze and there was a little bistro table out front with two seats.

"Mom!" Marc called from somewhere. Cadence turned this way and that and beaming, rose her arm to wave back at him. He was down the trail setting up his tent, a brother from another chapter helping him out, a teen girl standing by as her daddy threaded fiberglass tent poles through the pocket it belonged in.

"Looks like Marc's made a new friend already," I said with a chuckle.

"I'm not sure if I like that," Cadence said through a tight smile as she looked her son's way. "Hormones are gonna start raging any minute."

"He's a smart kid," I said.

She turned back to me with raised eyebrows and a faint smile and mused, "So was I when I was his age."

"Ooo, touché," I said. "Want me to talk to him later?"

"Talk to him how?" she asked, stepping up into the little trailer past me once I'd gotten the door open.

"Man-to-man, condom use, making sure he's set... you know the drill."

She looked back and took her little suitcase that I handed up to her.

"You'd do that?" she asked curiously.

"Figure it might be easier coming from me than his mom," I said.

She smiled sweetly and said, "It's been handled. Marc *does* know better, but I do appreciate it."

"Speaking of some sex education," I said with a lascivious grin. "Trailer's rockin', don't come knockin'."

She threw back her head and laughed. Shouldering my pack, I got up into the small space with her and shut the door firmly behind us.

"Holy shit," I muttered, and she turned and smiled, working the window nearby open. I went to the other one on the opposite side of the trailer. It was hotter than Satan's hairy asshole in here.

"Should cool off with the breeze," she murmured, and I palmed her hip and drew her closer to me.

"Mm-hm." I dipped my head and kissed her, and she kissed me back. The bed was a pretty good size in here, but that was all there really was to this trailer. A bed, a place to set up our bags to get in 'em, a little two-seater nook, and the tiny kitchenette, which was really just a mini fridge now, the stove gone and converted to counter space. Other than that, it was just some funky retro art and a clock on the wall. The sleeping area, clearly upgraded to a bigger bed, ate up the rest of the renovation.

It was the bed I was interested in and getting Cadence in it.

Her lips were like silk underneath mine, her curves sexy and sleek where my hands wandered over her tee beneath the leather jacket that I'd bought her. The jacket looked as good as I thought it would on her, but it was about to look even better off of her and puddled somewhere on the narrow floor.

Her hands were like butterflies against me, plucking at my clothes, landing softly against my chest, her touch sweet and light. We pulled the leather and fabric from each other's skins a piece at a time and when she pressed herself against me, even with the trailer being hotter than Hell, it was like the pearly gates opened.

So soft, so smooth, so beautiful and goddamn did she smell so good – sweet and pretty, like champagne and candy, decadent and feminine at the same time. I kissed her, tongues twining, and my cock was so hard it ached.

She wrapped a delicate hand around my dick, and I moaned into her mouth. Shit, fuck, it took everything in me not to come right then and there. She stroked me lightly, teasing, her touch almost cool. My cock was so hot against her palm. She gripped me a little more firmly and I grunted, thrusting my hips unconsciously, my precum slicking me through her grasping fingers.

"Jesus *fuck*, baby," I breathed against her mouth and felt her lips curl in a little smile beneath mine.

"I love that I can make you feel good," she whispered and *holy shit*.

I captured her face between my hands and devoured her mouth, kissing her fiercely, wanting her so bad I wanted to crawl *inside her*. I wanted to slide my hands into her long tresses, but they were captured by the leather sheath to keep them from tangling.

"Turn around, I want to let down your hair," I told her, and so obediently, so *sweetly*, and so trusting, she gave me the long sweeping line of her back.

There wasn't anything about this woman that wasn't sexy.

I undid her hair, pulling the elastic off of it and turned her by her shoulders. She turned around, all that silky, ebony perfection foaming around her face, and I buried my hands in it, knotting my fist at the back of it and pulling her head all the way back. I kissed her fiercely, my blood heating to a slow rolling boil in my veins as the volume on my desire was turned all the way up.

I loved how she reached for me. How she stepped into me. How she pressed her body as close to mine as she could get, and how she was content just to make out with me until I was so worked up, I was practically throwing her onto the bed.

She hit the mattress and I pulled her to the end, going onto my knees at the edge of the bed, shouldering her knees apart and grasping her hips as she fell all the way back in surrender. I tasted her and fuck, she was so good – musky and sweet, fresh, and womanly. I could spend fucking *hours* eating her out. So wet and dusky pink, if sunshine had a flavor, it would taste like Cadence Mitchell did.

"Oh!" Her voice was breathy and high, sounding as though she were in awe and fuck, that was a turn-on. A big one.

"I'm going to make you feel so fucking good," I growled against her cunt, and she shuddered provocatively against me.

I sucked on her clit and lapped at her opening, teasing her slowly, working her up steadily.

I loved how she gasped. How she fisted the covers at her hips. How I had to hold her thighs, fingertips digging in to hold her still so I could give her the attention she deserved.

She yelped and gasped as I slid my first two fingers inside of her and then moaned and whined, pressing the heel of one hand against her mouth as I teased her clit and made that come-hither motion inside her, teasing that spot inside her. But I had another slight trick up my sleeve. I took my free arm and pressed just above her pubic bone, bringing her G-spot in closer contact with my questing fingers, and she made this wonderful animalistic sound, her hips trying to jerk, but I had a hold of her firmly, now and I was about to put her into some beautiful agony.

It was exquisite torture, making her come and not letting her up, bringing her so hard, so fast, and holding her *right there* against the heat of the sun of her orgasm. I held her there until her doubts burned away and then I held her there a little longer until the panic swept back in, and she was so overwhelmed I had to relent. I wanted to push her every limit, but I didn't want to scare her, or push her over the edge of what she could endure.

She lay panting, eyes closed, head turned, legs splayed and twitching, and I rose between her thighs with such a sense of *satisfaction* that it was my hands, my mouth, that brought her to this.

I smiled and watched her, such a beautiful mess below me. I stroked myself lazily, fisting my cock, squeezing, sliding up and down my shaft, over my head, waiting on her panting breath to slow, waiting for her to look at me and to know she was back with me, before I fucked her and sent her sailing over that cliff and plunging her deep into orgasm all over again.

She gasped and turned her head slowly and looked at me through heavily lidded eyes. I smiled – grinned actually – and asked her, "You ready for more?"

"No," she whispered softly but the flicker of a smile on her own lips told me she was a fucking liar.

I wrapped my arms around her thighs and dragged her bodily to the edge of the low bed. She slid easily over the covers, and I brought her ass slightly over the edge of the bed. It was the perfect height – with me kneeling on the floor beside it – to enter her and so I did. I wasn't gentle. I plunged into her wet waiting heat hilt deep and listened to her yowl half in surprise and half in pleasure.

I loved the feel of her silken wet heat around me, how she tightened up around my cock as I thrust, making it hard to pull free, as though she didn't want to let me go. She was so fucking beautiful, so natural, so giving of herself and submitted to whatever I wanted of her so beautifully. It was a special kind of high controlling someone as gorgeous and who had her shit together like Cadence.

She didn't *have* to give anything to me, but she gave her all and didn't hold anything back and that was *intense.*

I was just on that edge, that fine silver edge, balls tightening, that tell-tale tingle at the base of my spine when a fucking knock fell at the door.

Cadence jerked beneath me and scooted back on the bed. I swore as I slipped out of her. Whoever was fuckin' bothering me was gonna fuckin' hear about it.

"Cover up, baby," I said, and she slipped between the sheets, pulling the covers over her perfect breasts, and hid her face behind her long shining fall of hair as I went to the trailer door.

I opened it, not caring I was naked as the day I was fucking born, then cursed myself as the door swung out, the thought, *'what if it's Marc?'* coming a hair too late.

Thankfully, it wasn't Marc and there were no kids lingering out here.

"What the fuck do you want, Dipshit?" I demanded.

"Sorry, boss. Fish sent me to come get you. Says the big council's been called early and you need to be there."

"Where at?" I demanded, frustrated. Shit was up, shit had to be up. We didn't deviate from schedule like that often. Not unless it was really called for.

"Firepit area. Everyone's been told to steer clear."

"Got it, be there in two."

"Yeah, I'll tell 'em," he said. He wouldn't look at me, his face red as he decidedly tried to look anywhere else.

I hadn't dismissed his ass yet, and I let him squirm for a full minute before I demanded, "Anything else?"

"No!"

"Well then, fuck off!" I shouted and without a word, Dipshit beat a hasty retreat.

I chuckled when I went back in and looked back to Cadence who had her hands over her mouth, her green eyes as bright and vibrant as I had ever seen them.

"Duty calls," I said, and she blinked owlishly at me. I had to say, I loved putting that freshly fucked look on her.

"I am so glad that wasn't Marc," she said.

"Me too. I honestly didn't even think," I said, putting my hands on my hips.

"Sounded important," she said.

"Yep." I nodded.

"To be continued?" she asked.

"To be continued," I said with a reluctant sigh and started separating our clothes, finding mine and pulling them on.

"Ugh, I hate that you didn't get off," she complained, and I had to smile. The fact she cared was pretty fucking fantastic and just one more reason I liked her as much as I did.

"Oh, I'll get mine," I said. "I guarantee it."

She smiled and said, "What was that about the firepit?"

"That's where the council is meeting up, so if you could avoid it for the time being, that would be great."

"Sure thing. I'll go find Marc and we'll head to the beach," she said.

I nodded. "Good plan. I'll find you there."

"Okay."

I pulled my shirt over my head and leaned over her, kissing her soundly. She kissed me back, touching my face and I loved that she did that. Made shit special. More special than it had a right to be.

"I'll catch up with you as soon as I can," I promised and took my cut off my jacket and swung it on over my faded gray motocross tee.

"Okay." She nodded, and her posture was much more relaxed now that it was just us. I gave her one last long, lingering look, and popped open the trailer door and made a small leap over the steps to the ground.

I shut the door behind me and let me tell you, it took some fuckin' discipline to march my ass down the trail to the meet.

I frowned when I realized it was just Ps and VPs from each chapter.

"What's up?" I asked Mav.

"Word from Eulogy's Canadian connections. Shit's heavy, stay tuned," he said. "It'll all get laid out."

I nodded. "Thanks for the preview of coming attractions," I grated and wasn't thrilled. His tone brooked bad things were on the fuckin' horizon.

We were waiting on the president of the Eastern Oregon chapter who came up the opposite trail from mine with just his cut over his bare chest. Looked like I wasn't the only one indulging in his woman's body.

"Couldn't this wait?" he demanded. "I was just about to get off."

I laughed and he scowled at me. I held up my hands and shook my head. "Same, bro. Same. What's the big fuckin' deal?" I asked.

Fearless gave a nod in my direction for asking the question and posted up next to his VP, Armor.

That's how we all sort of stood, in a circle, president of their chapter shoulder to shoulder with their vice president. It had been too long, man.

There was me and Mav, repping Western Washington, and honestly with the biggest chapter by far, Mav was sort of the de facto leader to the entire five chapters when we all got together like this.

Then there were the new guys, Lone Wolf, or just Wolf and Ryder, repping the Eastern Washington crew.

Lone Wolf was a tall guy, six-three and in his forties, his long hair pulled into a low pony and looked like iron. It'd started out dark, but he had healthy swaths of gray in it, but it didn't serve to call it salt and pepper – no, *iron* was the descriptor there and his gaze was straight up steely through eyes as dark as coal.

By comparison, his second, Ryder, was a runty little shit at only five-six. Blond hair that curled like Tic's, he had it in a pony that went to the middle of his back. If it weren't for his goatee under those piercing green eyes, he would almost, *almost,* be as pretty as a woman. I wouldn't say any of that shit to his face, though. Guy had a temper, but it was cold as ice. He didn't get mad, he got even, and it wasn't always in a joking or prankster sort of way.

South of us in the land of Western Oregon, things were run by Gargoyle and River. Gar was one of those silent stony-faced mother-fuckers who sat or stood by and observed everything, the calculations going on in his brain unreadable on his face. He was a smart son of a bitch, though, just usually quite a bit more methodical than Mav. When he and Mav put heads together, you better watch out, though. His hair was close cut, a high and tight, and was mostly white with a slight sheen of silver to it. He was an ex-Marine and looked a shit ton like Steven Lang from his *Avatar* movie days. Cameron's, not Airbender or whatever the fuckin' cartoon was.

River was a thoughtful hipster-lookin' motherfucker with his dark hair and van dyke beard. Always wondered if he fancied himself some kind of revolutionary with how much he hated the U.S. government. He kept it to himself for the most part, but if you got him drunk and got him going, he would almost never shut up about it. I personally kind of wondered if he served and if it was something he'd heard or seen overseas that turned him out that way, but I wasn't about to fuckin' ask.

Eastern Oregon's leadership consisted of Fearless and Armor. Fearless was as his name implied. An adrenaline junky by nature, he ran a skydiving school out near Pendleton. He was a Patrick Swayze moth-erfucker al la *Point Break*, but he didn't have an ounce of surfer dude to him. In his thirties with no sign of slowing down, he was the man you wanted in extreme situations where the adrenaline was flowing – always cool as a cucumber and able to think like the adrenaline somehow streamlined his thought process rather than sent it into chaos.

Armor was a bigger dude, black hair, and dark eyes, he looked like he should be his club's enforcer or SAA. Not the VP. He also looked like your typical chip off the eastern block dumbass, shit for brains, all brawn and nothing upstairs asshole – but you'd be wrong. The guy threw off all kinds of mixed and just plain glaringly wrong signals. Standing here among the rest of us, he had his arms crossed over his barrel chest and was glowering, but it didn't mean a goddamn thing. That was literally just the dude's face.

You'd never guess that he was his high school's chess *and* weightlifting *and* wrestling champion back in the day. Ask me how I know? We'd gone to school together – but we hadn't been friends. Not even close. We might as well have been worlds a-fuckin' part back then. Now, he was giving me the chin lift I always got in recognition that we were the same age and came from the same place, if not from wildly different demographics at the time.

His mom and pop were immigrants and ran a little Eastern European deli and convenience store until the day they'd been robbed and both of them shot to death while Armor had been away looking at colleges. The pigs hadn't even really tried to solve his folks' murder and he'd spun out in a big way, using his grief like armor against the world's apathy. Nobody had given a fuck about his immigrant parents, and no one had given a fuck about him, except us which is why he was here.

That shit was still unsolved. Best believe we ever found out who did it, we would have his back, though.

Ain't no justice like street justice, I thought to myself looking at him. I hoped he'd find some, or at least some peace.

The thought made a turn toward Cadence, and the peace I'd found in her arms. How much I wished this meeting were fuckin' over already so I could get back to them.

I sighed and looked up at something Hem was saying... speaking of which, last but not least, were Hemlock and his second, Nightmare, out of Idaho.

Hem was a chill, philosophical type and got his name from a comment he'd made after a brother had said something about if he could go back and meet any philosopher, it'd be Socrates and Hem had shot back something or other about going back to be the hemlock or shoving the hemlock down Socrates' throat. Hell, I don't remember the story exactly but the guys who had been there swore it was the funniest shit ever and that's how he'd gotten his name.

I guess you had to have been there.

Hem was a clean-cut guy with wavy, almost tawny, hair. He was an average sort of tall at six feet, and almost skinny as a rail but don't let that shit fool you. He was wicked fast and packed a hell of a punch. Dude was legit all muscle, not enough fat on him to grease a fuckin' cake pan.

Nightmare was, well, nightmare fuel. His face was all tatted up like a skull and a line of piercings through the bridge of his nose. He looked like the boogeyman just plain got tired of hiding in the dark and walked among us, no fucks given.

I think every inch of that motherfucker had tattoos, everything we could see did – scalp, face, neck, hands... all of it. All of it like he was decaying, and his skeleton underneath was coming out to the fore. There were even bugs, man. Dude had literal maggots tattooed on his jaw and the side of his neck like they were coming out of his fuckin' ears.

I couldn't begin to understand it, so I didn't try. Whatever made the dude fuckin' happy.

Rumor had it, even with the fucked-up tats, dude was drowning in pussy, and I guess I could see why. He had that classic, hot, bad boy bone structure, and he was indeed the baddest of bad boys among us.

He had spent time in juvie until he was twenty-one, institutionalized and shit for killing his own daddy when he was twelve.

"To order," Mav called, and we all straightened up and stopped standing around with our dicks in our hands. "So, what's up?" Mav asked Gargoyle. "You insisted it was important enough to discuss business out in the open like this, what gives?"

"It's important, alright," Gargoyle drawled. "Eulogy heard from one of his contacts up north over the border. Says dude's got good contact within the Canadian law enforcement departments up that way and well... I think it's best you hear it from the man himself, considering."

"So, why didn't you bring him down here?" Lone Wolf asked, looking amused.

"Didn't want to step on anyone's toes, Eulogy being just a member and all."

"Gotcha," Wolf nodded, sagely.

That was Gargoyle. Methodical. Logical. To a fuckin' fault.

"Well, get his ass down here and let's hear it," Fearless said.

Gargoyle himself wandered off and while I was thinking about it, "Anyone got their phone on them?"

"Oh, *shit!*"

More than one of them swore.

"Get 'em gone, gentlemen, and hurry your ass up getting back here," Mav said dispassionately.

I'd left mine in my jacket pocket back in my trailer with Cadence, so I was all good.

Men hustled off and back, everyone sort of just naturally reconvening when Jack showed up. I switched in my head from Eulogy to Jack the moment I saw him. Didn't want to slip up and bring up old hurts. I wished his chapter would just fuckin' change it already but no dice. For some reason, they were sticking to it.

"Jack, what's going on?" Mav asked, inviting the disgraced doctor to take the proverbial floor.

Turned out his Canadian contacts had gotten in touch and law enforcement was sniffing around harder than we thought. The whole operation was in peril, and we were too fuckin' obvious. The Smuggler's Inn may have been burned and Manny was looking at some serious prison time if we didn't change things up and figure it out.

"He's got a good stock up there hidden. If they search the place and find any of it, we're all fucked," he concluded.

"Goddamnit," I muttered and watched the wheels turn in everyone's head.

"Say nothing to no one," Maverick declared. "Take the weekend, relax, let your minds work and we'll come back to this table with what solutions we come up with before we fuck off back home."

Slow nods went around and really, in the grand scheme of things, it was all we really could do for now.

"Copy that," Ryder muttered and ain't none of us were happy with it, but what else were we going to do.

We broke apart, but none of us could even force a smile. The shit had officially hit the fan in a big way here.

21

*C*adence...

"Marc! Go take one of your allergy pills!" I called out after listening to my kid sniff and sneeze for like the millionth time. "Poor kid has the worst sinuses," I said to the women I was sitting with at a group of picnic tables in the shade. "He doesn't take one of those allergy pills with the decongestants in it, *hello sinus infection* and they are just the *worst*."

"Better than Mateo and his insulin pump," Marisol said, worry in her eyes as she watched her little brother and my much older son kick a soccer ball around the big clearing with a couple of the club members from other chapters.

"I can't even imagine," I empathized. I mean, there was no competition there.

Marc came jogging up a second later and said, "I forgot them."

"Shit, Marc! I just bought those! You know I can't get anymore."

"Wait, why not?" Little Bird asked.

I was upset. I didn't want this trip ruined for Marc with sinus problems, I really didn't, and it was *such* a pain in the ass getting those pills.

"They're a federally regulated substance," I said, rolling my eyes. "You have to get them at the pharmacy counter, and they scan your driver's license and keep track of how much you buy."

"Oh, because meth heads," Aspen said, making a face.

"Exactly."

"Oooh, is that the shit they used to buy in like bulk to cook their drugs with?" Kestrel asked, the lightbulb going off.

"Yup."

"I guess you're just going to have to suffer," I said, looking up to Marc just as Jared came walking up.

"Do what now?" he asked.

"I forgot my allergy meds at home," Marc said, and Jared frowned.

"There's a pharmacy in town. Let's go grab some," he said.

"You have to go to the pharmacy counter, and they track that shit. I can't buy him anymore this month," I said unhappily.

"Pfft! I got it, what's he need?" Jared asked.

I perked up slightly.

"Really?" I asked.

"Fuck yeah. He needs it, right?"

"Yeah, but it's not *that* big a deal. Mom's just being a drama queen," Marc said laughing at me.

I rolled my eyes. "Right up until it's 'Mooom, my head hurts! And Moooom, my ears hurt!' Then let's see who becomes the drama queen," I said.

"Okay, fair," my kid conceded, and Jared laughed at the two of us.

"Come on, we'll go get what he needs. In the meantime, let the kid go be a kid."

"Alright," I agreed. "Go, but be careful with Mateo."

Marc jogged backwards and said, "You got it." He gave the scout's salute which I didn't get where he'd picked that up from. He'd never been in Scouts.

Jared held down a hand and hauled me to my feet. "See you after a bit," I said to the girls who all waved and chirped their goodbyes.

"Thought you guys would be at the beach," he said.

I shook my head. "Everyone wanted to wait for you guys. Everything okay?"

"That's club business," he said with a crooked smile that didn't reach his eyes. I stopped on the path outside our trailer and put my hand on his arm.

"Everything's *not* okay, is it?" I asked.

"Everything's fine," he said, and the look he gave me was one of patience and practically begging me to let it go.

We went in and geared up for the short ride across town to the pharmacy and stayed silent until we reached our destination, all of three minutes later.

"Just tell me what you need," he said, and I smiled.

"The decongestant allergy pills, twenty-four hours, the pack of fifteen," I said. "Ask for them at the pharmacy counter and they'll get them for you."

"Specific brand?" he asked.

I shook my head. "Tell them the generic is fine if they ask."

"You got it. Go grab us a couple cold drinks?"

"Divide and conquer," I said with a smile. "I like that."

He gave me a swat on the ass as we parted ways, me wandering through what was more giftshop than pharmacy, and around into a different section. I spotted the line of coolers at the back and went and fetched a couple of cold drinks, the sport drink I knew he liked and a bottle of water for me.

"Babe!" I heard him call from the other side and I scurried up to the counter and set down the two bottles. The cashier finished ringing him up and we left.

"Thank you so much," I said out at the bike, and he shook his head.

"Some of the rules set forth by citizen society are just plain fuckin' stupid. That would be one of them."

I both agreed and disagreed, and I said as much. "Is it a pain in the ass? For people like me, *absolutely*, but I get it. It's *also* a major pain in the ass for the people looking to cook this shit into meth and worse."

Jared snorted like I was being funny.

"Baby, meth cooks gonna cook meth. They just switched to different materials and poisons. This shit? Didn't slow them down at all."

I sighed and had to concede. He was probably right.

We took some drinks out of our respective bottles and he twisted the orange cap back on his and slid it onto the bag around my wrist with Marc's pills in it.

"Ready when you are," he said with a wink.

We went back to the trailer park motel, and I got my baby taken care of. Truth be told, it was nice to have a few extra of these on hand.

Why did it have to be so complicated for the people who hadn't done anything wrong?

THE REST of the day was spent on the beach until the sun began to get low on the horizon. I spent most of it with the girls form the Western Washington and other chapters.

There was Kestrel, Aspen, Marisol, Dahlia, and Raven from the Western Washington chapter. Then there were several females from the rest of the chapters that I was told I would likely never meet again. *Club Girls*, they were called, and they were looked down on with disdain. I didn't completely understand why until Dahlia took me aside and let me know. She was, apparently, a club girl but different in that while she enjoyed sex, she said, she had morals and wouldn't fuck anyone that was officially attached.

I blanched at that and looked out over the sand where Jared was kicking the ball around with Maverick, Mateo, Marc, and several other guys and teens from other chapters.

Dahlia was smiling when I turned back and said, "Oh, I wouldn't worry about Glass, honey. We've never seen him so serious about a woman before. I think you're 'the one.'"

"What?" I asked, taken aback, not sure if it was good or bad that she had put 'the one' in air bunnies with her fingers.

"Pretty sure Glass would castrate himself if he even thought about cheating on you," Kestrel declared.

I looked back, and he caught my eye. his grin was something... I don't know... transcendent as he gave me a chin lift and one of the guys from the other chapters kicked the soccer ball into his face.

"Oh!" we all shouted in unison and cringed.

"Yo, what the fuck, man!?" Marc shouted at the other brother ,and I felt three things all at once – proud, a little scared, and annoyed that my kid was so casually dropping the f-bomb in public. I would have a chat with him about that later. I had a rule... he could say whatever he wanted *after he was eighteen*.

I would rather have *that* in his head as being his big eighteenth year milestone rather than what mine and so many of my generations was... it being legal for him to smoke. I had to give up on making it the ability to buy nudie magazines or porn for himself. I'd tried that one only to have him roll his eyes at me and tell me, "The internet is for porn," before he dropped the knowledge on me that he'd been jerking off to internet porn since he was thirteen.

Thirteen!

I relayed this to the women around me to gales of laughter and a slightly glazed look on Marisol's face.

"Oh, the things you have to look forward to," I said with a gusty sigh.

"Being a boy mom isn't for the faint of heart," Aspen said kindly.

"Speaking of which..." Kestrel murmured and we all sort of turned to her.

"What?" Dahlia asked, brow furrowing with concern.

"I'm not sure how to tell D.T., but I think I'm pregnant."

"Oh, honey! Congratulations!" I cried and the other girls made similar noises of delight too, but Kestrel? Kes just crumbled and started to sob.

"Oh, honey! Oh, honey, no, don't cry!" Aspen went over to her and hugged her tight.

"What's going on?" A shadow loomed over the group of us and we all sort of just froze.

"I think I'm pregnant!" Kestrel wailed and Dump Truck froze.

"For real?" he asked, and she nodded and just broke down harder.

Raven sort of grimaced and said, "I think you're pregnant too."

Dump Truck threw his cane to the side and got down on the ground with us and pulled her tight into his arms and kissed the top of her head.

"Holy fuck," he said grinning. "What are you crying for, baby? This is great!"

"Yeah?" she sobbed.

"Uh, *yeah!* But only if you want it to be great."

"I was so afraid you'd be unhappy!" she cried, and he shook his head and pressed his mouth to hers.

"No fuckin' way," he said.

"Can I tell 'em?" he asked, and she nodded and just sort of clung to him in the shelter of his arms.

"Guys! Hey guys!" he boomed and everyone in the vicinity turned. "I might be a daddy!"

I heard someone say, "What?" and it took nearly a full heartbeat before the whooping and hollering started up.

That night, after the kids and teens were squared away, the adults headed into town to a bar called the Captain's Quarters. When Dump Truck came through the door with Little Bird tucked under his arm and into his side, I kid you not – he held up a pregnancy stick and shouted out, "It's official!"

Wow.

The noise was *deafening*, and I grinned and applauded and gave Kestrel, who looked equal parts happy and scared, the best supportive look that I could manage.

"Aw, what's that look for?" Jared asked when my face fell when she was no longer looking.

"Oh, nothing," I said, waving it off.

"Seriously, spill," he said.

"I just remember how scared I was when I first found out I was pregnant with Marc," I said. "I didn't know how people were going to judge me, or how much it was going to hurt. I didn't know if Ben was going to stay with me, or if I was going to end up a teenaged, unwed, single mother." I sighed.

"You think Kestrel is afraid of the same things?" he asked, eyebrows raised.

"Oh, no." I smiled and shook my head. "Some of them, sure... but not being teenaged, or... I don't know is she unwed? Are she and Dump Truck...?"

"No, they're not married, and she doesn't have a fucking thing to worry about when it comes to D.T. being there. He was raised by a single mom, and I think he resents the fuck out of his sperm donor for leaving her that way. He grew up poor, and it was hard on his mom."

"I see," I murmured, and then said, "Still, it's a scary prospect growing an entire human being in your body."

He nodded. "When you put it that way," he said with a laugh. "She doesn't have a thing to worry about, though. She's family, and when you're family to a club like this, things may not always be easy but damn if any of us are going to let you fall. We help each other. That's what we do. We take care of each other, and that's that."

It was food for thought. A lot of this was just so overwhelming, and things were going on behind the scenes. The women knew it. Some of them knew more than they were saying, but none dared speak of it.

I worried about that to a degree but all of them that *did* know, swore up and down that it wasn't bad, whatever it was.

Still, I worried.

It was a worry that ended up getting put to the back burner and that was drowned in drinking, dancing, and some *really* bad karaoke until finally, Jared and I had both had our fill of alcohol and other people. Not each other.

It was a fun day and a fun night, but I just wanted to get back to our regularly scheduled program and finish out that *to be continued* from earlier.

We stopped just short of the big clearing with the firepit to listen to the kids telling scary stories and trying not to giggle. As Marc told a sanitized version of the plotline to *Jeepers Creepers* to the littler kids, we went up the path to our trailer.

"C'mere," Jared said. Catching me by my fingertips with his one hand, he towed me in against his body.

The kiss was wild and fierce, and the only thing that prevented the moment from being over-the-top magical, at least for me, was the lack of fireflies lighting up the dark. Sadly, that wasn't a thing here in the Pacific Northwest. I think it was honestly the biggest thing I missed about the south. The little sparkling golden glow of lightning bugs.

He gripped me by my ass and hauled me against his body, his other hand tangling in my hair and holding my mouth to his as we kissed in the dark outside our trailer door.

I let my arms twine around him and held him close as he pulled me in as tightly to his body as he could get me. I loved that about him. How he could never seem to get enough of me. How he held me so tight and so carefully at the same time.

"Inside," I gasped between kisses, and he chuckled against my mouth.

"Yes, ma'am," he growled, and he very reluctantly stepped back so that he could fish out the key from his pocket and unlock the door.

I waited giddy with the buzz I had going on mixed with the intoxication of just plain *Jared*. Once he had the door unlocked, he held out his hand to me and I took it, letting him tow me in and press me to the metal hull of the outside of the trailer. He kissed me, pinned me with his body, his hands wandering over mine over my clothes, squeezing my breast under the jacket, over the covering of the thin, form-fitting tee, and the cup of my bra.

He slid a hand down my body, over my clothes and dipped a hand beneath the hem of my shirt, pushing it up out of his way, pulling down the cup of my bra. My breast spilled out over it, and he ducked his head and took my nipple into his hot, insistent mouth.

I squeezed my eyes shut and put my head back and tried to strangle the throaty noise of *yes* that I made but it was barely accomplished. His other hand was at my pussy, rubbing me through my jeans and *holy hell*, that was smoking hot.

"Jared!" I gasped out his name.

"Mm?"

"What if someone sees?" I asked, gasping and giggling between my pants. I couldn't help myself. I ground my hips against his hand at my crotch and bit my bottom lip.

"Fuck 'em," he mumbled.

"The kids!" I gasped, and he grunted and let my nipple pull, captured between his teeth, the sensation sharp and yet not unkind, just intense and I gasped and squirmed harder.

God, I bet my panties were *soaked*.

"Up you go," he ordered. "Get those boots off."

I got up into the trailer, got my boots off as ordered, and when I turned around, we were crashing into each other, fervently kissing all over again.

It was a mad scramble for each of us to get the other unwrapped. My jacket fell first, then his cut was tossed aside on the counter nearby. His tee followed by my hand, and he worked at my jeans, unfastening my belt, fingers scrambling at my button and zipper even as I struggled with his.

"You do it," he growled and pulled his hands away from mine as we each slid pants and underwear down as one to get out of them.

He pulled me to him, and we kissed. He backed me up toward the bed. He turned me by my hips to face it and one hand on my shoulder, the other on my hip, bent me over the end. I still had my shirt and bra on, but I didn't care.

I *needed* him inside me.

"Jared please!" I begged.

"Oh, fuck *yes*," he muttered, and I practically yowled, pressing my ass back toward him and into his hand as the smack landed on it.

I was vaguely aware of him kneeling behind me, stroking himself.

"Let me see that pretty pussy," he ordered, and I arched obediently, opening myself up to his gaze. The lust in the small trailer was palpable, the air so thick with desire I could almost *taste* it. Musky sweet, a forbidden fruit, I clutched the bedding in front of me as he nudged my knees further apart with one of his own. With one hand on my shoulder, the other on his cock, he guided himself into me.

I couldn't wait, so desperate was I to have him in me, I leaned back, taking him deeper. He put hands on my hips and guided me into it.

"Yeah, that's it, baby. Fuck me. *Jesus,* that pussy's so good."

I fucking loved it when he talked to me like that. So sultry, so dirty, but everything that came out of his mouth was such high praise and I didn't know how much I *needed* that. How much I needed to be... just... *cherished.* That was what he did when he smoothed his hands up my back, under my shirt.

He worshiped me with his hands as I slid up and down his length and fucked his cock with my dripping wet pussy.

Fuck, he felt so good! There weren't any words for how fucking good he was to me. I arched low, and the heat rose between us, one of his hands on my hip, the other up under my tee, fingers curving over my shoulder as he grunted and with a hard thrust, fetched my body up against the bed.

He. Let. Fly.

Slamming into me with a bruising force, fucking me so hard, so fast, so *sweetly*, I happily died a little death and kept right on dying over, and over, and over.

His hand moved from my hip, the pad of his thumb teasing my back entrance, and I let out this throaty sound that was pitiful in its begging.

"You like that?" he demanded between panting thrusts. "You like your little asshole played with?"

"*Yes!*" I gasped, and it was true. It was absolutely a guilty pleasure of mine. One I remained silent about as it wasn't the sort of thing nice, professional, mothers did... at least not in the south.

Except I wasn't in the south. And fuck those people. Fuck them all for how they treated me *and* my son.

I let some of that go and brought myself back in the moment, a fresh orgasm hitting me all over again as Jared breached my asshole with his thumb to the first or maybe second knuckle.

My pussy was drenched, the sex devolving into one of those sessions that was going to make us both a beautiful quivering mess at the end and I needed it, I needed it so badly, a catharsis, a way of shedding my old skin and setting the burden of my past down behind me.

"Oh, fuck, *yes!*" Jared cried and thrust into me hard and harder, losing his steady rhythm as he took the shining fall with me.

"God*damnit*, you're so fucking good," he murmured in my ear after draping himself over my back.

"Oh, shit!" I whispered. "Did you remember a condom?" I asked.

He chuckled, and pulled out of me, and the familiar sensation of the condom dragging out of me past the head of his dick had me sagging with relief.

I did not want another pregnancy; one was enough for me. Plus, I couldn't fathom making Marc an older brother at eighteen.

"Mm, I'm with you," Jared said behind me as he disposed of the condom in the trash. "I'm good with just being Uncle Glass Jaw to everybody else's little ones."

"Ever thought of a vasectomy?" I asked jokingly.

"You know what? I am now," he said.

"Yeah?" I asked.

"Mm." He lifted my shirt over my head and threw it somewhere behind him, then he bent and unhooked my bra. "To be inside you raw? I am now."

Holy shit.

"Up you go," he said and drew me to my feet on shaking legs. He guided me up onto the bed and followed me. We settled in the dark cuddled into one another.

"You're serious," I said in awe.

"Why wouldn't I be?" he asked and kissed my forehead, and I didn't know. I guess I just never fathomed anyone going that far just for something so small, for *me*.

"God, you feel so fucking good," he murmured against my hair. "I want to grow old with you and die like this, right here with you in my arms."

I cuddled in tighter, pressing my ear over his heart.

"That sounds nice," I whispered, still drifting on the euphoria of my afterglow.

"Sounds perfect," he said with a slight chuckle, and with the long drive and ride, the activities of the day, and the drink and songs of the evening, we fell asleep in each other's arms quicker than anything.

I didn't have many perfect days to look back on for me, but this one? This one was probably the best one I'd ever had.

Still, with everything he'd given me to think about? I was surprised I was able to sleep at all.

22

*G*lass Jaw...

She slept, deep and dreamless, which was nice. The few times I'd stayed at her place, she'd shifted at points in my arms, and across the sheets, moaning out in her sleep, her lovely brow furrowed as she wrestled with whatever demons she had.

She was opening up to me, telling me more about the fallout and how she was feeling; what some of those fucks had put her through back in Atlanta with their fake-ass polite, genteel bullshit, their silence a damning one.

Letting a good person needlessly suffer when you could say something to stop it didn't make you a good person. It made you a steaming shitbag, just like her fucking ex.

I watched her sleep, worry gnawing at my gut that I honestly wasn't any better for her in that regard.

I was a club man, and the club had its secrets. I think, on some sort of sublevel, she knew that, just like she'd known on some sublevel that things with her ex weren't quite right.

It gutted me, really, knowing that if shit went any further on the skids with our operation, and the LEOs sniffing around, I could be eating asphalt in a whole different way than how I did every time I looked at her beautiful face.

I was worried it would be just as devastating, just as bad for her if I ended up gone by way of being locked up for an extended stay – or *life* – as it would be if I died.

I wrestled with that, knowing that things were still relatively new, that she might not be all-in. That I should stop this, protect her and Marc from more heartache but… I was a selfish fucking prick, and I didn't think I had the balls to do it.

The only thing worse than thinking about how this could all crash and burn for me and her was the way my thoughts chased their own damn tail around in my brain over this whole prescription drug running scheme we were in and how I couldn't for the life of me figure a work-around.

We were caught between a rock and a hard place. We were way too far in, and we couldn't fuck these people over who *depended on us*. There wasn't any alternative for them. A lot of them would literally fuckin' *die* without the drugs we supplied and none of them had the where-withal to get those same drugs in an above-board way. Some of them were too poor to be insured. Some of them made too much for government assistance, but not enough to afford healthcare or the drugs they needed outright.

It was bullshit, how the healthcare system just expected these people to die.

How many Americans had no recourse and just had to do without. You shouldn't be expected to sacrifice your home, food, or being able to reliably get to and from work just to get the medicine you needed.

It was fucking barbaric, and yet *we* were the barbarians according to the cops and the politicians and the fucking bureaucrats.

Cadence stirred, her deep and even breathing interrupted by a shuddering inhalation of breath and a long luxurious stretch. Her green eyes opened, and I only just barely got a smile on my face in time.

She didn't need to know about the dark night of the soul I was having over here. I didn't think I could keep it off my face forever, but I damn sure would work on keeping it away from her for now.

"Good morning," she murmured, voice husky and seductive from sleep and by the fact that she was just painfully sexy as fuck.

"Good morning," I rumbled, my own voice rough from sleep and the hours of disuse between when we'd passed out and whatever the hell time it was now.

I smoothed some of her long silky hair behind her ear and just stared at her in the late-morning light cutting through the window back here.

She was so fuckin' beautiful, and if I *were* to get put away, I wanted to remember this moment.

"What?" she asked, smiling after I stared at her a hair too long.

"You're just the most beautiful creature I've ever seen," I said. "Now c'mere."

She drifted toward me and I kissed her, rolling her onto her back and posting up between those wonderful thighs of hers.

I had it, didn't want to waste it, so I put my fucking morning wood to use.

~

THE REST of the day was like having an instant family. We made love, cleaned up, got dressed, and then it was time for breakfast. We all scattered for the day, the clubs people breaking up into their little families or couples and fucking off around town to do all the touristy type of shit.

We were no exception. We ended up at the kitschy little oddity museum in town after our seafood omelets at a little diner in town. We laughed and took pictures with the weird things inside, got some squished pennies which I found funny since it was like, a total obsession of Little Bird's, and then we hit the main drag and the little merry-go-round and go-kart track.

"Now, how you gonna say you're gonna whoop my ass when I've been driving for like as long as you been alive and then some?" I asked Marc.

Cadence laughed and Marc said, "Just let it happen, old man. Just let it happen."

"Old?" I cried, turning to Cadence. "Did you hear that? Since when am I *old?*"

Cadence laughed, head back, sun glinting off the rims and lenses of her sunglasses and it was another one of those perfect moments.

We got onto the track with a few other guys and Tic-Tac from our chapter and let fly. Cadence stayed outside the fence and recorded things with her phone.

It was fun. Marc didn't win, but neither did I, and despite my best competitive efforts, Marc did come out ahead of me.

Guess the ice cream was on me.

23

*C*adence...

    I hadn't seen Marc so happy in a long time. I guess deep down, I always knew he needed that male influence that Ben was never really there to provide him, but it was something else watching how much he opened up and smiled at the go-kart track.

I was standing at the black iron fence, my phone out, video recording this because Lord, I needed these memories committed to some type of media, when two of the girls from another chapter started talking beside me.

"I overheard my old man say the club's in deep shit," she said and I immediately homed in to what she had to say.

"The Canada thing?" the other girl asked.

"Yeah, we're talking RICO, smuggling, the whole works. It's international. I swear to God, my man goes back to prison, I don't know what I'm gonna do."

"It's not gonna happen, Carly. The guys are smart. You just wait and see."

They moved away from me, and I smiled at Marc who waved at me on his way by, Jared skidding around the bend in the track right behind him. I laughed, but I wondered if I asked him if Jared would say anything about what the 'Canada thing' was.

I pushed it to the back of my mind for later when the boys got off their ride and came toward me.

"After that, I think I need some ice cream," Jared said. "What do you guys say?"

"Sounds good!" Marc declared, and I pasted on a smile.

"Sounds perfect," I agreed, and Jared threw his arms around my shoulders and turned us toward the old-fashioned general store and ice cream counter across the street.

The shop was crowded, a popular place on the main drag, and so rather than stay within the crush of people or even on the crowded street, we ate our ice cream and started walking back toward the trailer park motel and campground to change to go to the beach.

"I have a feeling I'm not supposed to ask," I said when Marc got ahead of us to talk to a couple of other teens.

I glanced sideways at Jared, and he cocked his head, taking a lick off his ice cream cone.

"Spit it out, baby. What's up?" he asked me.

"I overheard something. What's the 'Canada thing' and what kind of smuggling?" I asked once I knew no one could hear me.

Jared stopped in his tracks and put out a hand to grasp my arm firmly but gently.

"That's club business. Where did you hear that?" he demanded, and he was suddenly earnest.

"A couple of the girls from another chapter. One of them said they overheard their old man talking about it. I don't want to say who because I don't want to get anyone in trouble. I just... I don't know if I can handle anymore secrets especially something as big as whatever *it* is." I bit my lips together for a moment while Jared searched my face. "I don't want to lose you," I said, and I felt my shoulders drop.

"Oh, shit, hey." He pulled me into his arms and pressed a hand to the back of my head and said, "You're not gonna lose me, babe. We've been in stickier situations, and I promise everything is going to be okay. You don't get to worry about that stuff."

"So, you are in trouble," I said against his shoulder, voice muffled.

"I won't talk about it," he said. "It's club business, but I swear to you, you ain't gotta worry about a thing," he said, drawing back to look at me.

I searched out his hazel eyes and wanted so badly to believe with the sincerity that shone in them but... Ben had been just as fervent, just as convincing, something like a thousand times over and yet here I was, only spared the divorce by his death, and a whole other shattered family left behind him.

I hated myself for it, in a way, the fact that I swallowed all of my misgivings and chose to believe him... for now... but I wasn't done digging. I needed to know what they were doing. I couldn't be with someone smuggling illegal drugs or worse, *people* over the border and The Sacred Hearts? They had *such* a reputation... had been involved with *cartels*... I nodded and Jared smoothed a hand over my hair and pressed a kiss to my forehead.

"Let's head to the beach, huh?" he asked, and I nodded again.

We went back to our trailer, finished our ice cream, got changed and gathered our beach blankets and towels.

At the beach, the ol' ladies and women of the Western Washington chapter were in a tight knot, their boys off throwing around a frisbee.

"Mom, can I join 'em?" Marc asked.

"If it's alright with them," I said nodding.

"Of course, it is!" Jared declared, and I gave him a kiss.

"You guys go on. I'll get us set up," I said, and they left me with their things and jogged off to join the game.

Little Bird and Raven got up to help me. Aspen, coming across the sand from the direction of the restroom, hurried to help. I set up with them.

"Why the long face?" Dahlia asked from behind her big, bug-eyed sunglasses, her body gleaming with oil where the retro pinup yellow, blue, and white bikini didn't cover.

"I overheard something," I said, deciding to make the brave leap with these women and hoping it didn't backfire.

"Oh?" Marisol sat up, her interest definitely piqued.

"I may have it recorded," I said. "Hang on."

I brought up the video at the go-kart track and played it, the girls all huddled around my phone giggling at the boys when the woman's voice, Carly I think her name was, came out from my phone. The girls around me all froze.

Marisol lit off in a string of colorful Spanish curses.

"Do us all a favor and delete that," Dahlia said, and she suddenly looked ashen beneath her tattoos.

"On one condition," I said finally, already bringing up the command to delete the video while they watched.

"What's that?" Raven asked, looking apprehensive.

"You ladies let me in on what's going on. I know you know something, and I don't want to be in the dark anymore." I deleted the file, and they all exchanged worried looks.

"We know," Marisol said.

"We *always know*," Aspen said and looked unhappy. "Even when we don't want to."

I nodded and said, "So what is it?"

They all looked scared and a little guilty.

"It's no offense," Dahlia said. "We like you—"

"A lot, actually," Marisol said with a sniff.

"We just don't want to lose our men, either," Raven said unhappily.

"Look," I murmured. "I..." I looked across the sand at Jared who leaped and caught the frisbee flung by someone else. He laughed and knocked shoulders with Marc, and I felt nothing but fear for him.

"I think I love him already, and Marc and I have already *lost* so much. I don't know if we could bear it all over again so I just need to know... should I stay or should I go? Just what are they smuggling – hell, don't even tell me what, just *promise me* it's nothing like heroin or worse... *people.*"

"No, no! It's nothing like that!" The girls all traded alarmed looks.

"Listen, let me tell you how *I* met the club," Marisol said, and she took a deep breath.

Her story was eye-opening to say the least. I stared at her wide-eyed for a very long time and thought about just yesterday and what Jared had done to secure the medicine I needed for Marc, and that had only been a *minor* inconvenience due to the federal regulations.

"I... I'm shook," I finally declared. "I have never been so underprivileged as to even consider..." I stared across the sand with what had to be a veil lifted off my eyes at these rough men and *holy shit...* "Marisol," I said. "Out of all of us, you have to know the most... how can we *help?*" I asked.

"The short answer is we *can't*." Dahlia leaned back in her lounge chair and sighed. "This is all club business, and the women aren't supposed to get involved for a reason."

"*Dios mios*, we're involved," Marisol said, rolling her eyes.

"Whether the menfolk like it or not, Marisol is right," Raven declared.

"I can't lose D.T., so I feel like we'd better do *something*," Kestrel declared, her hands fluttering to her abdomen.

"I agree. Sometimes it's better to beg forgiveness than to ask permission," Aspen declared.

"So, let's put our heads together and figure it out." Raven looked at each of us in turn. "We are strong, capable, women."

"Starting point," I said. "What do each of us know?" I asked.

"Point of fact, we shouldn't be saying *any of this* around any open lines or phones and we need to figure out our own code if we do happen to have to text or say anything near an open line," Dahlia said, leaning forward.

"Looks like we're all in," Marisol said grimly.

I looked back at Jared and Marc and said, "I've finally gotten a taste for what it's like to have the family for my son that I always wanted him to have. Yes, I'm in. We can have drinks at my house next week after we get back. We'll figure everything out from there. Until then?"

"Gather what information you can," Dahlia said, looking across the beach blanket at me and I nodded.

"Precisely what I was going to say," I said.

"Anyone spills this to Mav, I swear to fucking God, I'm cunt punting you into next week," Dahlia declared and most of us broke into smiles and a bit of laughter.

"I'm surprised you're not fighting against this tooth and nail," Kestrel said, and Dahlia smiled into the sun.

"I know when the boys are outmatched and need an assist, especially Maverick. We grew up together. He's stuck on this one," she said.

"My house, next week, leave your phones in your cars," I declared.

"Sounds good," Aspen said with a nod, and I could tell that she, like me, didn't want to be in this position and yet... here we were.

24

*G*lass Jaw...

"Shit, this has to be the easiest church we've ever held," Dump Truck said, grinning like a fool. He was taking this whole news he was about to be a daddy like a fucking champion but on the flip side, his Little Bird was awfully fragile and a bit needy as a result. I couldn't blame her. It was a lot being a mom. I saw it with Cadence every day. I had to grin too. It was because of Cadence things were so smooth this time around.

"You can thank my lady for that one," I said. "Seems like she and the rest of the girls hit it off really good at the beach. She's got 'em all over at her place."

"Thank fuck for small favors," Mav said and sighed. He'd had to have a talk with the other presidents about loose lips sinking ships, which is never a pleasant convo to have. Less so when it turned out that Carly was the girlfriend of one of the other VP's. Not for long, though. Sounded like that slipup right there torpedoed that relationship.

I felt bad for River, I really did, but a broad like that was absolutely a liability.

I'd kept a careful watch and an even more careful ear out where Cadence was concerned but she had my back. Dahlia had even let me know that she'd talked to the rest of them and had deleted the video of me and Marc at the track because it'd caught the audio of Carly mouthing off.

I knew how much that must have hurt her, losing the recorded memory, but I couldn't tell you how much faith it put in me where she was concerned that she'd done that for me.

"Well, brothers. We got any ideas on how, or where to go from here?" Mav asked.

"As far as I can tell, Manny's place is burned," Dump Truck declared, and that was something I think we all knew but didn't have the fucking heart to say out loud.

"So, what needs doing then?" Deacon asked.

"That's the sixty-four-thousand-dollar question, now, isn't it?" Derry let out a gusty sigh and leaned all the way back in his boardroom chair.

"How much does he still got stashed?" Nine asked.

"A lot," I said. "Enough to get us through for two or three months but..." I sighed. "Can't get that amount of supply out on short notice on the bikes, and if we go up there now?"

"Way too sus," Maverick agreed.

"I would sure as shit hate to cut my losses on that much product," Dump Truck said.

"I think all of us can agree on that," Maverick declared.

"Not just for the money out of our pockets," Cipher said.

"But for all those *people*," Blackjack finished for him.

"Fuckin' feds," Fish muttered and there were a bunch of mutterings that swept around the table.

"All I can think to do is shut it down and wait for the Federales to get tired. Let them piss off back to wherever they fuckin' came from," Maverick said.

"Yeah, but how many are gonna fuckin die without those meds in the meantime?" Major asked.

"Too many," I said. "But I don't see another way, either. We can't help anyone ever again if we're locked up for life."

Mutterings and assents went around.

"So, is that it then?" Fenris demanded.

"Do you see another way?" Maverick asked.

A heavy silence hung over the chapel.

No, I thought to myself. *No, we do not.*

～

I DIDN'T GO HOME. I rode to Cadence's, pulling around back and feeling only slightly shitty I was crashing her girls' night.

I went to the back door and knocked. She answered after a few moments.

"Hi!" she called out, laughing, a glass of wine in her hand. I smiled up at her and said. "Hi," back.

"I know I'm interrupting, but I just really wanted to see you. Mind if I crash here? I can just fuck off to your room and let you ladies be."

She cocked her head, searched my face and asked me, "Everything okay?"

"No," I answered with a bit of a scoff. "But they will be. Shit's just extra heavy right now."

She nodded slowly and murmured, "Get in here." I slipped in past her to five sets of questioning eyes from the kitchen.

"Hi, girls." I waved tiredly at Dahlia, Marisol, Aspen, Kestrel, and Raven.

"Hey, you alright?" Dahlia asked.

"Yeah, yeah, I'm good. Don't let me interrupt. I'm just gonna crash here," I said, and I went into the kitchen.

"Want a beer?" Cadence asked behind me.

"Yeah, that might be good until I can have you," I said.

"Gross," Marc said from the bottom of the stairs, and we all had a chuckle at that.

Cadence handed me a beer out of the fridge and raised an eyebrow at Marc. "Soda please," he said, and she handed him a bottle of something with a pink label.

"Thanks." He went back upstairs double time.

"Too much estrogen down here," Aspen said with a wink.

"Not for me, but g'night," I said, moving past the counter and dining room where they were mostly gathered.

"Hey!" Cadence called, stopping me. I turned, and she came up and kissed me.

I smiled at that. "You're something else, you know that?" I asked.

"Oh, you have no idea," Dahlia said with a smirk. The rest of the girls giggled.

"And on that note, I'm out," I said, and they all laughed.

I knew when I was outmatched and five on one weren't odds I was in favor of. Still, I went into Cadence's room with a smile.

I shut the door, drowning out their conversation to a low hum and their bright giggles and fits of laughter to a dull roar.

I stripped down to nothing and crawled into bed, plugged in my phone on her charger and took a swig of my beer. I fucked around on the book of faces and yet, before I knew it, I was opening my eyes, the house dark and silent, the bed shifting beneath me as Cadence drew close into my side.

"Hey, sorry, didn't mean to wake you," she said softly.

"No, it's alright," I said, voice gravelly with sleep. "I'm glad you did."

"You looked so tired when you came in," she murmured and kissed me softly. I smiled against her lips and nodded slightly.

"Exhausted," I confessed.

"Sleep, then," she whispered, and I put my arms around her and held her close.

"K, I love you," I said groggily. It just slipped out. I didn't even think about it.

She froze for a moment in my arms, and I was about to curse myself when she murmured, "I love you, too."

It was like she put my soul to rest. I slept like a fuckin' baby after that.

I woke up to her lips wrapped around my cock, looking down the length of my body into those hallowed green eyes. Her lips wrapped around me as she slid my dick across her velvet pink tongue had me swallowing mine.

I made a strangled noise in the back of my throat as she smiled around me and slid me to the back of hers and *holy fucking shit,* I loved the way she gave head.

It was fucking porn-star worthy but sensual at the same time. She was making love to me with her mouth, and it had to be the hottest thing I had ever encountered. Definitely, watching her go down on me took the top spot on hottest, sexiest, and most meaningful sexual encounters I'd ever had the pleasure of being a part of.

I gathered up her hair gently and held it so I could watch her, and heat curled through me, making me groan. I breathed, letting the feeling of her mouth on me carry, washing over and through me until I didn't think I could take anymore.

I wasn't one of those guys that could come easy from a blowjob, but Cadence had me close, so very close.

Fuck!

"Slow down, baby," I ordered, voice tight, and she was such a good fucking girl. Always did just what I told her when we were like this, and it just made everything that much hotter.

"Aw, yeah, just like that, *just like that,*" I murmured and traced some of her hair behind her ear as she bobbed eagerly, sucking me so sweetly.

"Come up here and ride me," I ordered gently, and she worked me in and out of her sweet, sexy mouth a time or two more before moving to comply.

She was completely nude and looked like a goddess wreathed in the muted morning light filtering through her bedroom curtains.

She straddled me, an unreadable look in her eyes that was oh so very serious as she lifted my throbbing cock off my stomach and situated it at her entrance.

"Condom?" I asked.

She cocked her head slowing and asked me, "You want one?"

"No," I answered her honestly.

"Okay, then," she said and slid down over the top of me and *Jesus Christ!*

She was so wet, so fucking hot and slick and she took the length of me at this sharper deeper angle like a fucking champ. Her body meeting mine, my cock nestled inside of her, so deep, so *perfectly* deep, and I panted, fighting not to go off too soon.

She put her hands on my chest, her eyes closed, her head tipped back slightly as she savored the sensation of me inside her bareback like I was. God, she was beautiful like this – breasts perfect and heavy in my hands as I teased her nipples with my fingers, hair loose and wild, framing her face. Her beautiful face bearing a stricken look that was at once beatific, as though having me inside her raw like this was the way she'd found God and *holy Christ,* she had no idea how hot that was to me.

I smoothed my hands down her sides from her breasts, thumbs following the curve over her hourglass shape as she began to move, grinding her hips, keeping me seated *deep* inside of her and *oh, God; oh, fuck!*

I grunted and pulled her down onto me even tighter as she writhed against me, as much for her own gratification as for mine, and damn I was desperate to hold off. I wanted her to come with me inside her. I wanted to feel that warm gush and her ripple around me so bad, and I was determined to hold it for as long as it took.

I took a hand from her hip, licked the pad of my thumb, and delved it between us at the top of her sex, finding that little rosebud, teasing it as best I could and delighting when she threw her head back and moaned like some sort of wanton sex goddess.

I loved that in the month or two of us getting serious that she had really begun to let go. She'd gone from nervous and anxiety riddled anytime the clothes came off, to bold and sexy, just as willing to take what she wanted as much as she'd been to give me what I asked. She was so sweet, so sexy, so smart and cool.

God, I wanted to keep her for all time. I wanted the time I had her like this to never end. I wanted to burn every moment of watching her stiffen above me, listen to her cry out, and feel her shudder against me as her pussy rippled around my cock while she came.

I wanted to just live and exist in this moment for all fucking time with her.

But life? Life didn't fucking work like that. It never did, and I had to face the fact that each and every time like this with Cadence in my arms, on my cock, wrapped around me, on me, under me as I laid her on her back... that it could be the very last time, leaving me with just the memory of her to sustain me in lockup.

I turned her on her back, and thrust deep, raising her leg, pressing a hand behind her knee, and driving into her in long, smooth, even strokes.

She panted, grabbing at me, pulling my mouth to hers, desperate to kiss me, and I lost my shit.

My balls tightened, I didn't even have time for that building tingle at the base of my spine, and my world was exploding in flashing lights of multicolor wonder behind my eyelids as I squeezed them shut and came deep inside her shuddering, every small movement sending a pleasurable shock through my system that was almost, *almost*, too much to fucking bear.

She pulled me down on top of her, hugging me, holding me, with arms and legs, and we both just lay there sweating, panting, silent for the moment in a perfect harmony that I don't think I had ever allowed myself with anyone else.

"Whoa, God, that was good," she said with a little laugh when we'd both calmed down some.

"Only gets better," I promised her. Adding silently, *you know, if I can keep my ass out of jail.*

25

*C*adence...

I could tell he was tense. That he worried about something, and I knew that *I* knew what that something was, but he couldn't know I knew... and that was so *hard.*

I *hated* secrets. I *hated* not being able to communicate with him about this, to allay his fears, to tell him I was here for him and to help but the rest of the women of the club had cautioned me against it.

They'd said that in order for our plan to work, we needed to be *business as usual,* and it was imperative to feign innocence and appear we knew nothing about anything as it related to the club's side operations. *Darker operations?* Honestly, I didn't know what to call them. I definitely knew it fit the definition of an anti-hero, which was Marc's new favorite trope of superhero thanks to several of the men of The Sacred Hearts and an overly complicated discussion about superheroes over the long weekend.

"Hmm." Jared slipped from my body and we both shuddered, still overly sensitive from our mutual orgasms. He vaulted my leg gently and collapsed onto his back on the mattress beside me, though he didn't hesitate to reach for me and to pull me close. I loved that. He held me so tight, so well, I found a real peace and a joy in how he clutched me to his chest.

I laid my head on his shoulder and cuddled close.

"You have fun?" he asked.

"I always have fun when I'm with you," I said slyly, and he laughed at me.

"Okay, laying it on a little thick, but that's not what I meant. I meant with the girls last night."

"Oh! Oh, yeah! We all decided we need a girls' weekend and started planning one."

"Oh, yeah?"

"Mm-hm," I said, and he chuckled and squeezed me a little tighter, kissing the top of my head.

"What 'cha gonna do?" he asked.

"Haven't *exactly* decided that yet, but we'll think of something," I said, and he cleared his throat slightly and hummed thoughtfully.

"What're you going to do about Marc?" he asked, and I snorted.

"Marc is seventeen, almost eighteen, and should be good for one or two nights without me," I said.

"Yeah, stock the freezer with enough hot pockets, he might not even notice you're gone with his head buried in that computer monitor upstairs."

He said it with a grin and his usual lighthearted sarcasm and I just sort of giggled and carried the joke.

"Why, Jared, do you have a case of the *olds?*"

He laughed and hugged me a little tighter and kissed me soundly and said, "You want I should look in on him whenever you take your weekend?"

I smiled and said, "Got anything left to fix around here so you don't make it seem like that's what you're doing?" I asked.

"Ahhh, uh-huh, I see what you did there, and yes. I'm sure I can come up with a thing or two left to do around here. Make sure he eats at least one nutritious meal while you're gone."

"I would appreciate that," I said. Not that I didn't trust my kid, I did… implicitly – he was a *good* kid. He was certainly better than I thought I deserved, and the type of kid that I would forever be grateful for.

"When you guys planning on going?" he asked.

"Oh, sooner rather than later," I said with what I hoped sounded like a light and whimsical sigh.

"Okay," he said, and he tipped my chin up to kiss me. "You just let me know," he said, and I smiled and nodded.

"WELL, I WANT TO MEET HIM," my mother argued, and I rolled my eyes, tucking my phone between my shoulder and my chin as I juggled things out of my fridge to get them to my counter and it's cutting board.

"Mom, I'll be gone *one night*, and Marc is old enough now. Jared's just going to stop in and check on him for me without invading Marc's space. It's the perfect plan."

"Except for the part where you're leaving my only grandson alone with a man that I haven't met who, might I add, is dating my only daughter. Before you go haring off to Canada, *I want to meet him!*"

I was laughing by now and trying not to lose my phone as I dumped my armload of slick produce bags laden with produce on the kitchen counter.

"Alright, alright!" I cried. "Uncle! I cry uncle! I'll see if he's down to come meet my parents."

"Lunch on Saturday?" my mother asked serenely.

"Sunday might be better," I said, thinking of the job Jared was currently on which was taking a lot out of him. He said he might have to work on Saturday.

"Brunch it is!" she crowed triumphantly.

"I said I would see!" I cried.

"Honestly, Cadence. Mimosas or Bloody Marys?" she asked.

I frowned slightly and asked, "Who are you and what have you done with my mother? Why not both?"

"That's fair, I just wanted to make sure that *you* hadn't done something with my daughter – honestly, I *am* a bit worried, you've only just met this man."

I rolled my eyes and said gently, "Mom, I hate to break it to you, but you just *loved* Ben so maybe give it a bit of a rest?"

"Well, shit. When you're right, you're right and I hate that you are!" she said and let out a huffy breath on the other end of the line.

My back door opened, and I heard Marc call out, "We're back!"

I held my breath and both my son and Jared stepped into the kitchen. Jared held out the box of cream cheese in my direction and I lowered my phone and asked, "How did it go?"

He grinned at me a bit tiredly and said, "Just fine, mother hen."

I rolled my eyes and my mom said, "Let me talk to my grandson!"

I held out my phone to Marc and said, "It's your grandma."

He rolled his eyes, gave me a bit of a dirty look then brightly said into the phone, "Hi, gramma!"

Jared fought to suppress his laugh so she wouldn't hear him, and I said, "My mother wants to meet you! Brunch, at her place, on Sunday?" I cringed as I asked the last, knowing it was a longshot.

"Not this Sunday," he said, shaking his head with a sigh. "Next Sunday is your girls' thing, so Sunday after?"

"She can take it or leave it," I said over Marc's chatter from the dining room. He wandered my way.

"Uh-huh, I love you too, Gramma. I gotta go study though, so here's Mom."

Slick little shit, I thought, taking back the phone.

"Hey, Mom."

"Well?" she demanded with bated breath.

"No go this Sunday, Jared has to work – next Sunday is the trip, but he said the Sunday after that so…"

"Well, all I say is that you better not be found in trash bags on the side of the freeway like so many other girls!"

I laughed, and she was chuckling too. I could hear it in her voice.

"Did you listen to the latest podcast too?" I asked.

"I sure did!"

We talked about the true crime podcast we shared, and she told me a bit about the latest true crime novel she was reading. We talked a bit more about how Marc's driving lessons were going – something *else* Jared was taking off my plate and heaping on his already full one, and then we said our goodbyes.

As soon as I hung up, I let out a whoosh of a breath and leaned forward, letting my arms dangle, deflating a bit with relief.

Jared leaned back against one of my counters, arms crossed and smiling at me, he unfolded his arms, leather of his jacket creaking and beckoned me with his fingers, holding out his hand.

I put my hand in his and let him tow me into his arms, turning my face up for the kiss I knew he would have waiting. We pecked lips two or three times and he wrapped his arms around my shoulders tight and held me close rocking me a bit.

Do *not* get me wrong. I loved my mother more than life itself, *but* she could be a little intense sometimes, and also sort of a drama queen.

"How did it go, really?" I asked, my voice a bit muffled by his jacket and cut.

"*Fine,*" he said a bit exasperated. "He's just like every other seventeen-year-old that's learning to drive."

I sighed. "You have nerves of steel," I complained.

"Jealous?" he asked.

"Yes," I retorted, and he chuckled.

"He did great. I'd take him out the weekend you're gone, but no way is he driving my truck."

I blanched. "Oh, God no!"

I heard Marc thumping down the stairs from his room and he hit the bottom with his house shaking thump.

"Mom, when's dinner gonna be ready?" he asked.

"Half hour or so," I answered. He nodded and shook his hair back out of his eyes. That was *another* thing I needed to get handled, he needed a haircut.

"You have a good talk with Grandma?" I asked, and he nodded.

"Yeah, but you know her, if you don't keep it short, you'll be on the phone all night."

I laughed and nodded. "I think she's just bored in her retirement," I said.

He rolled his eyes. "She's only ever *been* retired!" he said and snatched his bottle of sports drink off the counter and walked backwards to head back upstairs.

I rolled my eyes at *him*. "She was a housewife, and a house doesn't clean itself," I pointed out.

"She doesn't clean her house either!" he said with a grin. "She pays someone else to do it."

"Now!" I called back to his footsteps thumping back up his steps.

I sighed.

"Oh, to be young." Jared grinned and moved out of my kitchen to go sit at one of the counter stools in the dining room so we could still talk while I cooked.

I gave a long-suffering sigh and started on the crack chicken in the pressure cooker to get it going before I fixed the salad that would be the bed of greens and vegetables that it was served on.

"So, you ready for me to meet your parents?" he asked me with a sigh.

It was one I returned but for a totally different reason. He knew, we had already discussed it.

"Yes," I said. "But as much as I love my mother, as you already know, she can be a lot."

He nodded slowly while I worked. "So you and Marc have both said, but I can take it," he shot back with a wink and that devilish grin that almost always made my ovaries explode. It was a good thing Marc was a one and done. I had an IUD and I wasn't about to have another – I did my bid with my son and as much as I loved being his mom, I did *not* want to do it again and start all over. A decade more, if I was lucky, I would have grandchildren to spoil. If not, that was okay, too. I was content either way.

"I'm not worried about if you can take it," I said with a slight laugh.

"Hey," he said and his voice was soft. I looked up from my cooking and he fixed my gaze with his.

"You can take it, too because your mother or not, she oversteps, I'm on *your* side and depending on what you say? I won't let it slide."

I carefully nodded my understanding.

"I love you," he said when I didn't speak, as if I needed the reminder.

I smiled, I had to, what else could I do?

"I love you, too," I told him and that was really all there was to it, wasn't there?

 lass Jaw...

"Hey, man. Good to see you," Fenris said, and we clasped hands and pulled each other in.

"Feels like I haven't since the Long Beach run," I said with a sniff.

"Yeah, well, the cats are away the mice will play," Tic called out from over by the bar and we all had a laugh.

"Wish we could all relax and enjoy it more," Dump Truck said with a bit of grim resignation, taking a pull from the neck of his bottle of beer.

"All we can do is wait for the hammer to fall, if it does at all," Mav said with a sigh. "We've done all we can to insulate ourselves. Manny wouldn't give us up, not in a million fuckin' years. He's hidden everything as best that he can."

"They search his place, we're all fucked," Major said.

"We ain't got no way of getting his stores out of there," Nine agreed.

"All we can do is wait," Maverick reiterated. "Quit borrowing trouble – don't put any of that shit out there. That's when the universe starts getting ideas and then we *are* fucked."

A bunch of us chuckled and exchanged looks.

Mace shook his head. "You're starting to sound like Raven and Dahlia when they start getting onto one of their astrology tangents," he said.

"Yeah, well, there might be something to some of that witchy woo woo shit of your girl's," Dump Truck told him.

I laughed. "What the fuck ever, bro." I shook my head. I didn't believe in a lot, if any of that shit. "I'd like to say we've been in darker places and worse positions, but it doesn't feel like we have," I said soberly.

"We have," Maverick declared. "It's not sticky or a shitshow until the lawyers get involved."

"Which, the lawyer's retainer is already paid, and we've been keeping up on it. That's a whole different bag of bricks separate from everything else, and everyone's dues are paid," Cipher said, and I nodded. Sometimes you just needed the reminder, you know.

"That certainly makes me feel a lot better," I said and nodded.

"Me, too," Deacon agreed.

"We gonna play some fuckin' poker or what?" Fenris demanded and some nods were exchanged. It was the first time the majority of us had been together since the Long Beach run a couple weeks back, and we had the intention to low key cut loose – meaning stick together, keep our heads down and out of trouble, and keep our noses clean for the time being until the heat was off of us.

So, poker and beer were the order of the evening. We broke up into a couple of groups, some of us around the pool table out here, and some of us in the chapel. Too many of us now to make one big game.

"What'll you have, Glass Jaw?" the prospect asked me. Momma Kat was with the rest of the girls.

"Gimme a Batsquatch, Dipshit."

"On it, boss." The kid was alright. I didn't know if he had the balls to stick it through, but I'd honestly thought the same thing about Fish a time or two.

I settled at Mav's right hand in the chapel along with Deacon, Fen, Dump Truck, Blackjack, and Cipher.

Blackjack was shuffling cards, Cipher doling out the chips, and the feeling in the chapel, around the table, was just plain *heavy*, man.

"You guys think about what to do if the worst does happen?" Dump Truck asked.

"Got it all handled, brother," Maverick drawled. "Your lady and your baby will be taken care of, bro. You don't *have* to think about this shit. That's what I'm here for. That's my fuckin' job," Maverick said.

"Taken care of how?" Dump Truck asked curiously. Fen looked interested as well likely thinking about Aspen. She'd been through some heavy shit a couple three years back to the point we all had to believe for a while there that if she didn't have bad luck, she wouldn't have any kind of luck at all. I mean, *Jesus fuck*, her whole family and her marriage crumbled inside like a *month*.

It made what Cadence had been through seem like child's play in a couple respects and what Cadence had been through was fucking *awful* in its own right.

I was thinking about Cadence and was sort of half hoping that if the worst was going to happen, that I was glad she could take care of herself and Marc no problem. That she was independent enough that she didn't *need me*, but the fact that she *wanted me* knowing all of that? Shit, if the worst did happen and I ended up locked up? I could go knowing I'd been a blessed man just for the time I did have with her.

Shit was *depressing*, and I was trying real hard not to spiral down into my fucking misery over it but these sad fuckin' pandas around me damn sure weren't helping with that. I didn't say anything, just tuned them out and focused my thoughts on my one big ray of fuckin' sunshine which was Cadence. Well, Cadence and her kid. I enjoyed Marc's company, too. Kid was a real firecracker just like his mom.

This is why you fought so hard against a fuckin' relationship in the first place, I reminded myself. *Just this eventuality.*

Which was shitty when you stopped to think about it. Real fucking shitty.

I cleared my throat and cut whoever was talking off and said, "Bottom line, we all got shit to lose. Some of us before it even had a chance to get started and some of us..." I shook my head. "We all signed up for this shit knowing it had to end at some fucking point. We need to stop fuckin' talk about it or all we're gonna do is end up more stressed out and more depressed than when we started. Enough with the misery circle jerk already. Let's play some fucking cards." I coughed and took a drink out of my beer that Dipshit had set at my elbow when I had been lost in my own thoughts.

"Your lady and her son will be taken care of, too," Mav said. "I know it's new, but—"

"Thanks, man. Won't save my business," I said. "But that helps." I nodded.

"It's no problem," he said and sighed. "We all see the way you two are good for each other."

We tabled the discussion and played cards, and it helped, some. About and hour or two in, Dipshit came in from out at the bar.

"Mav, your burner is blowing the fuck up," he said, and Mav looked up. We had a rule, no phones in the chapel at any fucking time to help keep any of the boys from ever fucking that up. He checked with all of us at the table with a glance and we all nodded.

"Hand it here," he said and took it from the prospect who leaned in the door and held it out.

"What's up?" he asked by way of answering and a few seconds later his brow crashed down into one stormy fucking frown.

"You're fucking kidding me, right?" he demanded.

We all waited, and he finally said, "Put her on the phone…"

27

*C*adence...

I was nervous, all of us quieting down from the excited cheerful chatter we'd maintained all the way north as I made the turn into the drive of the Smuggler's Inn. A subdued hush fell over the car, Kestrel, Aspen, and Raven quieting. Dahlia and Marisol pulled in right behind us. I put my car into park and pulled the handbrake and we all just sort of sat, staring at the front door of the working bed-and-breakfast.

"Well," Aspen said. "Are we sure we're ready for this?"

"I can't lose D.T., so *absolutely*," Kestrel said.

"Same," Raven declared with a sniff.

"Smiles on, ladies," I said and plastered one on my face.

"Right, they could be watching." Aspen nodded. We opened our doors, got out of my small SUV, and squealed with delight, rushing to Dahlia and Marisol – everyone trading excited hugs and so much chatter about inane lady things – hair, makeup, how we were going to make the absolute most of this weekend.

All in the guise of one wickedly wonderful bridal party which was only half a lie. We *were* planning a wedding. Kestrel's. Even though Dump Truck had yet to propose, we knew it was on the horizon, especially with the baby on the way. Aspen had it on good authority; Fenris had caught him looking at rings.

We all made a great show of unloading our very heavy excessive luggage, just like we planned and piled in the open door of the grand old house, the owner, a kindly older man by the name of Manny holding it open for us as we 'lugged' our empty luggage sets through the door.

Nothing to see here, just a group of flighty women who classically overpacked for an overnight trip.

We were careful inside, too. This place *was* still a working bed-and-breakfast and there was no telling, Dahlia had said, that the law enforcement agencies in play hadn't bugged the place, having gone undercover as a previous guest or set of guests.

Manny greeted us warmly, none the wiser that we were here to save the proverbial day. My level of paranoia was through the roof thanks to Dahlia and Marisol, but they had impressed upon the lot of us that it wasn't paranoia if they really were out to get you, which while they weren't out to get *us*, they certainly were out to get our boys which was why we were doing this insanity in the first place.

We played our parts, and Manny was none the wiser, right up until Dahlia handed him the sheaf of papers that we had written up, explaining why we were here and how this was going to play.

If we were lucky, I thought to myself.

"What's this?" Manny asked.

With a wink Dahlia said, "We wanted to tip up front for putting up with our asses, and we heard you had a *fabulous* wine cellar so there's some extra in there for a chance to raid it."

In the papers was a 'wine' key, different varietals and vintages to their prescription drug counterparts so we could get everything out and we did mean *everything.*

Manny was reading and for the time that he was silently skimming the first few pages of explanation, we were hoping he would play it off as speechless.

He looked up and said, "We're safe to talk. I've swept the inn for listening devices and cameras thoroughly. I do after every guest leaves."

I think we all sagged with relief. "You're sure?" Marisol asked with apprehension and Manny nodded.

"You can check with Mav, he doesn't know we're here." Dahlia pitched her voice low a barely audible almost hum, not quite a whisper. I didn't know how she did it.

He looked at us all in turn and his eyes held suspicion. He nodded reluctantly and said, "If you don't mind, I think I'll do just that."

"By all means," Raven said.

"We absolutely prefer that you do," I added.

"You're taking a wild risk," he said.

"So are we, talking so frankly. They might be sitting outside with a parabolic microphone or something," Dahlia said in that weird almost subvocalization. "Make your call and see for us please?" she asked pleasantly at a normal tone.

"What was that?" I whispered, and she smiled brilliantly at me, her expression saying 'shut the fuck up, Cadence.' I wisely, shut the fuck up.

Manny left the room, and we could barely hear the subdued buzz of his end of the conversation from the den or office he had stepped into. He came out after a time and nodded, saying, "Your credit is good, and we do have that particular vintage, but I would be *very* curious to know how you heard about it."

We all traded looks and watched some of the tension leave our backs and shoulders.

"Well, ladies," Dahlia drawled, smiling her brilliant if fake smile, an edge of deviousness to it. "Let's get lit."

We all laughed, nervously to my ears, and Manny, looking somewhat relieved, said, "Right this way, mind your step, the stairs leading to the wine cellar are pitched steep and one or two are loose."

We followed him into the basement, which was where my architectural mind started to pick out details of the old building and it *was* old. Extremely so, maybe one of the oldest buildings in the area.

The basement walls weren't even brick, but rounded river stones stacked and mortared into place, some of them clearly coming loose, some areas of the basement having been reinforced with brick sections in years past. A mishmash and hodgepodge of fixes from the old building's past to ensure it had a future.

Despite the, by all *appearances*, cracker-jacked together basement walls, the foundation was solid ensuring the building above's survival for years and years to come.

There was more than a wine cellar down here, which the wine cellar was indeed respectable, tucked back in the nook behind and below the basement stairs. What caught my eye, though, were the extra fridges at the back of the basement and the extra freezers lining the walls.

We set down our big suitcases, three in all, and had left our likewise empty carryon suitcases upstairs – there were five of those. We all carried big purses, and light clothing hidden in those. Silk or satin shirts, a change of underwear, stuff that would fit in with our wallets and keys, and little else.

Enough to make a good showing of coming out of the inn in a different outfit than what we had entered in.

Manny gestured for us to leave our suitcases and actually went through the wines under the stairs while we selected a couple of bottles.

"There are some fine things to do here in Blaine," he said when we returned upstairs. "I sure do hope you enjoy your stay."

"We certainly will!" Dahlia declared and Manny led us to a sitting room where we made ourselves comfortable while he opened and poured us all a glass of wine.

"A soda or something for me, if you don't mind," Kestrel said, laying a hand on her still flat stomach.

"Ahhhh, congratulations!" Manny declared, and we all laughed and smiled. He did go fetch her a soda. When he came back, he handed Dahlia a piece of paper. She passed it around.

Leave your empty cases where they are, it will take them all. I will spend the night loading them with everything and help you out with them in the morning.

You have no idea what this means to me. I hope your men feel the same.

It worried me that he worried for us, and we all traded looks.

"I know we all said we would keep our phones turned off for this girls' weekend," Aspen said nervously. "But you don't even know how much I want to check my text messages."

Dahlia laughed and said, "We all agreed! No cheating."

"No cheating," Marisol said and held out her wineglass.

"I'm with Aspen, but I agree. This weekend is all about Kestrel and our phones can wait."

"So," Raven said with a wink. "Something old, something new, something borrowed, something blue... Ideas?"

"I think a trip to the antique stores around here is in order," I said. "We could conceivably take care of all of those things with one purchase."

"Wait, how can you take care of all of those things with one buy?" Aspen asked laughing.

"Well, if I buy something old from the antique shop that is blue, it's new to me, and then I lend it to Kestrel for her wedding..."

"That feels like cheating," Marisol said with a laugh.

"That sounds like a damn fine loophole," Dahlia said also laughing. With as much as our nerves buzzed with anxiety, we threw ourselves into planning the wedding of Kestrel's dreams, asking questions and figuring out colors, daydreaming and talking venues all of which was a bit trying for Kestrel, Aspen, and I... all having been married once before and *yikes* betrayed by those men. As Marc would say, all three of our ex-husbands needed to be *yeeted* into the sun...

For me and Kestrel, that sort of had already happened, for Aspen, she still had to deal with her ex from time to time, which surprised Dahlia and Marisol, both of them seemingly having a deeper grasp of Fenris than even Aspen. Although they didn't outright say anything, I saw the traded looks and caught the whispered exchanges when behind or away from Aspen.

I didn't know if I liked that. It bothered me, maybe even triggered me to a degree, given my own past.

I reserved judgment for now, but it bothered me deep down. I liked Aspen; I liked her a lot. She and I had a lot in common to the point we were rooming together for this trip.

It was when we shut the door to that room, we both let out pent-up breaths we didn't know we'd been holding. We looked at each other and laughed nervously.

"Do you really think they're out there listening?" she asked carefully, almost whispering.

I shook my head. "Watching, maybe, but it's still probably a good idea to just not talk just in case."

She nodded and sighed. "When I got together with my man, I made the decision to accept him but at the same time, I also made the decision that I just didn't want to know, you know?"

I smiled, the final piece falling into place and relief flooding me. Dahlia and Marisol weren't talking behind Aspen's back – they were respecting her wishes.

That was a big weight off my shoulders.

"I mean, the men don't involve us anyway, but Mar and Dahlia are right – *you always know*. Things overheard, and it's our part enough to remain ignorant. Sometimes that's hard, you know?"

I nodded and said, "I hate it. After what happened with Ben, you know? I feel like I would rather know... you know?"

She sat down on the edge of her bed and nodded.

"We're different in that regard, I guess. I feel like ignorance is bliss. I mean, look at us right now!" she kept her voice low, and I nodded and smiled.

"Hopefully this is a onetime deal."

"Think they're going to be mad?" she asked and winced slightly.

"Probably." I nodded and sighed. "But they're just going to have to get over it."

"I hope this works," she breathed, and I nodded.

"Me too." I mean, I would be lying if I said I wasn't scared. While I felt as though I had lost everything when it had come to Ben and finding out the truth, nothing could honestly be further from the truth, you know? I had so much more to lose. So much.

I cheated. I turned on my phone while Aspen was in the bathroom to check for messages from Marc. He had checked in like he was supposed to, and I texted him back really quick, but it was the text from Jared that worried me.

Jared: Just what the fuck are you playing at? We're talking as soon as you get your ass back here.

Well, I guess that answered the question of if the boys were mad or not.

I sighed, an all-new set of worries gnawing at my gut.

I pursed my lips and turned off my phone, stashing it back in my purse before Aspen returned.

I don't think I slept a wink that night and honestly? I wasn't a teen or in my twenties anymore. Driving home was going to be brutal.

THE NEXT MORNING, our bags were packed and waiting. They were heavy, but not overly so, and we were changed and ready to go.

Manny served us breakfast, as this *was* a bed-and-breakfast, and my stomach really wasn't having any of it. I ate, but I was so nervous I think it went right through me. I ended up in the bathroom a couple of times before we left. Thankfully, everything stayed *down*, I just wished it didn't decide to stay so down that *out* followed.

Curse my nervous bowels, I thought as I came out of the bathroom for the second time.

"You alright?" Kestrel asked nervously, and I nodded and smiled.

"Just my body acting up," I said embarrassed.

"Happens to the best of us," Raven declared, bringing up the handle on one of the rolling carryons.

We'd made a great show of discussing and oohing and ahhing over fictional dresses the night before and discussing Dahlia's hookup at the bridal store, making it seem like we had been trying on different styles of bridesmaids dresses the night before and complaining about every sample dress size being an unrealistic diminutive size for us real women.

It felt ridiculous, but the wine had helped smooth the way, and if we got out of here without incident and without being stopped on the way south, it would have been worth it.

Aspen and I traded looks and I think both of us were sweating. We had discussed what we had discussed the night before and now? This morning? Back in the company of Dahlia and Marisol and the rest, it felt like a bit of a folly.

Please let me be right and let no one have been listening, I prayed as Manny shut the back hatch of my SUV with the majority of the drugs inside and held out his hand beaming.

"It was a pleasure having you ladies at the Smuggler's Inn," he said, and Kestrel hugged him.

"I am *absolutely* going to suggest it to my fiancé as a honeymoon destination," she said. "Thank you so much!"

"Of course, my dear. I hope you choose us," he said, beaming up at the old mansion.

"God, I'm going to miss you!" Dahlia declared hugging me tight. I laughed, a little startled, and played it up, hugging first her and then Marisol. I said, "We'll see each other before you know it!"

We all exchanged hugs like girlfriends saying a longer-than-average goodbye, even though we were heading pretty much right back down to my place.

I white knuckled that *entire* drive back south to my house, glancing in my rearview every couple of miles, looking for state patrol behind me, or county sheriff's office. *Or worse, an unmarked black SUV with government plates,* I thought to myself more than once.

I wasn't the only one.

Kestrel, Raven, and Aspen were just as subdued, just as nervous.

When we crossed back into King County with still over an hour to go until home, Raven let out a pent-up breath and said, "This is a onetime deal. I swear to God. I deal with enough adrenaline where these guys are concerned, I really don't need to add to it."

"What's that supposed to mean?" I asked, a little alarmed.

"In for a penny, in for a pound," Aspen said shrugging, and looking unhappy beside me in the passenger seat.

"We try to respect it when someone says they don't want to know," Raven said leaning forward. "But since Aspen has all but given me the go-ahead, I serve as the club's de facto doctor or medical personnel. Little things like patching them up when they get in a scrap."

Kestrel snorted. "More than little things," she said. "She saved Tic a couple years ago when he got stabbed by some idiot cranked up to the nth degree."

"What?" I asked alarmed, thinking about Jared.

"It only happened once," Raven said, rolling her eyes.

I glanced at Aspen who looked like I felt, nervous and worried; likely thinking about Fenris.

"Okay, let's not talk about anymore," I said, letting out a deep cleansing breath, my hands making an almost ratcheting sound as I gripped the wheel and nervously twisted it in my hands as though it was the throttle on one of the men's bikes. As though it would or could make the car go faster, even though I kept the speed steady at just a couple of miles per hour over the speed limit.

Dahlia had cautioned me not to go so fast as to get myself pulled over, but likewise she had cautioned against going exactly the speed limit or under it by any margin as that was almost *more* suspicious.

She'd also cautioned me that if we *were* pulled over to be polite, *'yes officer, no officer, I'm sorry officer,'* and what to do or say if they wanted to search the car which she said wasn't likely *at all*.

"If it goes that far," she said, *"They already know. You keep your mouth shut and if they ask you anything, the answer is 'I don't answer questions' or 'I want my lawyer.'"*

It hadn't been comforting, and my mouth was dryer than the Sahara as I pulled down the alley that ran behind my house, my heart sinking at the shiny black and chrome motorcycle parked at the end of that alley, and the stormy look Jared cast in my direction as he turned a wrench in the guts of what was his engine.

I wasn't sure what he was doing, but from his text last night? I knew why he was here.

"Shit," Raven muttered.

"We won't leave unless you want us to," Aspen said, and I pursed my lips. I pulled onto my back lawn off to the side of my driveway so Aspen could back out and take the rest of the girls.

"Just get this stuff into the storage unit and let me handle him," I said, and Raven nodded in my rearview grimly.

"Okay," Kestrel said faintly, and she sounded scared for me. I handed Aspen the key to the unit and taking a deep breath, I tried not to be scared too.

lass Jaw...
I kept going back and forth between being fucking *furious* at her and scared fucking *shitless* for her.

All the while, the same fucking question rattled around in my brain, *why? Why, why, why, why, why?* Why would she do this, *how* could she do this? She had her whole life, she had Marc, why would she take this kind of risk for *me?*

She got out of the car, and I stared down the drive with a baleful look as she turned in my direction. The other girls she had with her bailed out of the car and four sets of eyes fixed on me. They were all frozen like rabbits, but they had their own men to deal with.

I didn't envy Maverick. He had *two* women to put in their place between his best friend, Dahlia, and his woman Marisol. Dahlia I wasn't so worried about. She knew what this criminal enterprise shit was about. It wasn't advertised, but she'd grown up some kind of mafia princess. That's how she and Mav knew each other. Their respective crime families had some kind of a thing. An unholy fucking union between the Russians or Ukrainians or whatever the fuck Maverick was and Dahlia's Italian side.

Marisol and Dahlia pulled up and turned into the driveway behind Aspen's car and I pulled out my phone.

"Yeah?" Maverick growled into the phone.

"They're all here," I said.

"Tell Marisol and Dahlia to get their asses to the club," he said. "Let the boys deal with the rest of their women until we can all get together and figure it out."

"Copy that," I said and hung up. Dahlia got out of the driver's side of her car and cocked a hip, hand on it, eyebrow raised.

"Narcing us out?" she asked coolly.

"You know where my loyalty lies," I growled.

"Hmph, swear you got Mav's dick so far up your ass his voice just came out of your mouth," she declared, and everyone was frozen, staring at her, mouths agape.

"You're already on thin ice, *Princess*," I spat at her. "Disrespecting me is the definition of *'fuck around and find out'* at this point."

She rolled her eyes and turned.

"Let's get this shit unloaded, shall we?" she asked sweetly.

The back door popped open, and Cadence turned. "Marc, go back in the house," she said sharply.

"Whoa, nice to see you too, Mom," he said, holding his hands up as though in surrender.

"Back in the house!" she gritted out between her teeth and her kid was just like her, stubborn and didn't know when to quit.

"Fine!" he snapped, rolling his eyes and slamming the door behind him.

"Go," Cadence said to the rest of the women, and they started pulling out and handing suitcases down the line old-fashioned fire-brigade style, rolling them into the darkened pit of her storage unit.

She stalked across the grass toward me, and I seethed, Dahlia having gotten me properly riled up.

I was so fucking angry, and the defiance in her eyes was so fucking hot, I couldn't decide if I wanted to punch something or... yeah, the boner stirring in my pants told me just what I was going to do, the minute we were alone which fuck if I knew when that was going to be.

"You can't answer your fucking phone?" I demanded.

"I had it off," I said. "I only turned it on long enough to get the check-in texts from Marc, but I saw yours."

I got right up in her face and said under my breath just loud enough for her to hear, "I don't know whether to fuck you or kill you."

"You needed the help," she said, and her eyes were flinty, the green sparking like fireworks in the sky. I wasn't about to tread carefully.

"I didn't fuckin' *ask* you. *None of us did!*" I said lowly.

"You didn't *have to*," she fired back, stepping into me. "You needed the help and so did all of those *people*. We couldn't sit by and do nothing, so we did something! Now, you can take over and *get this shit out of my house and where it needs to go*, you ungrateful shit!"

She whirled away from me, and I snatched her arm and pulled her back. "What we do is *our* business, and fucking *none* of yours," I said savagely. "We go out of our way to keep you bitches *safe*."

"Bitches, huh?" she demanded, and I raised my eyebrows.

"When you act like this? *Yes.*"

"Go fuck yourself, *Glass Jaw,*" she said with derision. "It's all you're gonna get with that kind of disrespect."

The green fire of her eyes was extinguished by her hurt and I dropped my hand from her arm to rake it back through my hair.

"Fix whatever it is you need to fix on that thing and get the fuck out of my yard until you've had a think," she said, and I felt the corner of my mouth twitch.

Dahlia looked past my Cadence with a smirk in my direction and said, "Atta girl." Cadence went to her back door and opened it.

"Shut up," she said with disgust and slammed the door like her son had a moment before.

"What she said," I shot at Dahlia. "You and Marisol get your ass back to the club. Mav's there waiting on you. The rest of you, git on home. Your men are waiting on your asses too."

"Aye, aye, captain," Marisol said, rolling her eyes.

Fucking hell, it was a full-on mutiny!

I went back to work on changing my oil and a few minutes later, Marc came slamming out the back door looking pissed. He got his bike from where it was leaning against the back of the house and walked it past me.

"Save yourself, man," he said, rolling his eyes. "She's in a mood. Must be that time of the month or something."

"Hey," I said. "I know she's got you pissed off, but don't think you can disrespect your mom in front of me, again. I'm your friend, but I'm not one of your little bros. That's my woman you're talking about and disrespecting her ain't gonna fly."

Marc mounted his bike and rolled his eyes. "Whatever!"

"Hey! Where you going? Your mom know?" I shouted at him.

"The park! I got my phone!"

"Alright!" I waved him off.

"Making friends wherever you go," Raven declared with a flat, unfriendly tone. I turned around and looked up from where I'd kneeled back down by my bike.

She held out Cadence's keys.

"She, like all of us, did this for *you*. Because we're all fucking scared to death of losing you. Remember that and try not to be an asshole more than necessary," she said.

"Take that shit up with your own ol' man. Pretty sure he's waitin' on you." I raised an eyebrow, and she rolled her eyes at me and *Jesus, fuck!* There was a lot of eye rolling going on around here and only one fucking teenager. Was that shit contagious or something?

She went back and caught a ride with Dahlia and Marisol, which made sense with her apartment's proximity to the club. Kestrel looked out the back window at me from the back of Dahlia's car as they left. Her catching a ride with them also making sense with her and D.T. being right there on the way to the club. She would likely be dropped off first.

That just left Aspen out here with me, looking on as the rest of her girl posse left, standing at the open door to her car. As soon as the other girls were out of sight, her eyes started to well.

She was cracking.

Shit.

"Better get home to Fen," I said tersely, and she sniffed and nodded mutely, dashing at the tears starting to slide down her face.

I knew how fucking crazy the fucking Viking could get but I also knew what a fucking soft spot he had for Aspen. She was going to be fine. He would never hurt her in a million years, and I already knew, that when it came to punishment for her, it was going to be whatever hell confrontation she dreamed up in her skull and tortured herself with all the way home.

I watched her pull out, her bottom lip trembling, tears spilling silently as she held her shit together as best she could. As soon as she was out of sight, I pulled out my phone and called Fen.

"Yeah?" he answered, and he sounded pissed.

"She's on her way, bro, and she's scared shitless. Maybe go easier on her than even you were thinking," I said. "I mean, far be it from me to tell you how to wrangle *your* woman, but she's seen how you can get and it's written all over her that she thinks she's going to bleed when she gets there."

There was silence on the other end of the line and then, the call just *ended*.

He'd heard me.

I gave it a minute, staring at the back door of Cadence's place, willing it to open, and when it didn't, hung my head and cursed softly as I dropped my wrench all over again, got the oil pan draining and heaved myself to my feet, wiping my hands on an already dirty shop rag.

I went in the back door, through the laundry area and found her in the kitchen. The microwave was going, something heating, and I stood by the fridge and glared daggers at her back where she stood at the counter, leaning heavily on it, hands pressed to the stone, shoulders hunched.

I was half-afraid that like Aspen, she was cracking, but no... not my girl. She turned around, the fire in her eyes banked but there was a righteously hot coal bed still burning in them.

"Your attitude change?" she demanded, and the rage was back in me, just like that. I dropped the rag, strode up to her and pressed her back into the counter roughly. She made a noise of protest, and I grabbed her face, hard, pinching her chin, between fingers and thumb, hand almost at her throat.

Gloves were fucking *off*.

I kissed her, *hard*, pressing my mouth against hers, thrusting my tongue in her mouth, past her teeth while she pushed fruitlessly against my chest in a bid to get me to stop. I finally tore my mouth from hers looked her in those gleaming emerald eyes of hers and told her the truth.

"You scared the fucking *shit* out of me!"

The fire in her eyes went out, and she froze. We stared in each other's eyes from mere inches away, her half bent backwards over the counter, hands dropped from my chest, fingers curling around the edge while she *stared* at me, speechless for the moment.

Her position thrust the front of her hips against mine and I knew she could feel my raging boner pressed as it was against her.

"Congratulations," she spat. "Now you know how *we* feel."

I felt my brow crush down and some of the fire left my blood.

"I've done the whole secrets and lies thing, Jared. I won't do it again. We either find a way to communicate better, or we can't do this anymore."

I dropped my hand from her face and took a step back, staring at her. She moved her jaw around and looked vaguely ill.

I shook my head.

"I will *never* hurt you," I said.

"That hurt," she said, putting a hand to her jaw and coming away with a bit of grease on her fingertips from her face. "*Nice*," she muttered.

"I'm sorry," I said. "I thought it was hot. You've got me all fired up and *fucked* up, Cadence. I wasn't lying, you scared the fucking shit out of me when you wouldn't answer my texts or my calls."

"My phone was off. Dahlia said it was for the best. Tracking and listening, and all of that."

I nodded mutely and finally said, "I should have thought of that, but I couldn't think straight. Baby, you can't ever do anything like this again, you don't even know—"

"Oh, trust me, I know," she said and shook her head as though trying to banish whatever thoughts that'd been chasing around in her skull away.

"Can I ask?" She looked at me and I met her eyes with mine. *"What were you thinking?"*

She almost shuddered and said, "That I didn't want to lose you. That those people you all help, that they needed the medicine… that I had a choice to make." Her eyes did well then and she looked away. "That I could do the *right* thing or that I could do the *legal* thing and guess which one I chose?" She turned back to me and dashed at one of her tears.

"I'm coming back," I said. "And I'm going to kiss you just as hard as I did a minute ago only this time I'm not going to stop until you're naked and screaming my name underneath me."

She stopped breathing, her gaze where it met mine fevered and luminous as she tremulously said, "Okay."

Consent given, I crashed back into her and kissed her fiercely, her hands going to my face to cup it, and pull me into her instead of pushing me away this time.

I had to concede, she wasn't right, I wasn't wrong, the situation was a total no-win for either side but *fuck*, these girls had no clue how much of a dangerous precedent they'd set with this shit.

They were playing with fire, and they didn't know what they were doing.

29

*C*adence...

Jared crashed into me, his mouth crushing over mine, shoving me back into the counter again. The microwave on my lunch had gone off a while ago while we'd been arguing, but it was all a distant memory, my hunger for food replaced with a hunger for *him* like I'd never felt before.

The fact that he was willing to fight with me, willing to argue, and was seemingly *desperate* to keep me safe and to keep me with him... *God*, I had been so desperate for so long for someone to just... just... *fight for me*. To want to be by my side and be with me to the point of desperation!

I felt that from him. In the way his hands moved over my clothes. In the way his body pressed against mine desperate to be near me, in the way he lifted me up, onto the edge of the counter and simultaneously pulled me to the edge, urging my legs around him.

I clung to him, kissing him back with every bit of fervent need, trying to tell him without words that *yes! I choose you! I want you and I want to be with you! I just need you to want me too!*

Tears wanted to leak from the corners of my eyes at how desperately afraid I had been that doing this whole thing to protect him and keep him out of jail... at how it might backfire and break us. At how I knew deep down it had the power to break all trust between us and how it had all but been a precarious thing, fragile, a new hope, from the very beginning where we were concerned.

Trust... as invisible and as fragile as a soap bubble on the wind. So precarious in its structure that to even look at it wrong, it could burst, winking out of existence.

"Don't let me go," I breathed in desperation against his mouth.

"Never," he growled back, and he pulled me against him tighter and demanded of me, "Hold on to me."

I clung to him desperately, locking my legs and arms around him and he lifted me off the counter with a slight grunt and strode past my dining room table and around the corner, past the bottom of Marc's stairs and turning sharply again, down the hall to my bedroom.

He kicked my door shut with an impatient growl and threw me down on the bed, pulling his stained and greasy light-gray tee over his head from the back like men do and that just drove me nuts, laying back like that, him standing over me, muscles moving beneath his skin, coiling and bunching powerfully as he wadded the tee up and cast it aside.

I sat up and he flung me back down onto my back with a shove of my shoulder. I blinked in surprise, and he shook his head, going for his belt, toeing out of his boots as he undid it and I nearly swallowed my tongue watching him.

Every movement was strapped, precise, and measured. It was like he was an explosive personality and the only thing keeping the wildness in check was his own ironclad will and resolve not to hurt me.

He stripped and stood looking down at me, cock erect, a darkness in his eyes, but also a deep longing as he cupped the heel of one of my boots. He lifted it, never breaking eye contact and almost lovingly lowered the zipper on the inside.

He was slow about undressing me, almost tender, and it wall all round alien and frightening – no, *thrilling* watching him do it.

I propped myself up slowly, carefully, to watch him work, and there was a sort of savage beauty to it all.

The fact this man could be so angry with me, scared for me, and yet treat me so carefully. It was honestly an aphrodisiac like no other.

I was wet, craving him like he was my perfect drug, and maybe? Maybe he was.

That thrill, that edge of danger every time we fucked, I had to confess it was like loving a tiger or something equally as dangerous. Always that one change in mood away from being shredded to pieces.

It was so fucking hot, and the fact that a man like Jared could want and love a woman like me... so plain, so *boring*... that was even hotter.

He stripped me naked and vulnerable and any time I tried to rise with any significance he would push me back down. His hand was gentle but firm where he grasped my ankle now, his lips soft as he planted them in a kiss against my shin. I watched him climb my body one kiss at a time, his hands massaging my legs, parting them so he could kneel between them. His gaze was weighted and smoothed over my skin with an almost physical touch of its own.

He pulled me bodily down the bed a short distance, his cock thrusting up against my wet and waiting pussy, but not penetrating. Wrong angle. Still, he slid himself against my pussy lips, dry humping – if you could call it that – because I was so fucking wet and ready for him. I made a small mewling noise in my throat that I could hardly believe came from me, but I was prepared to beg him if he willed it.

He looked down at me, his eyes hooded with a combination of love and lust as he teased me, his thumb finding that bundle of nerves, slicking through my wetness and teasing me to greater heights but while it was nice, it wasn't what I *needed*. I needed him... I needed him to fill me, to go so impossibly deep I rode that edge between pleasure and pain.

"Jared, *please*," I begged, gasping, breathless with my desire and my desperation for him. He stared down at me, face imperious, unreadable, and he would not be swayed. He smoothed hands up my body, rocking against my pussy with his hips, sliding his hot, thick cock up and down my wet and waiting slit, pinching my nipples between forefingers and thumb, rolling them, causing such exquisite sensation, as he angled his cock to take over rubbing my clit where his thumb had been before.

It was kinky, it was bizarre, *why didn't he just fuck me?* But he would not be swayed, he just silently kept at it, relentless, forcing me closer and closer to the edge of that precipice without giving me the satisfaction of having him inside me which I so craved.

I bit my bottom lip, whimpering, moaning, close, so close, so *maddeningly* close; drawn fluttering a moth to a flame, captivated by the light and *wanting* to burn but with too much fear to venture that much closer to the flame and certain death by the incinerating heat and then all at once, it happened.

He smiled, wickedly, almost cruelly down at me and it was that final push I needed. I arched, shoving my pussy against him, and jolted; shuddering, as the orgasm he teased from me, *forced* out of me, consumed me.

It was all-consuming, too, and with a grunt of savage triumph, as my body rippled and convulsed with that white hot sensation that seemingly disrupted every electrical signal, plunging all muscle movement into chaos, he shoved himself inside of me. Thickly, roughly, completely, and I came all over again. The intensity of the new orgasm out of this world, overlapping the first, plunging me into a stream of wild colorful chaos as he slammed in and out of me, pinning my wrists to either side of me to keep me from flailing, to keep me from scratching as he pushed me way beyond my limits and left me a screaming, squalling, jerking mess beneath him.

He fucked me so hard, so fast, so thoroughly, I didn't think it was going to be possible to ever be the same woman I had been before this encounter.

With the way he fucked me, pouring every bit of savage, wild love into me; I honestly thought that this was it… this was how I was going to be somehow reborn. Stronger, surer of myself than I had ever been. Because if I could bring a man like this to his knees between my thighs? Surely, I was an all-powerful being.

Jared made me feel transcendent; an all-powerful goddess wearing a mere mortal skin. He made me love the skin I was in, just by virtue of the fact that he loved it, loved *me* for who I was.

30

*G*lass Jaw...

She was luminous, beautiful, and I had a penchant for loving to break beautiful things and make them whole again. From gutting a house and building it back better than before, to taking apart and restoring old hulks of cars and bikes. I fucking *loved* making that mess then cleaning it up.

It gave my little boy's heart a savage glee, like ripping the wings off a fly only putting them back better than before. She was like that now, whimpering, begging, nearly broken beneath me as I teased her slowly.

She took longer to break than I thought she would, and I delighted in every second of watching it happen. Then, when she finally did? I doubled down, pressed my way into her throbbing, tight, achingly wet pussy and I thrust so hard and fast I damn near broke myself.

Her?

I absolutely fucking destroyed her, pressing her past the point of exquisite anguish into a beautifully devastated *agony* that said a few more times bottoming out against her cervix, and I would have gone too far.

I liked to break things – but not to the point past fixing. That was a drag.

She was anything but a drag.

Fuck, she felt so good. So hot, so slick, so beautiful as she gripped the sheets once I could trust enough to let her go and that she wouldn't savage me with her nails.

Her voice was like a benediction, spilling from her lips in fevered and feral chanting, at first 'yes' then 'fuck yes' then just my name, over and over, and over again.

She blessed me, goddess to my god, and made me an all-powerful being with her supplication for whatever I was willing to bestow on her.

I took her to that sacred space where pleasure and pain were one and the same and the tighter she gripped my cock with that tight little pussy of hers, the closer she brought me to the stars until they starting going off behind my eyelids and covered my vision even when my eyes were open and my balls drained inside of her the likes I had never felt before – and I knew, I just knew, I would be chasing *that* particular high like a fuckin' unicorn for the rest of my days and if I were ever to find it again?

It would only be with her.

There wouldn't, *couldn't*, be anyone else.

I collapsed over her, smoothing her hair back from her face, my lips finding hers and kissing her deeply, possessively as I murmured against her mouth, "Good girl, that's my good fucking girl."

I felt something slick against my fingertips and pulled back, rubbing them at her temple, through the tears there as she broke emotionally – no, *crashed* – the adrenaline and fear, and all of that anxiety letting loose all at once. I gathered her close and did what any man should do when his woman cried, choosing to be vulnerable in his presence.

I held her close, kissed her tears away, and did my best to soothe the pain.

∿

WE WERE LYING TOGETHER, her emotional storm subsided, basking under the rainbow of our mutual afterglow when we heard the back door open, the alarm system belting out its chime that a door had been opened. We heard the door shut and a moment later, Marc pounding up his set of stairs.

Cadence sighed and made to pull out of my arms from where she was laying against my chest, and I tightened my grip on her hand and around her body.

"No, not yet," I said, and she rested against me. It didn't take much arm twisting.

"I don't want him to think I'm mad at him," she said gently. "And I owe him an apology for snapping."

"It'll keep, babe... just give me a little bit longer," I said and pressed lips to her forehead. She melted into my side, and I smiled even though it wasn't a full forced kind of a thing. No, it was watered down by worry and tinged a little with regret.

I worried about the position that she put herself in, because of me; and I worried about what it meant to stay with me. I'd never been with a woman in such a way that it shook my foundation this much. I had never, *ever* been in a position like I was now that my loyalty to the club was in question – and that was the position I found myself in now.

Holding this beautiful, fierce, brave and wonderful creature in my arms. I found myself questioning whether I should maintain a future with my brothers or whether I should consider giving it up... and *fuck* that was heavy. The heaviest burden I'd ever have to bear because I really wasn't sure if I could have my cake and eat it, too here.

"What are you thinking about so hard?" she asked me, and her voice shook, as though she were afraid to ask.

"Fuck," I said. "I don't know."

She pushed herself up, resting her chin on the back of her hand which rested on my chest. Fixing me with those hallowed green eyes as she said plaintively, "Liar."

I smirked and played with her hair, brushing it off her forehead, chasing it behind her ear, committing her face to memory in case I bet the farm and lost it all.

"I guess it's time for some kind of reckoning between you and me," I said softly and her slightly playful expression fell off her face, replaced with the most serious look I had ever seen her give me.

"What do you mean?" she asked softly.

"I mean, I feel like I have to choose, and I've never felt like it's been higher stakes."

"Choose what, exactly?" she demanded and pushed off of me, into a sitting position. "Are you breaking up with me?"

I shook my head. "No. No, I can't do that... but I do feel like it's you or the club after what you pulled because, baby, I need you to fly free. If either of us is ever gonna get caged, it *has to be me*, because I don't think I could survive the guilt of you getting locked up and I know I wouldn't survive getting locked up without knowing you were out here and free and living life for the both of us."

"I did what I did because I don't want *either* of us getting locked up. I didn't want to lose you and I *don't* want to go back to being in a relationship where I'm alone all the time again. Do you understand? I love you, and this?" She swallowed convulsively, "This was a onetime deal,

Jared. I will *never* do anything like this again but…" she looked off into the distance, pensive and I waited her out.

"But?" I asked when the silence had drawn on too long.

"But those people, they depend on that medicine and… and I hate to sound like a giant nerd but it's *Kobayashi Maru.*"

"It's what?" I asked, brow wrinkling in confusion as her cheeks colored slightly.

"My dad was a huge, and I mean monumentally huge original *Star Trek* fan," she said.

"And?"

"And the *Kobayashi Maru* was a fictional training exercise they would put *Starfleet* cadets through. A simulation that was an absolute no-win scenario designed to test a cadet's character."

"Okay," I said. I wasn't following, but I was trying. "Spell it out for me."

"If I tell you to leave the club, to choose me, I am being *incredibly selfish*. Not just to you, but to all those people that not so secretly depend on you. I would be doing the world an incredible disservice to my own ends, and I won't do that."

"Okay," I said, nodding slowly.

"But I am not so *un*-selfish that I am willing to give you up, you understand?"

A bubble of hope was rising in the center of my chest.

"I get that, baby." I reached out and touched the side of her face.

"So, it's a no-win situation for me," she said, turning her face into my hand. "Because I won't give you up, and I absolutely don't expect you to give up the club or helping those people because I can't let you do that. I won't let you do that."

"Let me ask you something," I said, and she opened her eyes and looked at me. I pushed myself up into a sitting position and leaned back against the headboard. I cleared my throat and asked, "What do you need from me?"

"I just need to *know...*" she said, and the desperation was clear in her eyes and the set of her expression.

I was silent for a long fucking time as my thoughts whirled like a kaleidoscope in my head, flashes of 'what if' and 'what was' a myriad of 'what could be' scenarios chasing each other around in my brain; some good, some really, *really* bad.

"I need to know," I said. "I need you to absolutely fucking *swear to me*, that *anything* I share with you is between you and me and *no one* else. Not Marc, not any of the other ol' ladies. Not Marisol, not Little Bird, not Raven or Aspen, and definitely *not* Dahlia under any fucking circumstance."

She searched my face, and she was thinking about it and thinking about it hard.

"You *have to understand* the consequences if I were to be caught spilling club secrets to my woman – because that," I swallowed hard, "that's a level of betrayal that *will* get me killed, and rightfully fucking so. My brothers can *never know*."

She took a deep breath and let it out slowly.

"Meet me halfway," she said finally.

I cocked my head to the side, and she twined her fingers with mine. I gave her hand a squeeze to indicate I was listening.

"Don't tell me anything that could or would get me in trouble. Keep the dirty details under wraps, but don't *ever* lie to me about how deep the shit is… *please.*"

Relief flooded my system.

"That's easy as fuck," I growled, hooking a hand behind her neck and dragging her mouth to mine. She kissed me back, fiercely, and I clutched her to me.

"I want to make this work, so badly," she whispered.

"Me too. You don't know how much."

"So, let's do that," she said. "Be my partner. Let me be your equal. Same team, always."

"I want that," I said. "You don't know how much."

"I think I do," she whispered. "I think we've both been desperate for the same thing for a long time."

"I know that's right," I said and held her close. She folded against my body so wonderfully, so sweetly, and it was perfect.

"I love you," she said. "And I don't want to fight anymore."

"I love you, too, and as much as I love a good fight, I'd rather do it with you by my side than as my opponent."

She snuggled in close. "So we're on the same page?" she asked.

"Chapter and verse," I agreed. "Chapter and verse."

31

*C*adence...

Maverick, Blackjack, Cipher, and Deacon showed up to my place late. After Marc was asleep, and with Jared at my side.

Blackjack and Deacon were in a pickup truck, Maverick and Cipher riding out in front of it like some kind of forward guard – except there wasn't anything valuable in it yet. No, the drugs (and I hated how awful that sounded to say it even if it was just in my head) were in my outdoor storage unit off my back patio.

I had talked with Marc, who was choosing to remain angry at the fact I had snapped at him for now, while Jared had gone out to finish the oil change on his motorcycle, getting it up and running so he could help the men coming move the prescriptions to a more secure location.

I didn't want to know. It was just enough that I knew, and he wasn't hiding anything from me anymore.

Maverick got off his bike as I stood, arms crossed and maybe a little defiant looking, but as he raked me with those dark indigo eyes of his I tried valiantly not to shrink.

"I'm sure Glass Jaw informed you as to why this was a monumentally *stupid* fucking idea on your part," he said by way of greeting. "So, I won't beat a dead horse."

"Appreciate it," I said clipped, but with no hint of sarcasm, just a tired relief.

Jared had indeed explained why the optics of our particular stunt were bad within inter-chapter and club politics. I swallowed hard and turned sideways as the men passed me by and went into the storage unit, flipping on the light.

"Holy shit," Cipher declared.

"Manny said the insulin was good for forty-eight hours packed like it is," I said and Blackjack just sort of stared at me like I'd done something interesting.

"Why do this?" Deacon asked. "You have a son, a house, a career..."

"And some people have none of those things," I said with a raised eyebrow. "They need those medications. All I did was flex some of my privilege to get those drugs *out* without a second glance. I didn't mean to step out of bounds, but Dahlia was right – it was better to beg forgiveness than ask permission and for once in my life, I have more than just my son, who is about to be a man and out on his own, to hold on to."

I fixed Jared with a look.

"I love Marc more than life itself, I'm his mother, but he's destined for a lot more than just being my kid and when the nest is empty... well, I found my other half and I wasn't willing to let him go. So, I did this for a lot of reasons, not all of them altruistic, not all of them selfish."

"*Kobayashi Maru*," he said.

"*Kobayashi Maru*," I affirmed.

Deacon raised his eyebrows. "Huh, I get that reference."

"Okay, Captain America Meme, get over here and let's roll. I don't want to be out here all night," Maverick declared, but he was looking at me with something like respect.

"They didn't throw you under the bus, per se, but informationally, Dahlia and Marisol let me know that most of this idea was yours. That true?" he asked me.

I raised my chin; I would take the heat. Perhaps if I did, I would get off easier under the guise of being the new girl.

"Yeah," I said. "It was my idea."

He nodded, raised an eyebrow, and tilted his head, mouth turning down in an expression of being impressed.

"I owe you without owing you," he said finally. "As much as I hate it, you girls out played us and saved our asses with this. Manny's place was raided a few hours ago. They didn't find shit."

Jared and I exchanged looks.

"Manny okay?" he asked.

"Yep, they didn't find shit and their whole case fell apart. They're stalled, and they ain't got nowhere to go from here."

"Except we're stalled too," Blackjack said grimly. "This is all there's going to be for a while."

Maverick nodded. "Manny's place is burned, for sure, but there are a couple other places under consideration. May take some time to re-org, but we can't stop what we're doing."

"Too many people depend on it," I said softly, and he nodded.

"And so it goes," he agreed.

"Well," I said with a slow nod. "This was the last part I was willing to play. You all are on your own from now on. I don't want to know it, see it, hear it, smell it – this was enough for me."

"That's just the way we like to keep it," Maverick said. "You girls pull a stunt like this ever again, there will be consequences and I would hate to mete them out. That ain't me – don't make me do it." He stared me down and his gaze was colder than I would imagine the outer reaches of space to be. It chilled me right to the bone, and I had to admit, he had *look terrifying* down pat.

"I don't want to fuck around and find out," I said softly.

"See that you don't."

"A more curious girl would ask," Cipher said, and I looked at him.

"Oh, I'm plenty curious," I said. "But I'm not asking. Sometimes the horror is best left to the imagination and sometimes, like I think this time, it's best left kept in the dark because I am sure whatever it is? It's worse than the things my sheltered mind could conjure up."

"Let's put it this way," Blackjack declared. "Feel free to fuck up this hard again. Pretty sure all the rest of us who aren't Glass would really like that."

I blanched.

"I catch your meaning loud and clear," I said through a throat gone tight with fear.

"The fuck, Blackie?" Jared scowled in his direction.

"Give him his one 'get out of jail free' card on that one," Mav ordered Jared with a hand on his chest and pushing him back. "That's not coming from me as your brother." He gave Jared a warning look.

"It's cool, Mav," Blackjack said. "For the record, we all like you, Cadence. We don't want to see anything happen to you, but as much as the citizenry loves to declare us a pack of animals – we aren't. We follow the rules, it's just a different set of rules. Animals have none."

"What he's trying to say," Deacon said gently, "Is that we want things to be clear. If you know the rules and the consequences, the likelihood of anymore transgressions is greatly reduced."

"What he said." Cipher lifted a carryon into the back of the truck, braced a boot against the back tire and heaved himself up and into the bed. "No mystery, nothing to decipher. You fuck up again, we fuck you – end of."

I paled, swallowed hard, and met Jared's eyes. His read that we would talk later. I nodded barely, imperceptibly and said nothing more while the guys loaded the back of the truck.

They finished, put a tarp over it all, and strapped it down with bungee cords.

Mav stood beside me watching the men do it, "Like I said," he murmured under his breath. "I owe you, but don't ever make me or Glass look weak again or like we can't control our women."

"I understand," I said softly. "I'm sorry not sorry."

"*Kobayashi Maru,*" he said. "I used to watch *Star Trek* as a kid too." I nodded, and he called out softly, "Saddle up boys, let's roll out. Glass, you're with me."

Jared nodded, came to me, and gave me a swift kiss goodbye.

"Lock up and set the alarm," he ordered, and I nodded.

It was a sleepless night without him.

"Are you okay?" I asked immediately upon answering the phone the next morning.

"Yeah, yeah! I'm good, question is are *you* okay?" Jared asked me.

"Yeah, I'm alright," I said and let out a breath I hadn't known I'd been holding.

"Guys were a little intense last night, I wanted to make sure you were good."

"Does that mean they didn't mean it and they were just trying to scare me?" I asked.

"No," he said with a sigh. "It means they meant every word of it and there wouldn't be a damn thing I could do to stop them because my ass would probably be beat to a fuckin' pulp – but babe, ain't ever gonna happen because you said it yourself this was the last time you were going to ever get this heavy."

I sighed. "I suppose. I mean, this is always how it starts in my true crime world podcasts. Girl falls for bad boy, will do anything for bad boy then eventually dies by bad boy's hand or the hands of bad boy and his friends."

"You want me to fuck off, I'll fuck off. You just say the word."

He was dead serious.

"It would be kind of ludicrous to do all of this to keep you only to turn around and tell you to fuck off now," I said with a wan smile.

"Yeah, well, I would understand," he said. "It wouldn't make me any kind of happy, but I would understand."

"*Kobayashi Maru,*" I said unhappily.

"To an extent," he said with a sigh. "But I promise you, it's not always this intense, or like this… this was just a rough patch in the road and you girls, as much as I don't want to encourage what you did, you kept all of us from eating asphalt and for that? Even though a bunch of these dipshits would never say it, we're all grateful baby and we all love you for it. Me more than anyone."

"I love you too," I said softly.

"Want me to come over tonight?" he asked.

"Please."

"You got it… how was Marc this morning?" he asked, and I smiled at that.

"He's good, we talked it out and I apologized again, and he cut me some slack," I said.

"He's a good kid."

"The best kid, I don't deserve either of you," I said.

Jared snorted on the other end of the line. "Now that's pure bullshit. We don't deserve *you*."

"Agree to disagree," I said.

"Babe, I gotta go. I'll see you tonight."

"I'll see you tonight," I agreed and hung up the phone with a sigh.

"Well," I said to the thin air of my office. "I survived his crazy-ass family. Let's see if he can survive mine."

BY THE TIME SUNDAY ARRIVED, things between Jared and I were much lighter as we started walking the path into our new normal together. Likewise, things with the club seemed to be good – which I sort of marveled at. I thought for sure more of the guys, especially the unattached ones, would be more hostile but nope.

I didn't understand that but held my tongue until *after* the party on Friday night and asked Jared when we were alone.

He'd simply shrugged and said, "That was squashed last Sunday. It's been handled, done and dusted. We don't hang onto shit if we can help it. Life is too short."

"Just like that?" I asked.

"Just like that," he'd answered and then he'd kissed me, rolled me onto my back and had pretty much dicked me down until I didn't have a single coherent thought left in my head.

I was good with that.

Now I had my hands wrapped around the steering wheel in a white knuckled grip to rival the one from the week before coming home from the Smuggler's Inn.

The weather was uncharacteristically sunny and bright on the drive to Gig Harbor and my mother and stepfather's house. The light filtering through the trees, dappled and beautiful on the final winding approach to their waterfront home.

Jared sat beside me, his jacket and cut across his knees, Marc behind me, head bopping to whatever music he had pumping through his headphones and with every mile put beneath my car's tires, my heart climbed further into my throat.

"You steady?" Jared asked softly at my side, and I nodded.

"Just remember, my mom can be super judgmental and doesn't always think before she speaks. Um, she also cares a lot about what other people think."

"Your call, babe. Do I go as myself or do I play to her finer sensibilities?" I blinked and looked over at him and he exclaimed, "Hey!" and put his hand on the wheel to keep us from crashing.

The swerve was enough to drag Marc out of his teenage wasteland back there and ask, "What was that?"

"Jared, shocking the shit out of me," I said a little more sharply than I intended. "Sorry! Sorry... you okay?" I asked. "Is everyone okay?"

Marc laughed. "Yeah we're fine, just breathe, Mom, okay?"

"She always get like this?" Jared asked.

"It's Grandma," he said jovially, "No one gets to Mom harder."

"I was a pure daddy's girl growing up," I said.

"There's a reason for that," Marc declared. "Grandma's... extra."

"Right, so play acting it is," Jared said easily.

"No! God no – no lies, no obfuscations, I'm a thirty-four-year-old, strong, capable woman. I can handle my mother," I grumbled the last under my breath.

"Damn straight you are," Jared said, squeezing my knee. "You can handle anything," he gave me a sidelong look reminding me with his eyes what I had only just done last week.

When I was sure Marc's headphones were back on and he was oblivious, I muttered for Jared's ears only, "You act like outsmarting several government agencies is like, *hard*."

He laughed at me then and dragged one of my hands off the wheel to wrap it up in his own.

"God, I fuckin' love you," he said.

"I love you, too... but this bitch is worse than the FBI – she's my *mom*."

He chuckled again at that, and a smile dragged at the corners of my mouth, my mood lightening some.

The hardest part about being a daughter to my mother was that I honestly wanted nothing more than her approval and it honestly felt like no matter what I did or how many accomplishments I achieved to impress her, I was always and forever deeply lacking somehow or some way.

It was exhausting, but for some reason? I just couldn't bring myself to not care anymore... her approval was just that fucking carrot on a stick for me and I didn't know why.

Maybe it was because daddy, who was always quick with his approval and to shower me with affection, was gone. She was the only parent I had left... and if I thought she was rough to get along with, my step-dad? Yeesh... he just had this knack for saying things meant in jest that just absolutely cut to the quick – but God forbid you say anything about it.

The man could do no wrong in my mother's eyes, and she was quick to side with him every time and point out that I was "just too sensitive."

Ugh... I hated putting myself through this but again, she was the only parent I had left and while she wasn't Marc's only grandmother, he was her only grandson.

Guilt swirled in my veins that Marc wouldn't see Ben's parents. It broke their hearts, but I respected his decision there even if I didn't agree with it, and I was bitterly certain their whole bevy of new grandchildren were keeping them occupied for the time being. I mean, we were back in their state, and we hadn't heard from them yet so...

"Here we go..." I muttered under my breath as I made the turn into my parent's driveway and Jared pitched a low whistle, impressed by the architecture.

"Like it?" I asked.

"Fuck yeah, I do."

"Cool," I said, pulling up in front of the house and putting it into 'park.' "Because I designed it."

Of course, my mother hadn't thought that. She wanted *Ben* to design her house since he was the more 'prestigious' but Ben was always and forever 'too busy' to the point he'd told me to do it and just put his name on it.

"Yeah," Marc said with derision. "Too bad *Dad* got all the credit."

I sighed when he used 'dad' like it was a dirty word.

"Not a word to my mother. She loves this house and doesn't know."

"That—" Jared just stopped and stared at me. "That just blows my fucking mind," he said.

"What? That she wanted my husband to design her house and not me?" I asked.

"That and the fact that he wouldn't do it. It's like the high-rolling rich white people's version of having to wrap your own Christmas presents or some shit. I mean, holy fuck."

"That's Grandma," Marc said, plastering on a fake smile and opening his back door as my mother came out the front of her house arms out, hands making a grabby gesture.

"Ohhhh! Oh, oh, oh!" she called laughing and excited. "My boy, my boy, my boy!" She grabbed Marc in one of her oppressive hugs.

"You look like your dad," Jared observed before getting out of the car and I snorted a laugh putting on my smile to please mom and getting out myself.

It's showtime, I thought as he swung into his jacket and cut but my mom was distracted right now, coming around to hug me and scold me at the same time for taking so long to bring Marc to see her... which she and my stepdad, Roger, had been in Europe when we got here soooo, yeah.

"You were in Europe!" I exclaimed, half to defend myself and half because I was stubborn enough to not make it my fault.

My mom turned and took in Jared, standing casually with his hands in his jeans pockets and my mother blinked taking him in. She didn't linger on the vest and it's faded and worn patches but she did lean back and ask, "And who is this? Cadence, why haven't you introduced us?"

I fought not to roll my eyes and Marc saved me by saying, "Grandma, that's Jared. Jared, this is my grandma, Maeve."

"Well, *hello*, Jared!"

Jared laughed. "Nice to meet you, Ma'am."

"Oh, ma'am! I like that," my mother laughed, and I went around the car to where Jared held out his hand to me. I took it, and he tucked me into his side. "Well come on in!" my mother cried, and she strode inside, her big floppy sun hat only outdone by her long white linen wide leg pants and matching long jacket. She looked like she was meant for strolling along some European veranda, but she also fit right in here, with her house of the many windows overlooking the bay.

I sighed and tried not to think about that too hard and let Marc lead the way, bringing up the rear reluctantly, hand in hand with Jared, my rock.

My stepdad, looked up from the bar on the deck and the tray of mimosas he was preparing. *His* eyes went wide at Jared's vest and patches and his gaze immediately became disapproving.

"Roger, meet Cadence's Jared, honey."

"Hello!" my stepfather called, and he strode forward hand out to shake Jared's hand.

I was surprised, brunch wasn't going badly at all. No cutting remarks, no backhanded compliments, Roger who what the worst at it was actually on his best behavior. The real shocker is that my mother was on her best behavior, too.

"Do you mind if I use your restroom?" Jared asked, probably three quarters of the way through the meal.

"Of course, not!" Roger cried, pushing his glasses up on his hooked nose. "Marc, why don't you go show him where it's at."

Oh, fuck. Classic ploy, here we go, I thought to myself. My sweet kid, ever eager to help, stood to take Jared.

"Stay with him, Marc!" Roger called, and I choked on the sip of orange juice I was taking.

"Why, so he doesn't *steal* anything?" I hissed.

"Oh, *honestly,* Cadence!" my mother cried. "It's probably so he doesn't get *lost,* isn't that right, Roger?"

"Yes," Roger said defensively. "That's right."

I pinched the bridge of my nose and tried counting to ten knowing that any second...

"Honestly, you're always so negative, darling, and so *sensitive!* You really need to work on yourself. People won't like you if you're like that."

I breathed slowly in through my nose, held it for seven seconds, and let it out for a count of four. It was an anti-anxiety breathing exercise and I would *not* let these two get under my skin or inside my head this time. I loved them, they did things for me, often nice things, often expensive things, but I didn't like the fact that they always seemed to have their price and the price being, well, *this...*

We sat in silence for a moment and just as I was going to speak, just as I worked up the nerve, my mother perked up and cried, "Oh, look. They're back!"

"Yep, and just in case you were wondering, I didn't steal anything," Jared declared, pulling out his seat, and I sputtered a laugh.

Roger laughed and the look on my mother's face was priceless and had me and Marc trading looks, eyes wide and not wanting to make eye contact with anyone else at the table.

"Oh, it wasn't that," my mother tittered nervously.

"Sure, it was," Jared declared, not letting them skate, adjusting his jacket and vest with a sharp tug as he leaned back in his seat. "You took one look at my cut and had your minds made up about me the second I walked through the door. It's okay, really, I'm used to it. That's one of the things I love about your daughter so much. She met me before she saw my bike or my cut, granted, but she didn't judge me. Not for being a contractor in her basement, none of my crew, and not a single one of my brothers when she met them, either. Also, in case you were wondering, I own my own contracting company, easily clear six figures a year, and I don't need your money or belongings. I have plenty of each all on my own and live quite comfortably."

I stared at Jared speechless and then looked back at my mother and Roger who stared openmouthed.

"And on that note..." my son cracked.

I reached out and took Jared's hand and stared at my mother and said simply, "I know this is awkward right now, and that there's a very real possibility that you may not like Jared after what he just said, but, Mom, you'd better get used to him because I love him dearly and he loves me. He's going to be around for a while."

My mother looked taken aback and Marc was grinning from ear to ear and said, "I like him too, and honestly wish he was my real dad."

My mother looked horrified at that, and I looked to Jared.

"He's shown us what a real family looks like," I said.

He grinned at me and leaned over and kissed me and I smiled against his lips.

"Well," Roger said, and did something that surprised me. He raised his glass and declared, "I'll drink to that."

I smiled and Marc and Jared held up their glasses. I followed suit and my mother recovered and looked at me suitably impressed.

"I think we can all drink to that," I said.

And we did.

EPILOGUE

*F*ish...

It was still a little strange for me, sitting at the table looking around at all the guys and being counted among them. I'd been a brother for something like a year and a half, pushing two years, but it still didn't feel real. I still thought that I'd wake up and that it would all be a dream or some shit. I'd honestly never thought I would get this far, but here I was and some other poor sod was where I'd been what felt like only moments before... except where I was uncertain if I would make it, I was damn sure Dipshit wouldn't make the cut – I mean *damn* this dude was stupid and not in the he was just sort of green kind of way, either. He was just plain dumb.

Listening to D.T. and Rusty bitch about him was something else. Rusty, the old parts puller over at the boneyard, was downright disgusted and the way D.T. said it, even Little Bird with the patience of a damn saint couldn't even educate his dumb ass.

"Look on the bright side," Blackjack said from across the table, flicking some ash off the end of his joint into an ashtray like it was a cigarette... old habit, I guess. "Boy's so fucking dumb there's no way he's the law trying to infiltrate the big bad biker gang or some shit."

We were all a little half-baked and laughed probably a little too hard at that one.

Our major brush with the law hadn't been more than six months back. It was heading into a wet and cold winter out there, summer but the dust of fuckin' memory.

I rode year-round, so it was all Gore Tex and a can-do attitude. Hot showers and hot coffee to warm up.

With how it'd been pissing down rain for like the last week straight out there, I was feeling like I needed to bust out the goggles and the fuckin' water wings from my little adventure through that car wash like four or five summers back.

I said as much when one of the guys commented on the weather and left everyone in stitches.

"We gonna have to start naming every new recruit things like 'fish.'" Major said.

"Duck," Blackjack declared staring off into space, mellow in his high.

"Find a real mean motherfucker? Goose," Cipher declared to another round of laughter.

We'd wrapped up business a while ago and were just chilling, none of us in any real hurry to get out in the weather.

"Y'all are some fuckin' dumbass losers," Nine declared over something I'd missed. My mornings started at like four-thirty, and it'd been a long day of shoveling ice and slinging crates of frozen fish down at the market. I had barely had the time to get my ass home and shower, change my clothes, before making church.

"Right, well, it ain't getting any better out there." I sighed. "I'm going home and pass out."

"Pussy!" Tic called, laughing at me and I shook my head.

"Man, you try getting your ass up at four-thirty every day slinging fish and shoveling ice and shit."

I worked four twelves down at the market, and had Saturday, Sunday, and Monday off. Today was Friday. I usually powered through Saturday and Sunday with the boys and did nothing but fucking sleep and catch up on laundry on Mondays. It was a whole lot of rinse and repeat but that was just life, I guess.

I went out to my bike, the night dark, the air cold, the sky pissing rain in a steady fucking miserable non-stop drip to the point I think we'd all give our left nut for a break.

I took the tunnel, would pay the toll, just for the chance to be dry for a fuckin' minute as I headed north to my shitty old hotel room turned studio apartment up on hooker alley, aka Aurora Ave N. in North Seattle.

I was riding at a good clip, taking the curve near Green Lake when something orange and white tumbled out from the Jersey barriers in place and stumbled into the roadway. I knew a cat or kitten when I saw it, and this was a bad stretch. It was pretty calm this time of night, so I pulled off, jumping the curb and stopping on the side there in the soggy grass right beside the sidewalk, the deserted Green Lake looping trail below to my right.

I waited for a couple cages to pass, a truck, the kitten struggling not to get hit, and finally as soon as there was an opening, I darted out and snatched the little guy up – barely getting my ass back to safety without getting taken out myself. Fuckin' crazy-ass cage drivers thinking they're the next Dale Earnhardt or some shit, *fuck!*

I got the cat under the light and he looked up at me, and it was *bad*. Half his little face and one eye was all raw hamburger, his fur wet and sticking up at odd angles, streaked with the rusty color of blood.

"Oh, shit. Hang on, little man," I said and with his pitiful cries echoing in my ears I thrust him into my jacket against my chest and zipped it up, trapping him.

He struggled, but there wasn't anywhere for the little guy to go, and he was pretty fuckin' weak.

"We gotta get you to a vet," I said. Straddling my bike, I looked up twenty-four-hour emergency vets near me.

There was one up past my place, *way* past my place, that specialized in cats up toward Bothell, shit – a good almost twenty miles north.

No problem.

I got back onto 99 and managed to not get taken out and twisted the throttle, shifting gears smoothly and hauling ass.

It was slicker than owl shit out here, and I was trying not to get us both killed as the little ball of injured fur squirmed like a mother-fucker inside my jacket.

I pulled into the well-lit lot in front of the animal clinic's doors that were marked with a bold red stripe, big white block letters going through it stating 'emergency' and I hopped off the bike.

Inside, it was well lit, but a little on the cooler side and a girl my age, maybe a little less looked up from behind the receptionist wrap in a set of cartoon unicorn pony scrubs.

"Help you?" she asked, looking at me confused as I dripped water on the non-slip gray mat in front of the wrap.

"Yeah, he's hurt bad," I said, unzipping my coat and dragging the unfortunate little furball out. "I found him just by Green Lake, the sharp curves there."

The girl took off her chunky black framed reading glasses and set them down, holding out her hands and taking him from me.

"Oh, God," she declared. "I'm the only one here. Come on back and help me," she said, and I went with her. She started doing things with swift efficiency.

"What's your name?" she asked.

"Fish," I answered automatically.

"I'm sorry, what?"

"Fish," I repeated. "Everyone calls me Fish."

"I need a legal name, for the paperwork?"

"Oh, Saul Masters."

"Okay, Mr. Masters, and what's his name?"

"Uh... Nemo?" I thought about the conversation earlier.

"And how will you be paying?" she asked.

"Wait, that's not my cat," I said. "Is this how you get a cat?" My brow wrinkled in confusion.

"This is how you get a cat," she affirmed, and I really looked at her, then.

She was beautiful, even with her face free of makeup, her nails natural and clipped short, her hair up in a messy sort of loopy bun thing, the ends spiky and at all angles. Her skin was smooth, her eyes calculating and focused and the most astounding shade of gray, an almost silver in her face. I bet if she ever let that tawny golden wheat blonde hair down, that her eyes would be out of this world framed up by it.

"Cash, card, what?" she asked.

"Doesn't matter," I said, snapping back with it. "I'll pay it. Just fix him."

"My pleasure. Poor little guy is in really rough shape. He's going to have to stay overnight, may need surgery. This could get really expensive."

"He's a little scrapper, a fighter. I'll pay it."

"We're talking maybe a couple thousand dollars here, you sure?"

"You trying to talk me out of it?" I asked with a half-smile.

"We can't take on another clinic cat," she said. "I'm making sure – I would hate to put all sorts of care into him, call the doctor and wake him up to come down here, just to have you skip out on the bill and little Nemo here end up in a kill shelter."

"Fuck that! This little guy fought way too hard to live, just look at him."

She looked up at me and fixed me with those eyes and I felt my heart do a barrel roll in my chest. Shit she was pretty.

"Let me get him stable, call the doctor, and get the rest of your information. Hand me that thing there," she pointed at a weird tube looking thing that looked like it went on the end of your finger, but I'm sure that wasn't what it was for. I obediently handed it over. "Okay, I think that's all I need you for. Please don't ditch," she said.

"I'll be right out here in your waiting room," I vowed.

I went out and took a seat, tired and fucking around on my phone just to stay awake. She came out a little while later.

"Doc is on his way, he's definitely going to need surgery for that eye, you want to get him neutered at the same time?"

"Yeah."

"Vaccinated against…" She listed off a bunch of shit I couldn't follow.

"Yeah, might as well do it all," I said.

"Alright." She nodded and said, "We can take care of some of this upfront and the rest when you pick him up."

Five hundred and eight-nine dollars later, I was damn sure hoping a blow job came with things. Yeah, shitty and douche baggy to say, I know, but all I could picture was her lips wrapped around my cock, her eyes rolled up and looking at me and *down boy*.

"Anything else you want to know?" she asked me and without missing a beat, I shot back, "Your name would be nice."

She fixed me with a flat look, those eyes giving away the calculations that she had going on behind them and I waited her out. Finally, she said, "Kinzleigh."

"Kinzleigh?" I asked, "Never heard a name like that."

"Yeah, well, it's East Tennessee for I was raised poor white trash," she said, and her tone was clipped. My eyes went a little wide and I laughed. She didn't have a trace of an accent. I wondered if she worked on that.

"Well, it's nice to meet you, Kinzleigh," I said.

"Nice to meet you too… Fish. Can I get your number?" she asked, and I grinned. "To call about Nemo," she added and my grin only grew.

"Sure thing." I wrote it down on the pad and paper she handed me, and she said, "I'll call you as soon as he's ready to go home."

I nodded, and it was halfway back down Aurora that it hit me, *shit, I don't even know if my apartments will allow a fucking cat… fuck me!*

I was going to have to figure that out, but it looked like I had a little time. What I couldn't stop thinking about was Kinzleigh of the efficient sharp wit and silvery eyes. I wondered what her story was. Didn't sound like it was a happy origin story by any means, but at the same time neither was mine; so many people's rarely were.

I barely dragged myself through a hot shower before collapsing into bed, falling asleep to the vision of Kinzleigh looking up over the rim of those smart little glasses at me, naughty librarian style.

I had some fucking dreams that night, I tell you what…

ALSO BY A.J. DOWNEY

Sacred Hearts MC Novella

Christmas with the Brotherhood

Indigo Knights

1. Her Thin Blue Lifeline

2. His Cold Blue Command

3. A Low Blue Flame

4. His Wild Blue Rose

5. Her Pained Blue Silence

6. A Cold Blue Call

7. Her Reluctant Blue Cavalier

8. Forged Under Fire

9. Under A Blue Moon

Sacred Hearts MC Pacific Northwest

1. Over the High Side

2. Wind Therapy

3. Apex of the Curve

4. Low Sided

Paranormal Romance (with Ryan Kells)

1. I Am The Alpha

2. Omega's Run

3. Hunter's End

Indigo City Darker (with Jared KingPacal Lain)

1. Triple Threat

2. Double Shot

Standalones

Synchronicity

ABOUT A.J. DOWNEY

A.J. Downey is a Pacific Northwest girl living in an East Tennessee world who finds inspiration from her surroundings, through the people she meets, and likely as a byproduct of way too much caffeine. She specializes in real and relatable romance stories featuring that real-life kind of love that everyone craves.

Stalker Information:

Website
www.ajdowney.com

Sign up for her newsletter at
http://eepurl.com/dkQiIH

Facebook Group - AJ's Sacred Circle
https://www.facebook.com/groups/authorajdowney/

facebook.com/authorajdowney
twitter.com/authorajdowney
instagram.com/ajdowney
bookbub.com/authors/a-j-downey